Also by Jose Yglesias

Novels

A Wake in Ybor City

An Orderly Life

Double Double

The Truth About Them

The Kill Price

Home Again

Nonfiction

The Goodbye Land

In the Fist of the Revolution

Down There

The Franco Years

TRISTAN AND THE HISPANICS

Jose Yglesias

Simon and Schuster
New York London Toronto Sydney Tokyo

Simon and Schuster
Simon & Schuster Building
Rockefeller Center
1230 Avenue of the Americas
New York, New York 10020

This book is a work of fiction. Names, characters, places and incidents are either the product of the author's imagination or are used fictitiously. Any resemblance to actual events or locales or persons, living or dead, is entirely coincidental.

Designed by Susan Brooker/Levavi & Levavi
Manufactured in the United States of America

10 9 8 7 6 5 4 3 2 1

Library of Congress Cataloging-in-Publication Data
Yglesias, Jose.
Tristan and the Hispanics / Jose Yglesias.
p. cm.
I. Title.
PS3575.G5T75 1989
813'.54—dc19 88-28628
ISBN 0-671-67335-1 CIP

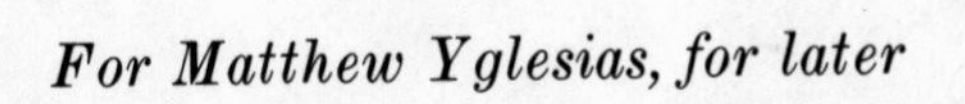

For Matthew Yglesias, for later

Tristan and the Hispanics

One

TRISTAN FLIES TO TAMPA, FLORIDA

One of those distant Tampa cousins called and told Tristan's mom (his dad was in the hospital for one more day) that Grandpa was dead. Dad's father. When the call came, Tristan was still unpacking the two duffel bags he had lugged home from New Haven. First year at Yale, so he had accumulated a lot. He was self-conscious about that and did not like to see Mom enter his old room the way she used to. He hadn't put everything away, and the hand weights were right there in the open. All winter he had practiced self-containment, and did not blink now when he saw her eyes catch on the weights momentarily. His ability to stand cool was to prove handy in the days to come, for the upshot of what Mom came in to say was that he would have to be the one to go down to Florida and cremate the old man.

To have him cremated, he said to himself. Yale was teaching him to be careful about his speech too.

She interrupted herself in the middle of all this news and pointed to the weights. "I thought I saw more muscles," she said and touched his right biceps and smiled, her way of hiding her nervousness about his mission. "You're not going to take up heavy metal, are you?"

Tristan frowned for a moment. "Those are not for muscle," he said. "They're for stamina. I carry them when I jog."

Six miles every day. Like Bruce Springsteen. But he did not tell her that. He might appear trendy—next week's performances at Madison Square Garden had been sold out in record time—and he was not that. Not at all. As Nanao said, self-knowledge was his thing.

Tristan knew that he must try to be calm. Mom was edgy, he could tell. His father was in the hospital to have his cast removed, his older brother Owen at Oxford, his uncle Crispin with one of his girlfriends on a Pacific island, and his kid sister Emily at Buxton. That was it: Mom had no family to speak of, only a gay brother in San Francisco; on Dad's mother's side, some distant cousins in Boston that you sometimes ran into summers in Maine, but with no connection to Grandpa. (Poor Grandpa.) For the moment he (Tristan) was their only option. He was happy about that.

He said to himself in explanation for feeling glad (he was given to explanations): I'm the middle sibling, I have never been the center of attention, so my pulse is running a little faster. Still, he should not go so far as to feel happy, for he had always liked this grandfather—years ago, in childhood, they had been buddies—and he was sorry, even before now, that he had never called him during the three years the old man had been living in Tampa. He looked forward to feeling nostalgic about him. Yes, that was it: he felt nostalgia, not guilt.

But why was Mom nervous?

She hadn't liked Grandpa and was feeling guilty about it? He put that thought away quickly; it was not fair. She was nervous about Dad more likely. Tomorrow when they removed Dad's plaster cast the doctor might decide to do more about the broken leg. Something about his knee, he could not recall just what.

"Lots of things to do," she said as if not for the first time. "I talked to your dad and he thought you might need a power-of-attorney. But we can Federal-Express that down to you after you leave tomorrow."

"A power-of-attorney?" he said.

"To act for him," she explained. "Dad's the older son, the natural heir." She laughed. "Sounds like a Trollope novel, doesn't it?"

She was nervous about him. That was it. It made him feel good. He would show her that she need not be.

He checked that the small notebook and pen he always carried in his shirt pocket were there, and led her to the living room. The first time she had ever deferred to him in this way. Macho, he thought, and told himself that he must think about this feeling of power later, when he was alone. Now he sat her down and took out the notebook and pen and told her, one at a time, the things that needed to be done. He listed them thus:

To do, before leaving:

1) Call the airlines and make a reservation.
2) The addresses and telephones for:
    a) Our New York lawyer.
    b) Grandpa's.
    c) Cousin who called. Marina?
    d) The hospital here.
    e) The hospital there.
3) Pack a carry-on bag with 2 (3?) changes.

4) A novel by Grandpa; the new book by Stephen Jay Gould.
5) Sony Walkman; cassettes.
6) Extra notebooks and pen.
7) Call Nanao; Skitch.
8) More cash?

To do, in Tampa:

1) Rent a car at airport.
2) Call hospital as soon as arrive.
3) Ask Marina for reputable funeral home.
4) Arrange for cremation. (Comparison shopping?)
5) Look for will in his papers.
6) Call home and report.
7) Payment of outstanding bills.
8) Call home.

He noticed the embarrassing repetition to call home, but he didn't cross it out; to save face he added, *for final instructions.* "Anything else you can think of?" he asked his mother and paused, as he had after each notation, to give her a chance to make a suggestion.

She had none. "Great," she said and looked proud of him. Indeed, she unaccountably giggled and became so relaxed that she called Grandpa the Old Spic, as she always had.

Before they went uptown to the hospital, he called Nanao at the off-campus house where she lived. She came on talking. "How'd you know I had definite news?" she said. "Charlie for sure is moving in with his lover in the fall and you're in—everyone agrees."

"Okay," he said and paused, wondering how to make the transition to announcing Grandpa's death.

She continued: "Aren't you glad you know an older woman!"

She was a year older and a year ahead in school and that was why she had been living off campus and he not until the fall.

Without leading up to it, he told her he would not be in New York when she came in a couple of days. "I'm gonna be in Florida. Sorry."

"Florida?"

Then he told her. "My last grandparent," he said. "The one I got my Spanish name from."

"Retired in Florida?" she said, not knowing whether she should, as she had heard it expressed, extend condolences.

Retired? It would take a long time to explain about Grandpa. He said, "Well . . . no, he was a writer."

"Hey," she said. "I'm very sorry." A pause. "You the only one going down? How come? In my family they spend all their time going to funerals. Everybody goes. Especially down South."

He said, "Well . . ." but did not add anything.

"Hey, I'm sorry. Maybe it's a cultural difference."

Then he said, "That's all right. Listen, I'll call you later. After I see Dad in the hospital."

"In the hospital!" she yelled. "God, you're full of terrible news."

"Really?" he said. It hadn't struck him that way. He was definitely a little elated.

In the taxi he asked his mother, "Did you read all of Grandpa's books?"

She shook her head. "None; I didn't want to give him that pleasure." She chortled. "I had no other way of getting his goat." She took his hand and said, "I'm not a nice girl, Tristan," and let it go when he only nodded. "I am *too,*" she added. "I hope you haven't got rid of your Oedipus yet."

He could be funny too: he said, "I'm working on it."

The rest of the ride uptown he thought about Grandpa in Maine. Summers, when he was a boy. He couldn't remember him in New York, though he had lived there until three or four years ago, when Grandma died. Her, he couldn't remember at all. Funny.

He caught his mother studying him.

In Dad's private room at the hospital, he took out the notebook before he began his questions, and Dad who was not neat immediately said, "You're going to have to play a lot of it by ear. You don't have time to take notes—they talk too fast. At least, that's the way I remember them."

Tristan did not take him up on that. He knew all about father-son rivalries: whether he took issue or agreed with him he would be sure to irk him.

Instead, he reviewed his schedule with him. "Today is Monday," he began. He figured he could get a morning flight (he had made a tentative reservation with Eastern before coming uptown), arrange the cremation tomorrow afternoon, see the cousins in the evening, and spend Wednesday and Thursday consulting a lawyer there (maybe Grandpa already had a lawyer) and on Friday morning, or perhaps even Thursday afternoon, come back to New York City.

"Dad," he asked, "is there something down there you'd like me to bring back?"

Mom asked, "What?" as if daring anyone to answer her.

"Something of Grandpa's?" Tristan insisted.

"Good boy," Dad said and shook his head, then changed his mind. "Maybe he was working on something—we'll talk."

Did he mean when Mom was not there? She must have thought so too: she had the alert look of a bird about to take off.

Tristan thought of more things. "Manuscripts?" he asked. "What about the old house?"

Dad grumbled. Tears suddenly appeared in his eyes.

His mother asked, "Is your leg itching?"

"Yeah, sell it," Dad said loudly, in one of his outbursts. "Who's going to stay in that run-down neighborhood? Your uncle Crispin doesn't care. A measly writers' strike and he flies off to the Pacific like Gauguin. Your mother neither."

"Me?" she said and looked around as if there were other people in the room. "Should I?"

"I'll call a real estate agent," Tristan said quickly, to stop the impending argument, and wrote in the notebook *real estate agent.*

He noticed the item about calling a reputable funeral home. What was that? He crossed out the adjective.

"We'll talk on the phone," Dad said apologetically, and the tears came back. "Once you get down there."

Mom said, "Get rid of it all. You kids were down there only once—it was all a Latin ghetto, and now blacks moving in."

Dad said, "What's wrong with that!"

Tristan had been trying to remember that trip. A big porch and cement steps to funny grass. The beach at Clearwater, the smooth smooth silky white sand giving to his flapping feet, so unexpected after Maine's rock-strewn waterfront.

Dad added, "He was only eight or nine."

"I'll look for a will," Tristan said. "And I'll call his lawyer."

Dad said, "If there is one."

Mom repeated, "Get rid of it all."

That seemed precipitate. Tristan frowned a small frown.

Dad said, "You sure you want to do this? Those miserable television writers will no doubt negotiate endlessly about creative control—ugh!—and I'll have plenty of time—for weeks!—to go down there."

Tristan nodded. "I want to go."

His mother said, "He's the only one available."

"There's that Marina cousin who called," Dad said.

"I have her name," Tristan said.

Mom asked, "You think she's competent?"

"And there's also the guy with the funny name who phoned me when Father . . ."

"That's Tom-tom," she said. "What a name! I don't think the Old Spic trusted him."

"Gail," Dad said and paused. Tristan saw him suppress his irritation, as if there really were an itch he could not get at because of the cast. "There's nothing to be trusting about—or not."

Mom said, "You're right, we could just call that Marina and give her instructions. That's all that would be necessary."

"I think they would be shocked." Dad tapped his cast to call for attention. "And I don't blame them."

Mom quickly said, "So?" Then apropos of nothing: "He went down there because he was crazy. What the hell does it have to do with—any of us?"

Tristan said quickly, "I'm going. I want to."

His father said, "You liked Grandpa, didn't you?" And he half smiled to show that that pleased him. "It'll make me feel better if you go now . . . you know. We'll confer on the phone after . . . I hate bumbling like this, but I'm glad you have that old feeling for him."

Actually, Tristan had not thought about his feelings. He could not remember Grandpa after he grew up. Nor anything he had specifically done. Or said. He could not even remember what he looked like. Only from below, from his little-boy height. Big eyebrows going up and down. He frowned. His father was staring at him. His father's eyes, brown and oval-shaped, bugged, bulged, and Grandpa's face suddenly took shape around those same eyes. Hey, his own too. Tristan remembered the old man now. They had walked down to Soho together—he still could not remember Grandma—and made many stops for treats that Grandpa enjoyed more than he.

"Yes," he replied to Dad, moved by an emotion he thought might be love. "Yes," he added, "I liked him."

"It's only natural," Mom said, less of an explanation than an excuse for Tristan. As for herself, she wasn't changing her mind about the old man. Dad signaled him with a lift of his eyebrows. (Grandpa's!) Tristan thought that meant he wanted him to argue with his mother. He sympathized, but he stayed out of it. Their bickering, that is.

He understood Mom: if people didn't like her?—she didn't like them back. Logical. No nonsense. Grandpa wasn't her father and her father was dead (a long time, he figured, because he could not remember him at all, no matter how he tried) and she must not have any unused kindly feelings lying around for Grandpa to inherit without having earned them. No, Grandpa was just another person with whom she practiced her sensible reciprocity.

He made two more phone calls when they got back from the hospital. The first one to that cousin who had called with the announcement. Marina. She was not at her home, so he called the old family house, as Dad called it, on the chance she was there.

She came right on. She quickly said, as if asked, "I didn't go home, I stayed here and I'm staying here tonight. Your folks can count on me to keep up the tradition. I met you when you were a little boy, you couldn't remember that. Are you coming with your folks, or they coming later?"

He told her why they couldn't come.

"And your brother and sister?"

He explained. She was silent. He noticed that he seemed to want her approval. It did not come.

"What airline?" she said.

He told her and again hoped for approval.

"The noon flight? I can't go pick you up. I don't want to leave this house. But there'll be somebody."

He reassured her. "I'll take a taxi," he said and repeated the address in his notebook to make sure. "Is that right?"

"Tell him it's in Ybor City," she said.

"Ybor City?" he said.

"You don't know about Ybor City?" Her tone changed. "My goodness," she said cheerfully. "It goes to show you can't take anything for granted."

He remembered. "Oh, where the Hispanic cigarmakers live."

"Where they used to live, honey. Everyone's darker here now." And she laughed. "I'll tell you about Ybor City when you get here."

"Wait," he said and then told her he might rent a car." "Is it difficult to get there on my own?"

She paused. "No, it's easy. Let's see—stay on the boulevard when you come out of the airport, and that becomes Columbus Drive in a little while. You go and go until—in Ybor City—you get to Fifteenth Street. Turn left and in two blocks you're there. And don't be scared of Ybor City—it's not so dangerous as they tell you."

The moment he put down the phone Mom asked, "What was that all about?"

"Nothing really," he said, not wanting to have to say that Marina did not approve of only him going down there. He had better go to his father's study to call Nanao. Mom and Dad sort of knew about her; that is, that he saw a lot of a girl named Nanao, but not much more. Did they know she was black? He didn't think so, but that didn't matter, not in his family. He wasn't sure he wanted them to know that she was getting to be so important to him. He wasn't sure that he wanted to know it himself, so he chose an out-of-the-way phone. Out of Mom's way, that is. Was he becoming overdependent on the phrase *that is?*

No confessionals, he told himself just before Nanao picked up the phone in New Haven. But to his surprise he told her everything that had gone on since he had talked to her two hours earlier, including his mother's feelings. She elicited it painlessly. She was interested in all the details and that surprised him too.

She said, "I wish I was with you now."

"There's no funeral or anything like that," he said. "Not in my family. I'm just going to arrange for the cremation and take care of a few other things."

"No, huh?" she said. "Your father doesn't want a burial?"

"God no, neither would Grandpa. They think it's barbaric, all that."

"You're sad?"

"I'm not mourning or anything like that," he said.

"Sure you are."

"How come you're sure?"

"Because I'm going to be very sad when my grandpappy dies." Her voice got thin. "Oh gosh, I'm crying!"

He laughed. "You're not logical."

"Who wants to be!" She laughed. "No, you're right."

"About what?"

"Oh, I don't know, don't be so logical."

"I gotta have all the phone numbers where you'll be." He opened his notebook and leaned on the long writing table and only then noticed the new word processor. "Hey, he's got himself the Toshiba 3100!"

"What kind of printer?"

He said, "He already had the laser jet," and looked around for a new one. "I'm surprised he didn't take the Toshiba to the hospital—"

"The hospital! I forgot about that—tell me. God, the things that happen when you get old."

"Yeah, like dying," he said.

She laughed along with him, and it was then that Mom looked in and was pleased he wasn't sad about the Old Spic's death.

"Is that your significant other?" she called, a passé epithet but very smart of her because he had no time to really deal with that if he hoped to get her out of the study quickly and thus she forced him to simply nod and admit to more than he wanted to. He nodded period, and no more. She was dying to talk but left when he would not get off the phone, and he was able to ask Nanao in private to stay one more day at Kim's in New York because he would certainly be back on Friday.

When she hesitated, he became inspired and said, "Do what you want to do."

That worked.

She cooed, "I made my mind up you're gonna be mine. Any trick in the book, babe."

But she spoke in her serious voice when she finally said yes, and since this Tina Turner talk aroused more feelings than he would be able to handle in his mother's presence, he went straight out for a walk and breathed deeply and looked in at the Lone Star Cafe. Only through the window, because it was filled for the Gang of Five, a new group he had not heard. Several guys offered him stuff, but the look on his face was such that he did not have to say no before they moved on. The opening act vocalist sang with no backup, playing both the guitar and harmonica, reminding him of Bruce on *Nebraska.* Yes, he said to himself as he walked back to the house, this is growing up. Someday Mom and Dad would die and there would be more duties like this to take on. He'd be entirely on his own then, full of responsibilities. He had not thought of it before, but it was inspiring—life.

It's only natural, he said to himself on the plane. I'm young. I've never taken on such a responsibility. It is only natural that I should be excited, even a little thrilled. Though Grandpa is dead, no happy event.

Like an intro by Bruce.

What will my refrain be like? He leaned back in his seat to let it come, but his eyes refused to close while the hostess swung down the aisle. What was she like underneath? It's only natural to have such thoughts, I'm young.

Tristan reasoned his way to the truth: he was enjoying the adventure of his grandfather's death.

Why didn't he know more about Grandpa?

He remembered then that he had forgotten to bring one of the ten books Grandpa had published. He had never read any of them and had meant to start on the plane. He looked in his notebook. He had written a reminder there—*a book by Grandpa.* He had even decided on the one called *Yours Truly*—how could he have forgotten? He must check his notebook often, but he put it away quickly now because the old man in the next seat was squinting at it, his body language sending out signals that at any minute he might start talking.

The only impromptu conversations Tristan welcomed were with Nanao, so he leaned back again and entirely closed his eyes this time. He opened them when the food was served. As usual, it was awful (when it came to food Mom had been a good influence) but he ate it all. I'm young, he said to himself, why not?

"Here we go," the old man said as the plane started to descend. "I done this so often I always know just when the pilot's gonna do it." He pinched his nose and said, a little too loudly, "This is how I take the pressure off the eardrums."

Tristan nodded and then looked out the window to unlock himself from the old man's eyes. He reviewed in his mind what he needed to do as soon as they landed. Take the bag from under the seat, sling it over his shoulder, and once off the plane head straight for the taxis. He was diverted by the sights in the window as the plane slowly came down all the way from Jacksonville on the Atlantic to Tampa on the Gulf of Mexico. A strange flat open landscape. He belonged to the New York islands, as Woody via Bruce said, and to the green up and down of crumpled New England. Did landscape get into the genes? He touched the notebook in his pocket and thought of again checking the address he would give the cabdriver, but decided to leave that for later. It might start the old man next to him talking again. Anyway, it was 1504 Nineteenth Avenue, he was rather sure. Landscape. Was that what made the difference? Between him and, say, Grandpa?

The rental! He had forgot his share of the rental for the fall. A check from Dad to Mr. Poindexter, the landlord. He must make a note of that, but the plane had come to a stop on the sunlit runway and there was no time. He'd do it in the taxi.

The old man lost no time getting out into the aisle.

"I like to get out fast, always did," he said and added, "You're traveling light," when he saw Tristan lift the bag from under his seat and hang it from his shoulder. "What the hell, you young fellas don't need clothes down here."

Several ladies turned around to look at Tristan and his bag. They were smiling. Everyone was. Not at him particularly. They were happy to be there.

"Have a good time," someone said, again to no one in particular.

"Have a good time," the old man said.

Have a good time, have a good time, have a good time.

He had not come to Florida for that, but it certainly did not look like a landscape for mourning. Why did he have the sense that Grandpa was a dour old man? Because in New York and Maine he was away from sun like this? Very likely. Its radiating warmth seeped into the passageway that connected the plane with the building and stubbornly fought the air-conditioning that flowed into it from the Eastern Airlines waiting room.

The passengers, mostly mottled old people, were drawn towards the cool air of the waiting room with wide smiles, and they pushed round Tristan, propelling him faster than he was used to going. "Have a good time, young fella," the old man said once more. He overtook and passed Tristan and spoke to a crowd around the door to the waiting room. "Hey, make way, make way."

The crowd paid no attention to him.

"What's the matter?" the old man said. "What's the matter? You waiting for Frank Sinatra? I'm not him."

In great good humor at his own sally he turned around and said to Tristan and the passengers behind him, "I can't sing." To the crowd, he said, "Let me through," and this time got round them.

They looked like a welcoming delegation. An old lady in the front rank yelled, "That's him!"

Tristan stepped aside, but she did the same and pinned him against the side rope that separated the passengers from the waiting room. She called to the others, "It's him, I reckanized him, I reckanized him!"

She hugged him without letup—he couldn't believe it was happening—and her floppy breasts pressed into his belly and her hand pushed his bag aside to make room for her arm to go well around his waist. A sweet penny-candy lavender scent rose from her blue-white hair. "It's Tristan! Tristan, honey!"

Tristan was too startled to catch his own name spoken in Spanish. *Tristán. Tristán!* The old woman spoke less to him than to the crowd behind her. She repeated *Tristán!* and then he got it. He smiled.

A wave of relief from the waiting group—exhalations emitted in unison—reached him: he must be the one they were there for. Immediately, he was pulled back by the strap of his bag and twisted bodily towards the group, but the old woman's arms did not let him go far. Like a yo-yo he snapped back to her yielding flesh and strong perfume.

He frowned. "Hey, someone took my bag!"

He was ashamed to say *he* and point to the culprit, for the young man didn't sneak away into the crowd like the thieves in the TV commercials, but stayed there holding the bag up to view, happy to have relieved Tristan of it.

"He'll be careful with it," said a young woman with red hair standing by him in the front line of the group.

"You kidding?" the fellow exclaimed. To Tristan, he said,

"Hi there, I work for Delta, you're in experienced hands. My name is—"

He was cut off by a squat wide fat man with a full head of gray hair. Rumbling and growling he headed for Tristan, bumping the others aside. He created ripples and waves like a speedboat and left a wake of exclamations. "Oh God, Tom-tom," the redhead said. He paid no attention to her and held up an admonishing hand to Tristan, calling before he reached him, "Let him carry it, don't strain yourself." His hand came down on the old woman hugging Tristan and yanked her away. "I'm Tom-tom. You don't recognize me?"

"Excuse me," Tristan said and tried to retract his bag. "Sir?" he said to the young man. "May I have it?"

God, it was like an early Hitchcock black-and-white, an innocent American in an exotic foreign country. Who were these people? Grandpa's relatives?

Tom-tom pulled away Tristan's outstretched arm. "Don't worry about it. You don't know me? Tom-tom?"

The old lady giggled, then jiggled Tristan's free arm. "Hello," she said, reclaiming him.

Tom-tom bumped his hard belly into Tristan. "I'm Pinpin's closest cousin. His partner, his buddy. The only brother he ever had." His voiced quavered, he dropped his eyes in mourning and remembrance.

"Aiee, aiee!" the old lady keened.

"No crying here," Tom-tom said brusquely and pushed her towards the others. Then to Tristan in a soft voice, "Tom-tom, that's who I am. Pinpin must have talked about me. We were very, very close."

"Pinpin?" Tristan said.

The old lady came back to his side. *"Tu abuelo, niño,"* she explained.

"Stop that," Tom-tom said. "No Spanish."

"Your grandfather, honey," the old lady said with as much

ease. "I'm your aunt Clemencia. Aunt Clem, I mean, cause Tom-tom don't want me to say anything in Spanish."

Tristan hung on to the first thing he had not understood; he would clear up the others later. "What did you say was my grandfather's name?"

He kept his eyes on this squat bossy man, but he felt and heard the others—they seemed fewer now, no more than fifteen or twenty, but still insisting on his attention, jumping up and down, calling his name, some in English, some in Spanish. Who were they? They couldn't all be cousins. In fact, they couldn't be real cousins. A couple of times removed, at least. It did not make him feel good to be thinking these unfriendly thoughts.

Then he remembered: the cousin with the funny name, as Dad said, Tom-tom.

"Antonio Granados, that was his name. Was!" Again the quaver in Tom-tom's voice. "There's no mistake, we're your family," he added and smiled a smile full of pure white dentures. His fleshy warm damp hands ran up and down Tristan's arm, squeezed his biceps, glided to his chest, smoothed down his pectorals, and switched to his back with a thump. "You're Tristan, I can tell. You think my cousin-brother Pinpin didn't talk to me about you many a night? I feel I know you like my own son. What am I saying! I *know* you."

"Pinpin, that's the name he wanted to know," Aunt Clem said. She hit Tom-tom. "Tell him that's his grandpa's name."

Tom-tom threw out one arm, meaty like Popeye's from the elbow down, to keep her and the others away. The crowd had moved in and now formed an enormous football huddle.

"I'm sorry about these barbarians," he continued. "I told them to stay home. They got nothing better to do during the day. But in this family—a bunch of hypocrites, but we'll talk about that later."

Tom-tom kept an arm on Tristan's back propelling him

away from the waiting area, and with the other waved forbiddingly at the relatives trying to greet him. In the corridor he stepped up his fat man's fast waddle and left them a few steps behind. "Later, later," he called back, "you'll talk to him at the house, goddammit."

"Excuse me," Tristan said. He wanted to ask if all these people were here to meet him but could not think of a modest way to put the question. He remembered Hertz from the list of things to do. "There's something I must take care of."

"You didn't pee on the plane? Ha-ha!" Tom-tom said. "You been in Florida before? Get ready to sweat. I know, I lived in New York once and weather don't change. The only thing in this world stays the same—look at me, I was a handsome fellow like you, once. A wreckpile, that's what I am now, but the weather's still the same."

A trim middle-aged man jumped in front of them. "Will you cut out the shit, Tom-tom. We're his cousins too." He smiled a wide debonair smile at Tristan. "Hello, I'm your cousin Jack."

Tom-tom whispered loudly, "There's sixty-six of those. I'm a cousin-brother."

Aunt Clem caught up with them breathlessly. "Jack is an engineer. He's with the water department."

Tom-tom said, "Oh, I thought it was the sanitary department!" and laughed and struck Tristan a blow that sent him forward faster than he meant to go. Aunt Clem kept up with him, however, and Tom-tom skipped and took little leaps on his short legs to stay ahead of the group.

Jack walked backwards and thus managed to face Tristan as he spoke. "He means the City Sanitation Department. I wish I were. Tampa is acquiring a complex sewage processing plant and it would be a challenge. Though I'd have to refuse it if it came my way."

Tristan nodded at him, then looked back for the young man who had taken his bag. The young man waved and called, "Hi!" and Tristan was sorry to have doubted, so he also said, "Hi."

He did not know where he was going or why. They were halfway down the wide corridor onto which all the waiting lounges emptied. There was no getting past them, coming or going. Passengers from his plane slowed down anyway, to look at him mostly. He felt he ought to tell them he was not a celebrity.

Jack still held out his hand and still maintained a smile. People must be getting the impression that he, Tristan, was a celebrity.

Tristan thought about this a moment longer.

There was no help for it. He shook Jack's hand and said, "Thanks for coming," and sure enough, some people from the plane stopped altogether and looked at him as if they too wanted to shake his hand.

"Let me introduce you to everybody," Jack said. He pointed to Tom-tom and Aunt Clem. "You met these two."

Aunt Clem hugged him again and this time she felt more like a pillow than a body. "I'm Tom-tom's kid sister," she explained and then laughed a laugh that caused a spectator to move off and a passer-by to step up his pace.

Jack beckoned the young man carrying Tristan's bag and the red-haired girl. "This is Dewey, my cousin's son. He brought Charlene into the family. Charlene's studying at the University of South Florida."

Dewey said, "I'm going to, too."

"Aren't they cute? And so smart!" Aunt Clem said. "Dewey is Dolores's son."

A man with a mustache looked over Dewey's shoulder. He said brightly, "Me too."

"That's Delio," said Aunt Clem. "Dolores's oldest, got the machine shop near Dale Mabry. He can take off in the middle of the day. Dolores gave all her boys names with *D*. *De*wey, *Del*io, *Der*by. Isn't that nice? Derby couldn't make it."

Delio said, "He'll come to the house, of course."

Aunt Clem quickly looked sad and said, "And for the wake too, you can count on him. And of course their daddy, Duran." She laughed. "Everybody in that family is a D!"

Tristan shook hands with Dewey and Charlene and when he reached for Delio's hand others intercepted it. "It's very nice that you happened to be here."

"You're kidding!" said Dewey.

"What?" he asked. "I'm sorry."

Tom-tom whispered hoarsely, "Whaddya apologizing for?"

Jack pointed to two elderly ladies whom he had signaled to come forward to be introduced. But first he said, "I want you to know for a fact, I want you to understand that we are all happy to be here and we wouldn't be anywhere else. Any service you need, as our grandparents used to say."

"Yes, yes," the elderly ladies affirmed and were echoed by murmurs, topped by exclamations from the others, threatening to break into embraces and more affectionate demonstrations. "Yes, oh yes!"

Jack took on a solemn look and shook hands again, "I accompany you in your sorrow."

His words both calmed and set the group in motion again. This time with reverence.

"My God, we forgot," said Dewey. He too shook hands again. "I accompany you in your sorrow."

Tristan looked beyond him and saw the others had regrouped and formed a line. "I accompany you in your sorrow," each said, and one old man, whom Jack had not introduced, added, "I am the more sorry because your father—"

"No, no, his grandfather!" Aunt Clem said.

The old man looked puzzled but continued. "He was the last memory left to me of Aunt Mama. You probably know that I was her bunchmaker at the Clock and that her memory is sacred to me. I cannot claim membership in this family by blood, but by all the claims of fidelity and comradeship I am as good as your grandfather—"

"No, no, great-grandfather!"

The old man brushed the objections aside. "This will be my last funeral. How can there be more? Who will accompany me in my sorrow?"

Aunt Clem protested, "For goodness sakes, all of us, Santo. Don't take on so."

"All right, enough," Tom-tom said. "This is getting outa hand."

Aunt Clem sidled over to Tristan and again reached around him. She poked him in the waist and he jumped. "Tristan, honey, I forgot to say I accompany you in your sorrow too. I just forgot, you understand, right? I was so excited to see you, honey." She gave him another poke. "We all so happy to see you, yes."

"Not me," said Tom-tom. "This is a sad occasion, Tris, I'm not good at pretending."

Immediately there were cries of agreement from the others.

Aunt Clem said, "No one said it was not sad."

"We are containing our emotions," one of the twin elderly ladies said.

A man at the back called out, "You are right, Tom-tom. It is a sad occasion."

"Whatever service Tris needs, *I*'ll do it," Tom-tom said with finality.

Tristan decided that the best way to show he did not share Tom-tom's . . . he did not know what to call it . . . his negative attitude? The best way was to shake hands all round once more. The men did shake hands but always accompanied the handshake with a pat—more often a blow—to his left shoulder. The women mostly hugged him while still managing to appear shy.

Santo, Aunt Mama's bunchmaker, said, "My last funeral!"

He would have said more, but Delio pulled him away. One girl, a little older than Tristan, whispered in his ear and her breath made him tingle, "Don't mind anybody, they're okay." She lifted her eyebrows at him and her frizzed hair seemed to rise and fall too. The elderly ladies patted his face. Their hands felt ghostly, but he was strangely cheered. "I'm Elvira," one of them said in a sweet Southern accent. "And this is my sister Elmira." She looked to the sides. She became confidential. "We want you to pay a visit to our house very soon. Just you."

She drew him aside with a look that made the others drop back. Not a mean look, a teacherly one. "I hope you don't mind Maximo—"

Elmira explained, "That's Tom-tom."

Elvira continued, "His family wasn't as fortunate as ours. Cuban on both sides and that is not the best ancestry."

Elmira nodded sweetly in agreement.

"Is Marina at the house?" he asked; inconsequentially, he feared.

Tom-tom heard that. "The libarian?" he growled.

Elmira and Elvira shook their heads and stepped back to be out of it. Their eyes signaled their alarm and their lips inaudibly mouthed in unison, "Remember, soon!"

Aunt Clem laughed, but there were no passers-by on the fringe to scare away anymore.

"Was," said Dewey. "Marina retired."

"Not at the main library," Delio said. "The West Tampa branch."

Aunt Clem said, "It's closed now."

Tom-tom grabbed his arm and took charge of him again. Tristan fleetingly saw the look of resignation on Jack's face. "How'd you hear about her?" Tom-tom said.

"I talked to her on the phone," he said.

"What did she say?" Tom-tom said with alarm. "What?"

"Sir?" Tristan said.

"You hear that?" Tom-tom turned around and berated the

others with his question. "Sir, the boy said. Did ya hear? He shook hands when he didn't have to. Especially at a time like this. In public. That's good manners. Learn from him."

Tristan shook his head; then, unaccountably, was reminded of the dean at Yale trying to head off their anti-apartheid committee's demands with good-natured talk. He still wanted to know about Marina, and although Tom-tom was a marvelous fellow, he kept his eyes on him, as their committee chairman had done with the dean, and waited for his answer. He stood cool and it worked.

"Of course you talked to Marina and Marina did not want to come to the airport, you know how she is," Tom-tom said agreeably. "She decided she should be the one to stay at the house. She said it was her place—"

Aunt Clem interrupted, "Anybody in the family coulda said that."

Tom-tom pushed her away irritably. "Somebody has to stay in the house. What else did she say?"

Tristan shook his head and took out his notebook and looked down the list. He said, "Do you know where the Hertz desk is?"

"You wanta rent a car!" Tom-tom was thrilled by the idea and he held up a hand like a traffic cop to keep the others away. He whispered, "You welcome to use mine. Go ahead. I'll drive you around. For the funeral you gotta rent a limousine anyway."

Tristan only shook his head: he didn't think he should correct Tom-tom now. "That's nice, thank you," he said. "But I couldn't do that."

"You couldn't rent a limousine?" This was the second time the boy had gotten that calm sure look. "Oh, you mean my car. Well, it's not in the pink, it runs. Of course, it's not a rented car."

"Thank you, anyway," Tristan said.

Jack got close. "What's the matter?"

"Nothing, nothing," Tom-tom said. "Sure, of course you

want to rent a car. In the main building, you and me. Listen, everybody." He waited until everyone caught up to prove to Jack he was not anyone special. Two passers-by stopped too. "Are they cousins?" Tom-tom said. "Somebody tell me who they are."

"It's a free country," one of them said, and left. The other looked around claiming his right to idle.

"They don't know they're down South—people are polite here." He pushed Aunt Clem's hand off Tristan's arm. "We're gonna have to break up after we take the subway to the main building. Tris, I don't care where you come from, nobody's seen such a phenomena anywhere. The Tampa Airport! OK, everybody, we take the subway car and then we split up. Tris and I will go separately. Dewey, you got no car. Here's my keys."

"What about me!" Aunt Clem yelled.

"Shut up," Tom-tom said. "You go with Dewey."

"I came with you," she insisted.

"Shut up," he said. "There's things this boy wants to get my advice on."

Tom-tom turned his back on them, discounting their complaints in advance.

"Hey," Jack began. The train arrived from the main building, so he stopped. He threw up his arms to show he was giving up for now. "I'll see you later," he whispered to Tristan. "There's some friends of mine want to meet you."

With an arm around his shoulder, Tom-tom led him away, into what did look like a subway car. "Wait till you see this." The group followed and flowed round him in the car. "It's a monorail thing. New York wishes it had a subway like this. Beats the Eighth Avenue."

Everyone became silent. A kind of aggressive propriety, in honor of the three or four strangers in the car. But in a moment Delio and another man whose name Tristan had not caught were confiding in the strangers what Tristan had come to Tampa for. Old Santo too. "It will be my last funeral," Tristan heard him say to a Japanese carrying a briefcase, and this time Tristan thought he should soon tell them there would be no funeral.

At the other end, with the wide-open spaces of the main building beckoning, Tom-tom pushed him through the doors. "Quick, quick. How did you like that ride? Wasn't it something?" He did not allow the others to listen to Tristan's response, but gripped Tristan's elbow and hurried him away. "You and me are going downstairs. They gotta take the elevators up to the parking." He waved them back. "Goodbye," he called, then whispered to Tristan, "I wish it was really goodbye. I guess you can already tell they're a pain in the ass, if you know what I mean."

Tristan said, "My bag."

"Let Dewey take it," Tom-tom said.

"They're coming to Grandpa's house?"

Tom-tom threw out his arms horizontally. "Who can stop them?"

"Are you coming too?"

Tom-tom grabbed him once more. "I wouldn't leave you in the hands of those vultures."

How to tell Tom-tom that he wanted to drive up the house alone? Up North he would simply have said so. It would have been taken for granted that he meant no insult, that he had good practical reasons for it. But here? He was not out of the airport yet, but he suspected nothing would be simple, that he couldn't just say what he was going to do period and be done with it. And not hurt their feelings, that is. He didn't want to snub all these newfound relatives. Real people, too.

He looked back to the group, as for inspiration, and saw Elmira and Elvira still holding themselves apart. They waved as if they had a secret compact with him. Their mouths opened in unison and he surmised they were saying, "Remember, soon!"

Tom-tom saw them too and whispered hoarsely, "They

think they're better than anybody because their father was a foreman."

Tristan still could not think of how to answer him.

"But those days are gone forever. Forever." Tom-tom searched Tristan's face, then gave his elbow a numbing squeeze. "Whatcha worried about? I'm here for you. Believe me, Pinpin wanted me to take his place. He said so. He had a suspicion, a presentiment. He practically said, take care of Tris for me."

"I do want to see Marina right away," he confessed.

"Even if you wanted to, you couldn't avoid it. Get away from Marina? No sir."

Without encouragement, Tom-tom volunteered another warning. "That mob's heading there. And God knows who else. They all wanta meet you, they all wanta hang around, tell you how they loved Pinpin when actually—but forget about that. I'll do my best, stick close to me."

Tristan cleared his throat.

"Okay, okay," Tom-tom said. "Maybe late tonight or early tomorrow morning we can get together alone with Marina. This afternoon and tonight God himself couldn't make a date. There's a lotta things to arrange and then there's them and plenty others." He threw out an arm towards the elevators, and an expression of anger overtook him. "Look—they're coming back!"

Aunt Clem announced defensively, "We wanta be with Tristan when he gets his bags."

Tristan knew how to act with them: calm and patient, as when Dad went in for an outburst. It was Tom-tom who was difficult.

"Thank you," he said, "but I don't have any other bags." He pointed to Dewey. "That's it. And I think I ought to take it with me."

"You don't have any other bag!" Tom-tom said. He grabbed the backpack from Dewey and squeezed and shook it a couple of times. "You didn't bring a suit?"

Aunt Clem said, "Sure, you gotta go to the beach. You never been to a Florida beach?"

That girl whispered in his ear, "Fort Lauderdale, with the rich kids, right?"

Did she blow in his ear? His body felt as if she had.

"I mean Clearwater," Aunt Clem said.

Jack laughed a mean laugh.

Aunt Clem gave Jack the closest to an angry critical look she could manage. "Whataya laughing for?"

"A bikini he could carry in his back pocket!" Jack said and laughed again.

"A suit, Aunt Clem, not a bikini," Dewey said.

Tom-tom tried to make it a conversation between himself and Tristan only. "That's okay, that's okay," he said. "We'll find a regular suit that fits you. There's enough cousins. Jesus, yes!"

"Oh, a suit with a jacket," said Aunt Clem. "Why didn't you say so? I got two grandsons could fit you."

"Uncle Tom-tom, I bet he didn't bring a tie either," Delio said. "That's the latest fashion—no ties."

Tom-tom glared at him and gave the bag back to Dewey.

Tristan stood cool throughout, but nothing came of it. No one stopped to hear if he had anything to say. A cultural difference, Nanao would have said.

Thinking of Nanao made him loosen up. Might as well ask. "Why do I need a suit?"

"We don't stand on ceremony," Tom-tom said, "but for a funeral . . ."

"What funeral?" The look he saw on sweet Aunt Clem's face made him wish he could take it back. "Oh, there's not going to be a funeral," he said, nevertheless. "I thought my mother told Marina."

Delio said, "That Marina plays it close to her—ha-ha!"

"No funeral!" One of Tom-tom's hands closed tight on Tristan's forearm; the other covered his own face; he was blotting everyone out: the thought was too unbearable.

Tristan kept his voice level despite the pain that ran up to his shoulders and neck. "Grandpa is going to be cremated and I'll take the ashes . . ."

Was Tom-tom falling?

Tristan felt the pull of the man's fat body folding into the fetal position—was he himself falling though Tom-tom had released the death grip on his arm? He took the karate stance for maintaining balance. It worked. Tom-tom instinctively reached out for help by grabbing Tristan's belt, and as he straightened he let out a rumbling groan that grew into a roll of thunder. Tristan heard the sound as if from a distance—an animal roar bellowing from the dark forest, as in the educational movies of his childhood. Yet Tom-tom's face came back into view with no reassurance for the kiddies in the audience: the moan was ended but the mouth remained open like a mask of tragedy.

Tom-tom was framed in the wide startled eyes of his cousins.

Something should be said. Tristan said, "Sorry."

Tom-tom maintained silence and he commanded it with his upraised arm and grimace of pain. An eerie silence, for it was not the absence of talk that caused it but awe. The group drew closer as if beleaguered. No one looked Tristan's way. No one dared speak.

Except for Aunt Mama's bunchmaker. He asked in his small piping voice, "What did the boy say?" He smiled and nodded although no one replied. "You know what I heard? I heard . . ." He became quiet because the idea was too unthinkable and inappropriate to mention now. Maybe later, at the wake, where one spoke about all sorts of things.

The ticket counters were a half block away in the wide space encompassed by the round building, and the insensitive tinkling sound of pleasant-voiced attendants reached them as a kind of affront. When Tom-tom spoke he seemed to be addressing them as much as Tristan. He waved his arm and clamped his rubbery mouth closed and then opened it again and cried, "In this family no one has ever been burned and you gonna have to burn me before I let you do it to Pinpin!"

Two

TRISTAN RENTS A CAR

It was a stand-off. Tristan knew how to steer past the reefs of his parents' angers. He was not one to boast—quietude had been (until Nanao) his most dearly won companion—but to himself he could say that he had always picked his way between Mom and Dad with such care that no one was bruised. Especially himself. (He did not know if he had inherited this trait or had picked it out for himself, as at a shop.) When he left for Yale almost a year ago he thought then that he had made it to the open sea. Like the time he first sailed alone in his own dinghy, the dinghy Owen had handed down to him, to the point at one end of their cove in Maine, and all of Penobscot Bay lay before him. What a calming sight, how purposeful he felt.

Not like now: here he was at the Hertz desk and he did not know how he had got there. How and when did he lose the helm?

Tom-tom was the difference. What would growing up have been like having to steer his way round this squat fat man?

A lifetime of being the innocent victim in a car accident, surely.

He got that image from his father's story of the accident in the Peugeot. Owen was in the backseat, he next to Dad. They were returning from Shea Stadium. Dad turned into Second Avenue after leaving the Midtown Tunnel and a car speeding away from a heist (the police later told Dad) hit them with considerable force. He had no memory of that, only of Dad's account, told throughout the years, of losing control of the car as well as of his temporal sense. The Peugeot skidded across the intersection in slow motion. It went on forever in silence, and the buildings at that corner that Dad knew so well, from trips in from Shea and the Hamptons, turned strange and more vivid—he read a small brass plaque he had never seen on that corner building—and also eerily dreamlike: was he hanging upside down as in a circus ride when he saw these things, skidding all the while? Dad's anecdote always ended the same: I used it in a script and it was dropped on the first rewrite, too much of a cliché. L.A., you know, the land of car accidents.

Was this a cliché?

This public embarrassment. Tristan had never experienced such an emotion. He had always known about privacy, always been shy, but shame was new to him. What was there to be ashamed about?

Tom-tom made him feel that no one should know that Grandpa was being cremated. Indeed, during the whole time he seemed to have been careening, like Dad in the Peugeot, before he came to a stop at the Hertz counter, there was only one thing Tristan remembered doing throughout. And that was stretching and looking about and then looking again to see if anyone in that airport was seeing or hearing Tom-tom. He was not sure. He was not sure of anything.

"What can we do for you?" said a very tanned blond girl behind the counter, and he held up a finger and pretended to look at his notebook. He was playing for time; he had lost his cool.

Tom-tom had lost his, too—in his way. Not about Pinpin being cremated—he had temporarily shelved that with a signal to the cousins to leave it to him—but about the Hertz desk. In the middle of it all, Tom-tom was overcome by this boy's ability to rent a car.

"Wait a minute, wait a minute," said Tom-tom. He pulled at Tristan's elbow, trying to draw him aside.

"Excuse me," Tristan said. "I will explain to you about the funeral soon, but now—"

"That's what I am talking about, this car business," he said in a confidential whisper. "Don't look so eager. They'll take advantage."

"Oh no," Tristan said. "It's a big company, they don't care." He took out his thick battered wallet, so changed from a year ago when Dad gave it to him for college. He took a deep breath and removed the credit card from it. The worst seemed over: Tom-tom had stopped talking about the funeral.

"You got one of those!" Tom-tom said. "Well, of course, it figures."

"Sir?"

"Is it a Visa or a MasterCard?" Tom-tom wanted to know.

Tristan looked at his credit card. It took him a moment to reply, "American Express."

Tom-tom's shoulders moved from side to side as if he were reeling from an assault. He stopped and appeared ready to wrestle a challenger. He looked back to the escalators, then the elevators. So did Tristan.

"What?" Tristan asked.

"They oughta see this," Tom-tom said. "A buncha small-town hicks. I lived in New York in the Depression, you know, I been around. I got Pinpin his first job."

Tristan waited to be sure he was finished. He knew already that it was not easy to keep one's balance with Tomtom if he were in some way unsatisfied. Physically, emotionally, the assault made itself felt. So he waited.

Tom-tom added, "He loved me like a brother." Then stared with an air of dissatisfaction and silently called for his due.

"Yes, sir," Tristan said.

"And now you, his grandson, is here—in Tampa!—with an American Express card. An American Express card! They watch TV. I want 'em to appreciate that—that's what I meant."

Tristan looked back over his shoulder for them. He did not know when they had disappeared. Disappeared? They had melted away as if he, Tristan, had turned into a leper. He took a second glance.

Tom-tom did not miss that gesture. "They left me to discuss with you—and we will, we will."

"Look," Tristan began in his reasoning tone, but stopped when Tom-tom threw back his head: he might start howling again.

But Tom-tom didn't. "We'll talk, you and me, we'll save Pinpin between us," he said, and poked Tristan's shoulder and added, "Go ahead, she's waiting."

"Hi," the girl said. "My name is Pat."

"Get up closer, Tris," Tom-tom said. "I can't hear from here." He pushed Tristan back along the counter and winked at the girl. "I don't hear so good but I'm still sharp—they can't put anything over on me."

She smiled and started over again. "Hi, my name is Pat."

"Hi," Tom-tom said.

"Do you have a compact car?" Tristan asked.

"Compact?" Tom-tom said.

Tristan explained, "I just need it for myself."

"Sure, sure," Tom-tom said and turned to the girl. "In good shape."

"Let's see," she said.

"Clean too," Tom-tom added. To Tristan: "Right?"

The girl looked up from her listings and smiled.

"Not dented or anything," Tom-tom said. "Okay, honey?"

"Sure," she said, humoring him.

"I'm gonna look it over before we go away, Pat," he said. "I was a mechanic for ten years, you know." He nudged Tristan. "You didn't know that, huh?" He smiled at the girl. "I'm his uncle, but he's never been in Tampa before. That's why he don't know." He insisted on her attention although she addressed Tristan. "About me being a mechanic. On American cars, though. I looked at a couple French cars—they had French cars too in those days—but mostly I worked on American cars. Inside out I know them. That's what you got, right? American cars?"

As soon as she could the girl said, "How long do you want it for?"

"A couple—" Tristan began, but Tom-tom cut him off.

Tom-tom grasped his arm above the elbow. "Don't answer that," he said. He looked at the girl and narrowed his eyes. "Why'd you want to know?"

"I—"

"What's the difference?" Tom-tom asked. "You gonna give him a good car either way?" He stepped back from the counter and threw out both arms. "Or am I wrong? Tell me, Pat. We might as well know now and not have a misunderstanding later."

"No, no," the girl said. "You're right—"

Tom-tom gave Tristan's arm a further squeeze. "You see? You gotta be alert."

"Let me explain why I asked," the girl said.

"Yeah, sure, honey," Tom-tom said. "We're friends here." He pushed Tristan further along the counter, so that he and the girl were face to face. "No misunderstandings; right,

Pat?" He looked sideways at Tristan graciously, as if he were generously including him also in the transaction. "Right, Tris?"

The girl now spoke only to Tom-tom. "Sometimes, if you're going to keep it three, four days only, it's cheaper to rent it for the whole week—"

Tom-tom said, "How about that!"

"Not only because of the price per day as compared to the weekly charge . . ." The girl paused to let her point sink in, but Tom-tom meant to interrupt her in any case, and did. With sagacity he asked, "The free mileage, are you referring to that, Pat?"

"You guessed it!"

Tristan saw that he need not have worried about the girl's feelings. She and Tom-tom got on very well. No one, very likely, had ever been as interested as Tom-tom in the niceties of car rentals. Still, he had better interrupt them. He had to get on. Let her know it was he (Tristan) who was renting the car and that all that comparative information about costs had no bearing on his intentions.

The two of them stopped talking and laughing simultaneously and he decided this was the best time to speak. "I'll take the compact then, if you have one. For two days, no more than three."

Tom-tom held up an arm as he had done with the cousins. "Not yet, not yet," he said and smiled at the girl to let her know his nephew was a precipitate fellow.

"That's all right," Tristan said and himself smiled, pleased at how equably he now could speak to Tom-tom. "I'm ready to go."

"There's three more these places," Tom-tom said. "At least. One of 'em may have a better deal."

Tristan shook his head and saw out of the corner of his eye that the girl was nodding at him and wanted him to sign up now. He also could hear Dad saying, Don't bargain, the most expensive *is* the best.

"Pat agrees with me, she's a sweetheart," Tom-tom said. "She said I could shop around. Am I right?"

"If you so desire, sir," the girl said.

"There is one called Budget Rent of a Car," Tom-tom said. "Get it?—budget!"

"That's all right," Tristan said. "I'm in a hurry."

"It's right here," Tom-tom insisted. "Budget is gotta be cheaper. They probably rent you a Ford, too." He turned to the girl. "Pat, Budget rents you a Ford?"

"I could not say for sure," she said. "You'll have to check with them what they have on hand."

"See?" Tom-tom said. "Let's check, Pat says so."

"No time, thanks," Tristan said, then added, "sir," in order not to sound unappreciative.

"I tell you what," the girl volunteered. "I'll give the gentleman a little better than a compact. A four-door Tempo. For the same price."

"Hey there, what'd I tell you!" Tom-tom exclaimed. He put an arm around Tristan and squeezed. "You're just like Pinpin, sure of himself, that's the way he acted with me all the time." He stopped and lowered his head in sorrow, shook it a little, then looked up at the girl first, as if he could not trust his emotions to look at Tristan. "His grandpa. My brother." He looked at Tristan, saw that he was somewhat preoccupied, and added, "Actually, my cousin, but we were close as brothers. You understand?"

The girl nodded sympathetically but did not allow her feelings to delay her work. She had taken Tristan's credit card, said, "Hi," when she read his name, as if they were being introduced, and began completing the sheaf of papers to draw up the order for the car. She asked solicitously, "And will you be requiring extra insurance?"

"Extra?" Tristan said.

Tom-tom was in favor of this. "You want every bit you can get," he urged.

"There is *some* insurance provided," the girl said.

"You know what these hick drivers are like?" he continued, ignoring the girl. "You never driven in Tampa—ha-ha! Course most of them are Yankees, right? Lots of new people down here, you know. It's a fast-growing area. Take it from me, you want to take all that insurance."

Tristan nodded and Tom-tom slapped him on the back. "Good boy," he said low. He watched the girl circle a row of entries on the form and he leaned towards her and asked conspiratorially, "What's that?"

She smiled and winked at Tristan: she understood the situation now. "That's where I'm going to ask your nephew to initial it." And she placed the papers on the counter and pointed to where he was to sign.

"Why?" Tom-tom asked.

"To show he accepts the extra charge," she said, smiled automatically, and turned away from them to get envelopes and more papers, all in a series of movements that should have been reassuring in their routinism.

Tom-tom reached out and stopped Tristan from signing. "Wait a minute, what's this gonna cost?"

Tristan said, "About five dollars a day, it says. That's okay."

"A day?" Tom-tom said. "You don't mind spending that?"

Tristan shook his head and signed.

"Yeah, you want all the insurance you can get," Tom-tom repeated.

"My folks would want me to," Tristan said, then wished he had not. It made him sound like a kid. He added, "I meant to, anyway," and that made him uncomfortable. It was not exactly a lie, but it was not true either.

The girl turned away again to check the credit card. Tom-tom squeezed him once more. "I'm gonna drive now. I know the way and how these hick drivers drive and that way we can talk on the way. We got a lot of things to talk about, you know." And his brows turned down and his look dark, but before Tristan could say yes or no to any of that, he exclaimed, "Hey, they still call bad drivers Jersey Drivers? I'll never forget that, Tris. Sometimes one of these hicks down here makes a wrong move and I yell after them, Jersey Driver!"

Tristan said yes and hoped that he had not said yes to talking about the funeral and whatever else was on Tom-tom's mind.

He had the feeling that all this fell under the category of family love and he was not sure he liked it.

"You know what we call em here?—*paragueros!* You know what that means? People that carries umbrellas. Isn't that something? I don't know why." He frowned and lowered his voice. "I didn't mean to say that—it's not good going round talking Spanish."

He made sure Pat was not listening. "You know Spanish?"

Tristan shook his head.

"Sure," Tom-tom said. "Sure." He frowned. "Maybe you oughta learn. A little, anyway."

Somehow he had said yes to everything Tom-tom proposed. That's what it felt like. The car's papers in his hand, thinking over whether there was any more information he needed from the Hertz girl, he called up the judicious statements he should have used with Tom-tom. He should have merely said, I'll think this over, I must think that over, let me think it over. In a neutral tone of voice, promising nothing, denying nothing.

No, those would have been cowardly responses, fit only for bureaucrats. Like the Yale administrators his committee had dealt with. Think over whether to divest? What finks.

He had, in any case, said no to changing the schedule for the cremation. But had he? Unequivocally? It had been Tom-tom who acted as if it could be put off. Wasn't that a presumption on his part? In which case he (Tristan) should have made himself clear.

But would that have been considerate?

All this went through his mind in an orderly fashion while that girl Pat awaited his goodbye with an eager questioning look. Tom-tom pulled him away. He was barely able to nod to her and call, "Thank you."

Three steps away from the desk, Tom-tom said, "Wait," and went back to the girl by himself. Tristan let him go and tried not to listen. Tom-tom whispered to her, but you would have had to be deaf not to hear. "If he gets into an accident, what's he gonna do?"

"Do?" she repeated, then recovered. "Report it to the police and call us."

"The police?" Tom-tom said in his normal voice, then whispered, "We gotta bring them into it?"

"Just call us," she said. "We'll let you know what to do."

Tom-tom thought that over.

"Don't worry," she said.

"Naw, naw, I'm not worried," he said. "I was just asking. He's a good driver, my boy."

The girl nodded pleasantly and waved a hand to Tristan that signaled him Don't be embarrassed, I understand.

That girl didn't really know what Tom-tom was capable of doing—wow. His contemplation of her innocence made him smile and she took it for agreement. He almost laughed aloud.

"Let's get out of here," Tom-tom told Tristan when he got back to him. "I think she's after you, she's sweet on you."

That, Tristan could understand—that old-fashioned adult way of thinking girls deliberately set out after boys.

That's what Tom-tom was—old-fashioned. He must remember that. And the cultural difference. And Tom-tom's good intentions. Yes.

Tom-tom squeezed him and he had to admit it made him feel good. In public and all, as Nanao would say. He even enjoyed knowing they must make a funny pair. He a foot taller, Tom-tom a foot wider. Hey, here he was in Tampa!

Oh, those tree-shaded lawns—middle America. Grandpa's hometown.

If Tom-tom held out one of his meaty hands and he took it in his own, it would feel natural. His hand up in Grandpa's, those summer days in Maine, walking in the woods looking for toads. He had had to teach Grandpa the difference between toads and frogs. The memory made him smile more broadly than usual, and Tom-tom was pleased, as if he had succeeded with a secret plan. Tristan saw that and let him think so.

Tom-tom winked at Tristan, then said, "This way," and gripped his elbow firmly and led him towards the arrival doors.

Tristan was glad to be led. "Were you a cigarmaker?" he asked.

"Are you kidding?"

"You were?"

Tom-tom stopped, held Tristan's elbow harder, and looked him in the eye, the way TV detectives questioned suspects. "I guess I'm gonna have to teach you about Ybor City. You came to the right guy."

"Why is it called Ybor City?"

Tom-tom did not have a ready answer. "We call it that," he said after a pause.

"Is it a name?" Tristan asked.

"Sure it's a name," Tom-tom said. "That's its name, Ybor City. We call it Ybor City, that's a name."

Tom-tom studied Tristan carefully, displaying a kindly look as he did so, as if the boy might, through no fault of his own, be intellectually deficient.

Tristan did not think he should in any way correct him. Instead, he said, "Yes, sir."

Ahead were the automatic doors leading to the broad sidewalk where cars unloaded and taxis arrived and where the Hertz bus would soon pick them up.

"Wait, wait, it's hot out there," Tom-tom said. "Listen, my

boy, that was very pretty. I mean that "yes sir" is nice to hear. But you gotta call me something else. Tom-tom. We're gonna be together a lot. Okay, I'm like your uncle, right? Call me Uncle Tom-tom. Okay?"

"Yes, sir," Tristan said.

"Come on, say it," Tom-tom said. "Uncle Tom-tom," and further urged him with a slap on the buttocks.

Tristan took two involuntary steps forward and said, "Uncle Tom-tom."

He let Tom-tom have his way. After all, letting people have their way was letting them have their freedom. So long as it did not, of course, restrict one—lose one one's freedom, that is. They had had long discussions at Buxton about this concept, so that by the time he had got to Yale last September it was already an axiom with Tristan.

In Tom-tom's view Tristan caved in, but he would have described it, to others, as his being a sweet boy. He tested his victory in several ways.

Before the Hertz minibus arrived he had gotten the rental papers in his hands and checked them out. "I forgot my reading glasses," he said after peering at them, and returned them to Tristan. "You know it's a waste of money. I got an extra car at my house. But that's okay. I was young once."

Tom-tom was only expressing his chagrin that he could not read the Hertz contract with ease, but Tristan felt the stirrings of guilt, an underdeveloped feeling with him.

Right after that Tom-tom said, "Don't you worry, we'll give your father a call." Then he winked and stroked Tristan's shoulder. What could he mean? What was there to talk to Dad about that involved Tom-tom? The funeral? Tom-tom repeated, "Don't you worry," just as he was about to ask. ESP?

A loud sigh from Tom-tom preceded: "I'll get this all straightened out. You sure your mother and father not coming? People can walk around in a plaster cast. He remembers me—he and me were pals. I only met your mother once." It sounded like a fault of hers.

Just before the Hertz bus arrived he got onto the subject of Grandpa's house. "I'm worried about leaving all those things in the house alone, but I couldn't let you arrive here all by yourself. On this sad occasion. I promised Pinpin. I promised him. Marina and the others go on about such things, but not me. I don't talk about it. In life we were close, that's all that matters. I don't have to inherit the things he said were for me. I am not mercenary. I hate people like that." He leaned over and looked close into Tristan's eyes and asked fiercely, "Don't you?"

Once, he muttered to himself, "I hope they're not cleaning the place out."

Tom-tom sat close to the bus driver. "Are you a Tampa boy?" he asked the man, a leathery fellow well past his youth.

"Memphis," the man said and volunteered a short autobiography. Tom-tom said, "Is that a fact," a couple of times and that encouraged the fellow each time to offer more details.

Tristan listened to the accents while looking out the window and worried about racism.

The road inclined leaving the airport proper, but it all looked flatter than any landscape he had ever seen. In fact, the slope looked man-made. It was hot. The air-conditioning did not entirely filter out the soggy heat. The strong sun shone from every direction; it came at you from all angles, not just from overhead, as if a theater lighting man had overdone the tropical setting. There were even ornamental palm trees, but he had seen those in California. They were more settled out there: here everything seemed to have been recently put together.

But that could not be, could it? Hadn't Florida been around longer than California?

At the Hertz parking lot, Tom-tom kicked at the car's tires, circled the car, feeling for dents in some spots, and checked that the inside was clean. He took the keys from Tristan to open the trunk, then slammed it closed to see that it caught properly, and went over to the driver's side and opened the door with a flourish.

"It's only got four hundred miles or so," said the attendant who at Tom-tom's insistence had come out to the car with them.

"We know there's ways of fixing that, right?" Tom-tom said and peered at the dashboard. "Course I believe you, I ain't doubting your word."

"You can always have another one," the fellow said.

Tom-tom snorted at that and said this one would do, reluctantly, as if it was too much bother to insist on a good car. But he shook hands before he dismissed him, and said, "Can't be too careful, you understand?" and winked and watched him leave before he turned to Tristan again.

"Tris," he said and paused. He paused only a second, but long enough for Tristan to think *what now?* "You get in next to the driver. I'm getting in behind the wheel."

"You think that's wise?" Tristan said.

"You don't want me to drive?"

"I told the girl back there only I would be driving the car," Tristan explained. "I don't mind you driving at all, Uncle Tom-tom."

"Then let's go," Tom-tom said. "We don't have to tell her nothing. I don't want you driving in these crazy streets until you get used to Tampa traffic. You know what I mean? Especially since you don't know the way."

Tristan watched him squeeze into the driver's seat and only then got in himself.

Tom-tom experimented with the position of the seat, sliding it forward, banging into the wheel with his belly and groaning, and then sliding it back and sighing. "I gotta get it just right," he explained and Tristan could see him jiggling his right foot to make sure he could reach the accelerator without stretching. "I like to be careful," he added.

"Sure," Tristan said.

"You got your seat belt on?" he asked sternly.

"Yes, sir," Tristan said.

"Push forward with it," Tom-tom said.

Tristan leaned forward slightly. "It'll be all right," he said.

Tom-tom grabbed the seat belt, banging Tristan on the ribs as he did so. The belt would not, when pulled forward violently all the way, have allowed Tristan to hit the dashboard.

Tom-tom grunted his approval. "That's how you check it," he added. "You ready?"

"I'm ready for takeoff," Tristan said and smiled, but Tom-tom remained serious.

"Okay, here we go," he said. "You gonna see I'm careful, I do *not* speed, I ain't no cowboy."

A car honked loud and long when he turned into the road without checking. It passed them and the man behind its wheel waved at them angrily. Tom-tom did not look his way. He glanced at Tristan and smiled. He was finally content.

To be sociable, Tristan said, "Cousin Marina said I should get on Columbus Drive until I get to Fifteenth Street and then turn left."

"What does she know!" Tom-tom said and hit the wheel for emphasis. "What business has she telling you anything? I could tell you things about her anytime you want to know. You just ask me, I'll tell you what she is really like."

Tristan wanted to avoid that, so he said, "That's not the way to get there?"

"There is many a way to go to any place; right, Tris?" Tom-tom said. "But we're not going there. We're going to my home. It's on the way. Olivia wants to see you and she can't go out."

"Now?" Tristan said and frowned. "Is this the right time?"

"No, later will be impossible," Tom-tom said. "I wouldn't let you take time off from all the important things we have to do. No use asking me later to take you to Olivia when we gonna have our hands full. Now is the time."

The only other occasion on which Tristan had come up against an immovable power was at Yale when he and others, after the arrests and the arraignments that had been fun of a sort, had been disciplined by the school committee. Probation for him and dismissal anytime during the next four years if he committed any offense. What you said to that committee had no effect. That's the way it was with mighty institutions, he had learned; you had to calculate all your movements in advance. But was Tom-tom a mighty institution?

Tom-tom changed his tone. "It will make Olivia so happy," he said. "She won't keep you, she just wants to take a look at you. Don't say no to Olivia." He turned to Tristan and looked at him so long that Tristan was afraid for the car.

Tristan frowned again. "Who is Olivia? Do I know her?"

Tom-tom smacked the steering wheel hard, startling Tristan, and turned full-face to him. He had an anguished look now, reminding Tristan of the sad frogs of his childhood television programs. "I told your grandpa that's what would happen!" he exclaimed. "And I was right. I told Pinpin, if you don't let your sons and grandsons come see ya down in Tampa, the day will come when they won't know their own cousins. And you don't!"

Tristan nodded; he didn't know why.

"Olivia is my wife," Tom-tom said sadly, his eyes still on him. He shook his head at two honking cars into whose lane he had drifted. "She's as good as an aunt, you could say. Practically a blood relation. We have been married fifty years and then some."

How best tell him to go on to Grandpa's house now?

Tom-tom threw out his right arm without warning and banged it across Tristan's chest. "There's Dale Mabry! Three, four miles of everything you can think of—stores, business, hotels, you name it. Who'd have thought, huh? One more block and we turn right—"

"Wait," Tristan said, but it came out so low he knew Tom-tom would not pay attention.

"Look over there! That's the Tampa Stadium! West Tampa! Who'd have thought, huh? I shoulda bought more than just one lot when I came back from the war. Here we go."

And he turned into a side street. No signs or shops or business of any kind, though the street backed up against Dale Mabry, a strip of what his Dad called New Jersey. The side street was also New Jersey. Another part of it: one-family homes, mostly clapboard, some stucco. Trees, but no shadows. Sunbaked America: the light reached into every corner.

Tristan rolled down the window and an unfamiliar heat and smell (as of overcooked air and grass) reached him and he automatically began breathing shallowly. If he closed the window again, would that look like criticism?

"Don't waste the air-conditioning!" Tom-tom said. He honked the horn and opened his own window and waved at an old man standing at the end of a short lawn planted in that funny grass. "Fried Eggs, look at my new car!" he yelled and the old man jumped and stared, a frightened half-smile on his face. "Wake up, you old thief!"

The old man continued staring and never waved back.

"He's failing fast too. He didn't recognize me—I think they gave us some bad medicine and it caught up with us," Tom-tom said. "And French Fries was the best shortstop the Tampa team ever had. Quick as a squirrel."

"What team?" Tristan said.

"That was sixty years ago, it's no use explaining," Tom-tom said. "Nobody remembers. Tampa Smokers. And Fried Eggs, he was the master of the double play. Look at him now—he can't make it to the sidewalk."

Why had he asked? He should be insisting Tom-tom go on to Grandpa's house.

"I'm turning," Tom-tom announced. He pointed. "To the right."

Tristan noticed that Tom-tom made wide turns as if he figured that the car needed as much room as his body to maneuver. A car coming towards them had to stop, and the driver leaned his head out and said, "What the hell!"

Tom-tom did not look his way or reply or twitch or anything.

Tristan did not know why, but he felt endangered.

He said, "I really think I should be getting on to—"

"We're right there, one more block," Tom-tom said. He pointed. "Right there at the corner. I got a corner lot. I'm turning into the driveway."

Okay, Tristan thought. It was a short block and an old American car was parked beyond the driveway. Red and highly polished.

"That's my other car," Tom-tom said and began his turn.

Why was he surprised the car was clean and cared for? Racism? Tristan relaxed, he could deal with that.

"The door by the driver needs fixing," Tom-tom said and was making the turn so wide it looked as if he might overshoot the driveway.

Tristan's fear returned. "Aren't you going in here—?"

Tristan did not know if he asked the question aloud. Tom-tom's right arm shot out and pinned him back against the seat. With his other hand he steered the car deliberately—Tristan was certain of this—into the red parked car, accelerating as they crashed. So astonishing a crash that it seemed to be happening quietly, as in a dream.

"Shit!" Tom-tom said, quickly backed up, and once more drove into the red car and again threw out his right arm to hold Tristan back. This time Tristan heard the bang—the rattled pots of his childhood games magnified—and saw that Tom-tom smiled all the while. "That oughta do it," Tom-tom said.

* * *

"You did it on purpose!" Tristan exclaimed. "I don't believe it! Why did you do it?"

"You all right?" Tom-tom said. "You not hurt, are you?"

Tristan wanted confirmation. "You hit it on purpose, didn't you? Your own car!"

He told himself he must be calm, but he needed to know: it was all too unreasonable. He could not get Tom-tom's attention. He repeated, "Why did you do it? We could've had a serious accident."

He heard in his own voice the tone of the Yale bureaucrats.

Had Tom-tom heard him? He turned away from Tristan, wriggling his broad body out the door in fast side-to-side motions. He skipped to his old car and bent over and looked closely at its side. He kicked it once. Twice. For fun, it seemed the second time. Was he crazy? Tristan started out but stopped when Tom-tom turned back to the rented car and bent once more and peered at its front fender. God, Tristan thought, don't let it be messed up. Tom-tom straightened and looked happily at Tristan through the windshield. He threw out his arms and called, "It's perfect now, perfect!"

Tristan managed the door of the car easily but was almost strangled by his seat belt. He was out before Tom-tom could say any more. The thick black fender looked okay. Its composition protected it. Those great new alloys. He had no esthetic objections like Mom and Dad.

He said, almost with a sigh, "Oh, at least there's been no damage."

"Yeah," Tom-tom said and threw an arm happily over Tristan's shoulder. "They only got to pay for my car."

"Your car!" Tristan said. "Pay for what?"

"Not the whole car," Tom-tom explained. "Just the dent on the door, etcetera."

"What do you mean?" Tristan said. "Who's going to pay? Why should anyone pay you?"

"Come on," Tom-tom said. He propelled him with his arm toward the cement-brick house. "You gotta tell them. Might as well do it now."

"Tell whom?" Tristan said. "Tell them what?"

Tom-tom did not let go of his arm. "First, you say hello to Olivia, then you call the girl."

"Olivia?" Tristan got that disoriented feeling that had overcome him when all the cousins moved in on him at the airport. Tom-tom's painful grasp of his elbow kept him from thinking things through. "That's . . . ?"

The hand let go. Tom-tom needed it to gesture. "You forgot! She's gonna be hurt. She's your cousin. By marriage, but your cousin."

"Oh yes, your wife." Things began to come into focus and he added, "I'm sorry," but thought, he banged up the car on purpose. He actually did. He was sure of that. He said, "I've got to get right on to Grandpa's home—"

Tom-tom stepped in front of him, leaned his face into his, and opened his eyes wide. "Wait a minute," he said. "Olivia is not right. But she is gonna appreciate your coming. What's there in life for her now?"

"Only for a moment," Tristan said and was pleased that he sounded so firm. It gave him the courage to add, "I'll be doing the driving from now on."

"Okay, okay," Tom-tom agreed. "But you'll call the girl first."

"What girl?" Tristan said, then tried hesitantly, "Nanao?"

"Nanao, what's that? Pat. Pat was her name," Tom-tom said. "Nanao's no name. It's not even Spanish."

Tom-tom opened the screen door of his home and motioned him in.

"The Hertz girl?" Tristan said. "Why should I call her?"

"You gotta call her," Tom-tom said. "She said so."

"Only if I got into any trouble," Tristan said and stepped into the house. "There's no need to."

There were two old women inside, one in a wheelchair. One said, "Tom-tom, she—"

That was all he heard or saw in the dark innards of the house. Tom-tom grabbed his elbow again and pulled him back into the sunlight. Tristan's head snapped back and he said more loudly than he meant, "What!"

Tom-tom answered urgently. "If you get into an accident, she said, remember? So you call her from here, I got a phone." He leaned his head back and yelled through the screen door, "Shut up!" Inside, one old woman continued to call for Tom-tom. He placed his bulk in front of the door and stood guard and waited. "You gotta report the accident to the police too."

"I haven't had an accident," Tristan said with composure. He knew now what Tom-tom was about. Rather, suspected. Damn, he thought, I shouldn't give him the benefit of the doubt—I know. He wanted all that extra insurance to pay for his dented car.

Tom-tom pointed to the cars at the curb. "What was that happened back there? Lookit my car. It wasn't an accident?"

A neighbor across the street stepped out of his house and stood at the top of his red cement steps. He wore an old-fashioned undershirt, shorts so tacky they were now fashionable, and no shoes.

"I didn't have an accident," Tristan said. "And their car's okay."

"Their car?" Tom-tom said loudly. "What car's okay?"

Tristan's reply was almost hushed—he did not want the neighbor to think they were arguing—but his voice did not quaver. "My car," he said. "The Hertz car."

For a moment Tom-tom's face—his wobbly jowls, the lined pouches hanging from his eyes, the folds of fat under his chin—settled into a look of apprehension and sadness. He had not foreseen defeat and now it was in sight. His fearfulness reached Tristan and he felt sorry for causing it. Felt guilt too, for being privileged.

"Who's worrying about Hertz?" Tom-tom raised his chin and called out across the narrow street, "Something bothering you?" and waited.

The man first looked away, then went inside slowly without answering, but slammed the door hard.

"The son of a bitch reported me when Olivia was in the hospital and I didn't have the time to mow the lawn."

"Oh," Tristan said.

"So I reported him for no top to his garbage can." Tom-tom chewed his lips. "Damn cracker, he ain't a Latin like you and me. In the old days everybody on the block was your own kind. You know." The thought that Tristan might not, indeed, know stopped him. "So you're gonna call Pat?"

"There's no reason," Tristan said.

"They'll fix my car, Tris!" He grabbed his elbow again. "You tell her first and then we report it to the police and that's that—they fix it."

"I can't do that," Tristan said.

"I understand that—you're shy," Tom-tom said and with his free hand patted him on the buttocks. "But you know Pat, she likes you, it's no problem talking to her. You call her and I'll call the police, I'll do that for you. After all, it's my car that was hit—it's me should call the police."

Tristan shook his head.

"I'll dial the number and say hello to her and then I'll put you on," Tom-tom said. "How's that?"

He patted Tristan's buttocks again.

Tristan emitted a strangled sound.

"Whatcha said?" Tom-tom asked gently. "How about it?"

"Sir," Tristan began.

"Uncle Tom-tom," Tom-tom said and placed a heavy hand on his shoulder. "Remember?"

"Uncle Tom-tom," Tristan said.

"So? Whaddya say?"

"I can't do it," Tristan said quickly.

"Do what? I said I'd practically do it for you."

"I cannot tell Hertz there was an accident and all that . . ."

Tom-tom peered at him.

Tristan added, "Uncle Tom-tom," but that did not seem to help.

"What I do wrong?" Tom-tom said accusingly. "I didn't say it nice? I didn't go to Harvard, you know."

Tristan shook his head.

"I mean Yale," Tom-tom said. He waited. "Whaddya say?"

Tristan looked down at his feet and saw that his loafers were properly scruffy.

"What are we doing here?" Tom-tom said. "Let's go inside and I'll explain it to you."

Tristan shook his head and Tom-tom exclaimed, "Don't say anything now. Nothing's working out! You go inside." He took Tristan's elbow again and turned him towards the screen door, reached over and opened it, and propelled him into the house. Tristan fell into the old woman's arms.

"I don't believe it!" she said to Tom-tom. She removed one of her withered hands from Tristan's back, leaned a little out of the close hug in which she had grasped him, and reached up to his face and stroked it with her bony beringed fingers. "You don't have to tell me, Tom-tom. I'da picked him out anywhere."

"Lila—" Tom-tom protested.

"I said you don't have to tell me, I tell you," she said and Tristan flinched at the feel of her rings. "The image of Aunt Mama. Lookit him. The same beautiful eyes, like those nuts. I forgot. Almonds! Ha-ha! You heard of almond-shaped eyes? He's got them. And that aristocracy nose."

Tristan smiled but said nothing: he could see beyond her the woman in the wheelchair staring at the floor and in slow motion reaching down for something. What?

The woman in the wheelchair was picking up her dress.

"Okay, Lila, make it short," Tom-tom said. "We have a lot of things to do."

Lila did not look Tom-tom's way. She brought her face

close to Tristan's and placed a cheek against his and smacked her lips in midair. Then she faced him in closeup and smiled and winked. "I don't want to mess my makeup. Or getcha into trouble with your girlfriend—ha-ha!"

Her lipstick ran into the valleys of wrinkles that radiated from her lips. He had never been that close to a lady that old.

"I'm Lila," she said and puckered her lips into an eruption of wet lipstick and brilliantly white dentures. "Your grandpa's cousin. He was so good to me. *Aiee, aiee!* He loved me!" she wailed. "I'm gonna ruin my makeup. The things he gave me, I never got a chance to pick them all up. Some are still at the old house. There's nothing he wouldn't do for me and now he's gone! What am I gonna do without him?"

"For crissakes," Tom-tom said.

"There are some things you can't hold back," Lila argued. She hit her chest with one hand for emphasis and caught a ring on one of her chain necklaces. "Oh God, help me, help me."

Tom-tom pushed her aside. "Here's Olivia," he said to Tristan and pulled him to an easy chair across from the invalid in the wheelchair.

Tristan bounced on its hard seat and noted a familiar smell in the air. He knew it from the doorways in the Village where the homeless slept. Urine.

"You smell it?" Lila said and rearranged the necklaces on her flat bosom. "Tom-tom, she's gotta be changed."

"Wait a minute," Tom-tom said.

"Who was at the airport?" Lila asked Tristan. "My sister Clemencia, I bet—Aunt Clem, she calls herself. She can get away for everything, but she's let herself go. Ugh, no shape whatsoever. Never mind, she's a good kid, I love her."

"I'm gonna ring them up," Tom-tom said, pointing to Tristan. "And I'll call you when she comes on."

Tom-tom waited a moment, but Tristan watched Olivia and seemed not to have heard.

"Who else was there?" Lila asked. Without looking she extended a hand and pulled down Olivia's dress.

"What about Maggie?" she asked. "Was she there?"

Olivia emitted a thin, muted sigh. She reached down again and picked up the hem of her dress between forefinger and thumb and slowly began to draw it up. To Tristan she looked mongoloid, but that could not be, he told himself.

"That's all she does. Pitiful. Allzetime, that's what the doctor says," Lila said. "Was Marina there? Oh no, I forgot she won't leave the house. I'm getting allzetime myself. She says she has to guard the house. Can you beat that! You better watch out for her—she'll take everything. Even the things Pinpin promised me."

Tristan did not believe they should speak about Olivia in her presence, but if she heard, she did not pay attention. She had once more got hold of the hem of her dress and lifted it past the midway point to her head, exposing gray underwear such as he had never seen. Her legs were mottled and bloodless.

Lila followed his glance, pulled Olivia's dress down firmly, plunked a worn teddy bear in her lap, and laughed. "It's no use talking to her," she said. She turned quickly to Olivia, leaned her head down, and shook her head so that her earrings flew. "Right, Olivia, you don't understand, right? You don't understand *anything,* right, honey?" She raised her voice to a shriek. "Tom-tom, you gotta change her!"

Tom-tom came to the kitchen doorway, the phone in one hand. "Tris, they got me on hold. You wanna take it now? They just playing music. You don't need me to introduce you and I can change Olivia, okay?"

Tristan got up, then sat down carefully and shook his head.

Tom-tom spoke in a reasonable voice. "Okay, I'll wait until she comes on. Then I'll call you."

"I won't do it, Uncle Tom-tom," Tristan said.

Lila laughed. "Uncle Tom-tom? Ha-ha! He's not your un-

cle. He's your cousin. Not even. Did he tell you that? If he's your uncle, I'm your aunt."

"Lila, watch out for her," Tom-tom yelled.

Olivia was bent forward from the waist. She still stared straight ahead, unseeingly, her jaw slack, her hands hanging at her sides.

"I shoulda used the strap on her," Lila said, "but I feel sorry tying her to the chair like that."

"For crissakes," Tom-tom said and stepped back out of sight.

Lila leaned towards Tristan as far as she could go, her necklaces and earrings dangling below her knees. She whispered, "What's Tom-tom up to? What's he want from you?"

"It's all right," Tristan said. "It's nothing."

"Don't give him the chased lounge," she hissed. "Pinpin promised it to me. I got nothing to lie on in my apartment."

She placed a finger to her lips for just a second and beckoned Tristan closer. "What's he up to? You can tell *me*."

Tom-tom was talking into the phone. He sounded jolly, but Tristan was so upset he could not make out the words. "Excuse me," he said to Lila, and got up and went out the front door.

The neighbor across the street was out again. He had walked to the edge of his short, coarse lawn and was staring at the rented car. He shifted his wary but inquisitive look to Tristan.

Inside, Tom-tom yelled, "Tris, Tris—did he go to the bathroom? Lila!"

"It didn't work, did it?" she said to Tom-tom. "You think I was born the day before yesterday, huh? I saw you banging away at your *fotingo,* ha-ha!"

"Shut up," Tom-tom said.

The screen door opened, pushing Tristan forward. He turned and Tom-tom's face glowered a few inches away. "I'm sorry," Tristan said automatically.

"You're just like your grandpa!" Tom-tom said. He saw

the man across the street standing at the curb and yelled, "Whaddya want?" The man gave Tom-tom the finger, turned his back on them, and slowly walked back to his front door. Tom-tom growled, then whispered, "Listen, I'll call Pat back. She's ready to be of service. Think it over—help me out."

Tristan shook his head.

"Okay, okay," Tom-tom said and hurriedly retreated into the house. "For crissakes," he said inside to Lila, "Push her in the bedroom. I'm not gonna change her here."

When Tristan went back in, Lila and Olivia were gone from the living room and Tom-tom stood in the kitchen doorway talking into the phone.

"You know how it is, he is not well disposed now," he said in his Southern voice. "He is shook up, honey. No, no, no, he is not injured, not at all. Just my car—an itsy-bitsy dent, but it'll rust if I don't do something about it."

He saw Tristan enter and waved at him as at a passing acquaintance.

"Uh-huh, yes, honey," he continued on the phone. He frowned. "Okay," he said and hung up. He banged the kitchen door with one hand. "Shit!" he said.

"I'm sorry," Tristan said.

"Let's not talk about it," Tom-tom said and waved his arms as if to erase all that had gone before. "We'll forget about it, for now."

Tom-tom opened the door to the bedroom, turned back and said, "Tris?," changed his mind, and closed the door behind him.

Tristan thought, it must be weird to change her. Even if they were doing it in this room he was sure he wouldn't look.

He could hear Lila yell, "Hold her up! Hold her up!"

Tristan got halfway up from his chair.

"Get out of here!" Tom-tom replied.

Tristan sat.

"You don't appreciate anything," Lila said, but she got out

of the bedroom eagerly. She stopped in front of Tristan, leaned down, and smiled at him, almost touching her nose to his.

He flinched but Lila did not notice.

Tom-tom yelled through the closed door, "Don't bother Tristan, you hear?"

"I hear!" she yelled back, but did not move away from him. She whispered, "I want a souvenir of Pinpin. Anything, honey, any little thing. I'm gonna die soon anyway, so I don't have any selfish reason."

"Sure," Tristan said quickly, then added, "I mean, about the souvenir."

"Ha-ha!" Lila said.

"Whatever he wanted to give you," Tristan said.

"The sofa and easy chairs," Lila said, cupping a hand over her mouth. "The linens and the wineglasses with the gold edge. And of course the chased lounge." With an effort she held her eyes open wide and waited for Tristan to object. "I won't ask for the curtains and the air conditioners," she added after a moment. "Marina's got her eyes on them."

Dad and Mom had said, get rid of it all. Did they want him to give it away? He said, "I have to talk to my family about all that."

"Sure," Lila said and patted his knee, but a film of disappointment veiled her eyes. "Sure," she repeated, certain of defeat, and seated herself across from him.

Tristan was not happy with himself.

She thought of something to cheer herself up. "What's your name?" she asked him.

"Tristan," he said.

"No, your last one."

"Granados?" he said.

"Oh, you're like everybody else. Spanish–ha-ha!" She winked and made a large arc through the air with one hand, dismissing the whole notion. "I got an American name now from my second husband. Dupee! Do you believe it!"

"It probably comes from the French," Tristan said.

"Is that a fact?" Lila said. "How about that! And I thought I was a regular American. I mean, you know what I mean. Poor Conrad, he didn't know it either. He was from New Jersey. Is there a lot of French up there?"

Tristan thought it over, but Lila did not wait for his answer.

"Conrad died last year," she said. "Just like that. Right in the middle of something I was saying. I haven't been the same since. I'm practically a charity case here. I live next door in one of Tom-tom's apartments. I came down screaming when it happened, they must of heard me all over the block. Tom-tom thinks I oughta move into here, so's he can rent the apartment. Can you blame him?"

Again he tried to reason out a reply, but she went on anyway.

"But I like to be independent. I really do. None of that living all in one house like the old Ybor City Latins. I mean, Hispanics. I don't worry about break-ins and muggers and rapemen, it's gonna happen, it happens. Even if I can't always pay the rent. Tom-tom is okay—don't go by appearances. You know, you never know. Right?"

This time Tristan simply shook his head.

Lila moved to the edge of her seat. She motioned him towards her for a confidential exchange. "Don't tell nobody I told you he owns those eight apartments. He don't want people to know. So many cousins and brothers and sisters and nieces and nephews, you know. They'd be all over him. But of course it's okay if you know, 'cause you don't need anything, right?"

Tristan did not answer. He was ashamed that he did not.

This time she did wait for him to respond, and when he said nothing, whispered, "Is it true your family is rich?"

"Rich?" Tristan said, and the bedroom door opened with a bang and saved him from answering her terrible question.

"Whaddya bothering him about?" Tom-tom said. "Tris, don't pay her any attention."

"He's my cousin too, you know," Lila said and turned to Tristan. "Isn't that so, honey?" But she placated Tom-tom by running to the wheelchair and maneuvering it back to the couch, and he sat and faced Olivia. She reached out and gently pulled the sleeve of the dress as if it needed straightening. "Olivia, you looking positively dressed up. Your Tom-tom did right by you."

"Why you talking to her for?" Tom-tom said.

Olivia looked up and saw Tristan. At least, he thought she did; her eyes stopped at him, in any case. The hand that had started to reach for the hem of her clean new dress came up and grabbed the inert other hand. Her face began a movement beneath the skin. Her jaw swung to one side and then back. She whispered in a sweet low voice, "You never loved me."

Tom-tom pushed Lila to one side of the sofa and sat by Olivia's wheelchair. "Here I am," he said to Olivia. He took one of her hands. "Your Tom-tom is right here. I love you, you know that."

Olivia looked across at Tristan again and said clearly, "Momma, momma."

Tom-tom laughed a young man's laugh. "No, no, Tom-tom's here. What do you want?"

Lila grimaced and pulled a long face. "Naw, she can't understand anything. I do believe she can't hear." She leaned towards the wheelchair. "Olivia! Olivia! What do you say to Tom-tom?" She clapped her hands. "See, she don't know anything."

"Momma?" Olivia said. A tear rolled down her right cheek.

"No, baby honey sugar, it's Tom-tom," he said in his youthful voice. "You hear, sweet baby girl?"

"Naw," said Lila. "She don't hear."

"Yeah, you're right," he said and got up, pushing himself

up with a groan and placing both hands on his knees to make a springboard. “Let’s go, Tris, we been farting around here long enough. We got a funeral to arrange.”

Tristan heard him but felt too sorry for him to remind him there was not going to be a funeral.

Lila exclaimed, “Tom-tom, I’m surprised at you, you never talk dirty.” She edged up to Olivia to ward off the hand that reached once more for the hem of her dress. “And in front of you,” she said to Tristan. “I hate people who say dirty words. Conrad never did and . . . and . . .” She bent over and laughed hard. “Tom-tom, I forgot my first husband’s name—what was it?”

Tom-tom did not seem to believe in answering Lila, and Tristan could not stop watching Olivia. He had become used to Lila, but with Olivia it was as if he had been warned not to look and consequently could not help himself. Tom-tom had to tap him on the shoulder to rouse him.

“Coming,” Tristan said, as he had responded all winter at the dorm when Skitch, his roommate, woke him. God, would he fall into a coma like that too?

“You gonna meet the rest of them at the old house,” Tom-tom said. “I better warn you.”

“Ha-ha!” Lila said. “Warn him, is right.”

“You seen the best of us,” Tom-tom said and touched himself on the chest. “And that’s not saying much.”

Lila waved a hand at Tristan. “Don’t listen to him. Tom-tom, you know we’re pretty good.”

“Yeah?” Tom-tom said. “Name one.”

“We’re just folks,” Lila insisted. “Except for my granddaughter Tamara—she’s special. How old are you?”

Tom-tom tapped him again, still looking defeated. “I’m gonna tell you what your grandfather thought.”

“That’s not fair,” Lila said.

“My grandfather?” Tristan asked.

“Pinpin thought . . . maybe I oughta tell you in the car going there.” Tom-tom sighed and became quiet. “He thought . . . well, we were a big disappointment to him, him being a writer and all that. He was right too." He pointed to Lila. "And don't you contradict me."

"Okay, okay," Lila said, but she grimaced and winked at Tristan. "Who am I to say anything?"

"I'm disappointed in myself," Tom-tom said. "We're just a bunch of Americans now."

Tristan got up. He said, "Of course you're Americans. You're as good as anybody else."

Tom-tom sighed again. "I didn't mean that. I mean we're as bad as the crackers."

"Oh," Tristan said. How terrific, he thought, but he did not know what to say himself.

Tom-tom looked at him as if he knew what was going on in his head. He threw an arm over his shoulders and pulled him towards him. Then said, trying a new tack altogether, "We can't call your father now, huh?"

"Dad?" Tristan said.

"That what you call him?" Tom-tom said, not dropping his arm yet. "We gotta wait for him to come home from the hospital?"

"What's that?" Lila asked.

Tristan nodded. "I'll be speaking to him."

Tom-tom dropped his arm and looked at him earnestly. "We gotta speak to him about this cremation business."

"What cremation?" Lila said.

"There's gotta be a funeral for old Pinpin," Tom-tom continued. "It's not right."

"What! What!" Lila looked back and forth between the two men. "Pinpin cremated?" She opened her mouth wide, but it took a mesmerizing moment for a shriek to emerge. She tried to get up and instead fell forward against Tristan's knees.

"You see! You see how people feel?" Tom-tom said.

Tristan leaned down to pick her up and she grasped his hands to be helped, but on the way up her necklaces became entangled in his belt buckle and she fell backwards onto the sofa. The necklaces tautened and to keep from snapping them Tristan moved his pelvis forward, almost into Lila's face.

"I'm fainting, I'm fainting!" Lila announced, and one bony hand pushed at his crotch.

Tristan felt the blood rush to his head. It was like the airport all over again.

Three

TRISTAN VISITS THE ANCESTRAL HOME

A film of perspiration covered Tristan's body. Hard work extricating himself from Lila. He had fled the house. He didn't try to say goodbye to Olivia; she had finally managed to pull her dress entirely over her head and Tom-tom and Lila were struggling with her when he got out the door. And then there was the heat. The rented car had turned into an oven too. God. He sat behind the wheel and turned on the air-conditioning and waited for Tom-tom.

Tom-tom came out and first went over to his old red car. He stood in front of it like a mourner and Tristan was forced to look away in order to keep steady in his resolve to be honest with Hertz.

Tom-tom returned to the Hertz car, gave Tristan a questioning look, his eyes pleading, jowls loose, but when he saw it was no use, he half-turned towards the house across the street. He squinted and said, "You know, I suspicion that son of a bitch over there has his eye on Lila—and she is encouraging him! Would you believe it!"

The man in the loud shorts stood at the top of his steps watching them.

Tristan shook his head slightly, ridding himself of Tom-tom's worry rather than taking it in.

"If she thinks I'm gonna let him move into my apartment with her—" He stopped short and pointed to the small stucco building next to his home. "I take care of those apartments. I'm the manager. A little job to keep me going."

Tristan decided that he should say firmly, without sounding aggrieved, "You didn't tell me that your wife—"

"Aunt Olivia."

"Aunt Olivia would not be able to recognize me."

"Oh, she knows," Tom-tom said. "She knows."

He opened the glove compartment and took out the literature inside. "Lookit, this is a nice map," he said and began folding it to the size of his shirt pocket. "Tampa and Surroundings, I can use it. Tampa is not the little town it used to be."

"She can't recognize anyone, really," Tristan insisted.

"No, no," Tom-tom said. "The doctor is giving her a medicine for her nerves . . ."

"Her nerves?"

"It's called Hall Door, something like that. And another one called Hyderdine—I'm sure about that one—for circulation in the veins around her head. She's gonna be able to remember everything you said to her today. One of these days. Maybe not right away, of course, but she'll remember and appreciate everything you said, you can count on that."

Tristan did not tell him that there would be nothing to remember: he had not spoken to Olivia. He put the car in drive and carefully stepped on the accelerator.

"Stop!" Tom-tom commanded and reached for the steering wheel. "How could I have forgotten?"

Tristan stopped, meaning to tell him it was not wise for a rider to handle the wheel, but Tom-tom quickly opened the car door and with moans and wriggling side-to-side motions got out surprisingly fast. He went to the trunk, slapped it once, came over to Tristan's door, asked for the keys, and returned to the trunk. Tristan could not see what he was doing back there, with the trunk's door up, but the neighbor across the street took the opportunity to cautiously raise a hand in greeting.

Tristan could hear Tom-tom cursing even before he slammed the trunk shut. He cursed again when he handed the keys to Tristan.

"What's wrong?" Tristan said.

"They didn't leave the tool kit, would you believe it?" he said. "What we gonna do if we have a breakdown? Those Hertz bastards are too smart for their own good."

"We don't really need it," Tristan explained. "They expect me to call a repair shop if I need help. They pay for it all."

Tom-tom grumbled all the way back to his seat. Tristan noticed a streak of red lipstick on his chinos not too far from his fly. God. Again he blushed. The odds on its happening again were one in a million, he figured, but he decided he would buy a belt buckle on which nothing in the world could catch.

Tom-tom waited quietly until Tristan looked his way; then he smiled and winked. "I coulda used the tool kit," he said and again winked. "They come in handy when something breaks down in the apartments. I'm like a super in New York."

"You don't own the building?" Tristan said, thinking that,

given his knowledge, remaining silent might be classed as dissembling.

"Who told you?" He stared at Tristan. "Why'd you ask?"

Tristan pondered whether a lie would be venial.

Tom-tom cut him off. "Well, you could say I do," he conceded. "Forget it, let's not talk about it." He pointed to the wheel. "Let's go, we got other things to talk about."

Should he look at his notebook? No need to until he got to the house. He could remember Marina's instructions. Stay on Columbus Drive until you get to Fifteenth Street. And he thought he could remember how to get back to Columbus Drive from here. Moreover, the wheel was in his own hands. Consequently, he felt that he was armed against any onslaught from Tom-tom, frontal or otherwise, that might deflect him from heading for Grandpa's house.

Grandpa's house. He remembered again the seriousness of his mission down here, the important responsibility his parents had placed on his shoulders, and it made him feel good.

Indeed, he was satisfied with himself. This side trip with Tom-tom had taught him a lesson. Not to be deflected. It would not happen again. He was back in command.

"Don't hurry," Tom-tom said. "There's lotsa things we gotta talk about before we get there. And things I wanna warn you." He shook his head from side to side to indicate how many. "Turn right at the next corner. That's Columbus Drive. Get into the right lane. You gotta think ahead. They made a right lane to accommodate the traffic to Tampa Stadium. I guess you heard about Tampa Stadium. Be careful. Stop!"

Tom-tom reached for the wheel, but Tristan caught hold of his arm and prevented him. "Not a good idea," he said.

"I thought you wasn't stopping," he said. "Listen, I don't remember. Where is your grandma Nora buried? I was always gonna ask Pinpin and I always forgot."

"Grandma Cora from Boston?" Tristan said.

"A slip of the tongue," Tom-tom said. "Watch out for the light coming up. She and me hit it off the first time she was here, so I know her name all right. We was good friends."

"Grandma came to Tampa?"

"Sure, when Aunt Mama was still alive," Tom-tom said, pronouncing "Aunt Mama" in a high, reverential tone. "Pinpin brought her here to meet Aunt Mama. You too and your brother, when you were kids, remember that?"

"Aunt Mama?"

"You don't remember Aunt Mama!" Tom-tom leaned down from the waist and brought his face close to the steering wheel and looked up at Tristan with eyebrows raised all the way. "Your grandma! I mean, your daddy's grandma—what's that?"

"My great-grandmother?" Tristan said.

"That's it. I only know it in Spanish—*tátara abuela.* Funny, huh? Better to say great-grandmother. And she *was* great! I wish we was going to see her at the house now and she was cooking the meal. She would call, Tom-tom, come on over, I made some flan for you. God bless her and I don't believe in God."

"Flan?" Tristan said. "Is that crème caramel?"

"What the hell's that? I'm talking flan. The flan she made was pure as pure, like a cigar made with real Havana leaf. None of that stuff the women make now. They put in condensed milk, they don't have the patience. Or worse—cream cheese. A stiff hard piece of shit they serve you and they tell ya it's flan. See that, that's the Hillsborough River."

They were crossing a bridge that arched at the center and Tristan could see the ribbon of water on either side, small piers and small boats at the end of small lawns.

"And at the other side is Ybor City?" he asked. Did he expect suddenly to come upon shanties like the one they put up at Yale to protest apartheid? "I mean, does it begin there?"

"Aw no, there's no dividing line now," Tom-tom said. "It don't matter—there's Latins everywhere. They got Spanish last names, anyway."

Tristan looked at him with interest, hoping he would say more about that. He wanted to ask about the moss he saw on some old dying trees, but sociology was more interesting than landscape. Moss would have to wait.

"In the old days," Tom-tom said and sighed, "this was all cracker country."

"And so it's integrated now?" Tristan said.

"Listen, I don't want to talk about that now," Tom-tom said. "So where was your grandma buried?"

Tristan had to think about that. "No place," he said after a moment.

"What about the funeral?" Tom-tom said.

"The funeral?" Tristan asked.

"You gotta bury them if you got a funeral," Tom-tom said. "Or something."

"I remember there was a memorial," Tristan said.

"A statue?" Tom-tom could not believe it. "You put up a statue! Hey."

"No, no, a memorial meeting," Tristan explained. "That's also a memorial. People come together and remember the person who died. There are also speeches."

"Without a body?"

"Right."

"She was cremated, huh?"

Tristan could not remember, but he said, "I guess so."

Tom-tom shook his head at that. "So there's no reason," he said, brightening, "that Pinpin—listen, pull over to the side."

"What's the matter?" Tristan looked ahead and then in the rearview mirror. Nothing. The street was too narrow at this point to park. "Something wrong?"

"Pull over," Tom-tom insisted. "We gotta talk."

Tristan slowed down. "I can't park," he said. "I'll block traffic."

"What traffic?" Tom-tom said. "There's no traffic. Everybody takes the freeway. I gotta talk to you. Pinpin would want me to—he wasn't the one to keep quiet, no sir."

Really? Tristan thought but said nothing. Why didn't he know these things about Grandpa? Was Grandpa bad-tempered? Wasn't it more that he was a rebel? Hadn't he been a Red or something when he was young? He did not like the phrase "when-he-was-young": older people denigrated the young with it. As if what you were when you were young was not to be taken seriously. Why had he let it creep into his thoughts?

"You hear me?" Tom-tom said. "Whyn't you stop?"

Tristan had slowed down, not in response to Tom-tom but because he had allowed his thoughts to wander off. "OK," he said and stopped the car.

"Some things we can't talk about in front of those people—" Tom-tom began.

Tristan thought he should ask who. "Who?" he asked.

"Your relatives, of course," Tom-tom said. "They'll be at the house all the time. But that's not what I thought of—I just figured it out. Whyn't you tell me? Your grandma's not buried no place so's natural you figure your grandpa won't either."

Tristan gave him a quick nod to show he understood and waited for him to finish.

"That's right, isn't it?" Tom-tom said. "That's how you figure, but you forgot your grandpa's got his own people buried right here. They been dying since a hundred years ago. The cemeteries are full of them."

Tristan shook his head. "Tom-tom—" he began.

"Uncle Tom-tom, Tris."

"Uncle Tom-tom, my dad told me what to do," he said. "It's not for me to say."

Tristan thought that over. Why wasn't it for him to say?

"We'll talk to him," Tom-tom said.

"He doesn't believe in all that," Tristan said gently. "Neither does Mom."

"*I*'ll talk to him," Tom-tom said.

Tristan decided it was only fair to add, "I'm not sure I do either."

"What's the matter with you all?" Tom-tom said. He smacked the dashboard with one hand. "Don't you understand?"

Tristan waited a moment deferentially before he put the car in gear again.

"Pinpin didn't want that," Tom-tom said loudly. "He didn't want to be burned up!"

Tristan unintentionally accelerated, and a car swerved by and honked at him.

"Here I am worrying about the pallbearers, ready to help you pick them," said Tom-tom, "and you don't even want a funeral!"

"Pallbearers?" Tristan said.

"Think of all the older cousins," Tom-tom said. "They expect to be pallbearers, yes. They're gonna be mad. How are they gonna explain to people?"

"What exactly is a pallbearer?" Tristan asked.

"You never been to a funeral?" Tom-tom said.

Tristan shook his head.

Tom-tom fell back in his seat. "My God," he said. After a moment, he added, "They carry the coffin," but he seemed too weary to say any more.

Tristan decided the best he could say was, "I see."

Tom-tom lay back in the seat gathering strength. He breathed in and out, inhalations and exhalations full of air and saliva and old cigarette smoke and more living than Tristan could imagine. A tornado was in the making.

"What can I tell you?" He sat up, and as he talked he gestured without a stop, a hand sometimes hitting the window or the ceiling or the dashboard. "It's an honor to be a pallbearer. You can hurt a lotta people's feelings. That's why I am offering to help you—you wanna go through life with grudges? They hold a grudge about that, you know. Lookit Arturo, he never goes to a funeral, his nerves will not take it, but if you don't make him an honorary pallbearer—"

"And honorary pallbearer?" Tristan said. "What's that?"

Tom-tom hit himself on the forehead. Hard. It startled and worried Tristan.

"My God, he don't know!" Tom-tom threw himself back on the seat. "Of course he don't know. He don't know what a regular pallbearer is, he don't know what a funeral is! What kinda Latin are you? What do they teach you at that Yale?"

Tristan's ears were hot with embarrassment. He could not have said why. Not with exactitude. He could not straighten out his feelings about Tom-tom and Olivia and all that back there. Then there were all the things Tom-tom had said about the funeral. Accusations, actually. He had stopped Tom-tom by saying he (Tristan) had nothing to do with it—he was only doing what his parents decided. But that was not entirely true; so he told him that he did not believe in funerals either. Not that he had thought much about it all. He wished he could get Tom-tom to discuss this, but already he was onto something else.

"Lookit that," Tom-tom said, and he pointed to the car ahead of them. Its bumper sticker said *How's my driving? Any complaints, call 1-800-EAT SHIT*. "Wouldn't you know, it's from New York."

Tom-tom sneaked a look at Tristan, saw he was red in the face, and added, "There's no respect nowadays. But you're not like that, Tris, I know, I can tell."

Tristan wished he could disagree.

"You saw that cemetery back there?" Tom-tom said.

Tristan nodded. He wasn't going to start in again, he hoped.

"That's the Colon Cemetery," Tom-tom said. "All West Tampa Latins there."

They had passed it on the right, its headstones threatening to fall onto the sidewalk in a good rain.

"My father and mother are there."

"Oh."

"That's not where we'd put your grandpa. I know it's not dignified enough for Pinpin. The Centro Asturiano for him. Not good enough for my folks either, I want you to know, but nobody knew that all those *boliche* places would start up a block away."

"That's not the point, Uncle Tom-tom."

"There's no more room, anyway. Forget it. It's all filled up. It was good enough for a lot of people."

"It's a fine place, I'm sure," Tristan said, surprised that he had thought of something to say.

"Unless you bought a plot a long time ago and you didn't use it. You could buy it from somebody like that."

Tristan decided to say nothing about that.

"I bet you don't even know what a *boliche* is."

Tristan shook his head. He had been doing a lot of that, and wished that words came easier to him. He stopped at a red light and that gave him time to think.

"I'm sorry," he said.

"*Boliche* is just a cut of meat," Tom-tom said. "Don't feel bad. It's nothing much. But Aunt Mama stuffed it with little bits of ham and olives and only she knows what else."

Tristan saw the long red-brick building two blocks to the left. "What's that?" he said, forgetting about Tom-tom's argument. "What do they do there?"

"A pants factory. Nothing down here worth looking at. But you oughta see the new buildings downtown—reflecting glass like mirrors on the outside. As good as New York."

"I thought it was a cigar factory."

"It was, it was. Forget about the cigar factories, they all gone." He prodded Tristan with a fat, hurting forefinger;

the light had changed. "Tris, you know, Pinpin was your grandpa but he came down here to die. You can't just turn him to ashes and take him away. It's his hometown."

"Yes, sir," Tristan said without agreeing.

"I'm gonna die too, you know," Tom-tom said. "I'd feel better if my brother Pinpin was nearby. Right here with the rest of us Latins."

That was nice, Tristan thought, but not reasonable.

"Wouldn't you want to be buried with your own kind?"

Tom-tom menaced his side with the forefinger to make him answer.

"My own kind?"

"With other Latins," Tom-tom explained. "Wouldn't you?"

What could he say? Tom-tom had already made him hesitate more often than in his whole life, but this was the ultimate. How could he answer? Would he want to be buried with other Hispanics—his own kind!

Tom-tom chuckled.

Tristan looked at him quickly. Why had he chuckled? Mom had had a good laugh when she discovered that the Grace Church School had entered him on their rolls, for statistical purposes, as an Hispanic. He had never forgot. They had probably also thus listed Owen and his sister Emily, flat blond hair and all, but only he had heard Mom report it to Dad. Her laughter had bounced down the oak staircase to the kitchen where he, Tristan, was preparing an English-muffin pizza to eat while reading *The Prince and the Pauper* in bed.

What would happen to him if he really turned into an Hispanic? Would he become a pauper?

He had never discussed it with anyone. Easy not to with Owen and Emily. He never told them anything important. The way Mom had laughed was not encouraging: she'd just laugh some more if he brought up the subject. But he sometimes thought of perhaps reasoning out this Hispanic business with Dad—especially during the commercial breaks when they watched the Mets games by themselves—because, after all, Dad had not laughed when Mom told him upstairs in the master bedroom. He never did talk to Dad about it, but he guessed now that he must have worked it out on his own although he no longer remembered. He liked that name Granados.

A surprise: he suddenly recalled Grandma. He saw her long face smiling at him. "Isn't it wonderful what a melting pot we Americans are?" she was saying. "You're part Spanish!"

"Whatcha smiling about?" Tom-tom said.

It would take too long to explain that he had thought then that Grandma was Spanish too, when she was, of course, all Boston. Old Boston.

"I was thinking . . ." Tristan began.

Tom-tom interrupted. "Me too. I get all my pleasure outa thinking nowadays. I think about me and Pinpin playing on Nineteenth Avenue, there was many empty lots there for a baseball field, and the double feature and serial at the Ritz on Saturday afternoon. And other stuff." He laughed and elbowed him and winked. "You know what other stuff."

Tristan said, "Why was he called Pinpin?"

"That was his nickname," Tom-tom said.

"Yes, but for what reason?"

"Who knows?" Tristan said. "We don't have to know everything." He jabbed him with his forefinger again, angrily now. "Whatcha gonna do with him when you burn him?"

Tristan opened his mouth but nothing came.

"Tell me that, huh," Tom-tom gloated.

"I don't know," Tristan said.

"You know what I heard? They give you a little vase and that's it. That's all that's left and you gotta take it away. And you don't know for sure—take it or leave it. It's uncivilized, that's what it is." He covered his face with both hands and groaned. "Only Americans got such little feelings."

Tristan took his foot off the accelerator. He had been speeding.

He took a deep breath to calm down. Maybe Tom-tom was right.

"Your grandma," Tom-tom said. "You couldn't a done that to her, no sir!"

He nodded, yes. He remembered now. Tom-tom moaned again. So loud that Tristan was glad that no one seemed to walk on Columbus Drive.

"I don't believe it, I don't believe it!" Tom-tom said. He grabbed Tristan's elbow. "What, what did you do with the . . . you know."

They had scattered the ashes in Maine. Dad announced at dinner, after Uncle Crispin arrived for a weekend, the first time in years, that they should leave the next morning—Sunday—open for that. They went out into the woods past the barn, where she had liked, on walks by herself, to follow a stone fence a couple of centuries old, but they had to send Tristan home for a can opener. That did not work, and Dad handed Uncle Crispin the metal container and went back to the barn for a hammer and awl; finally, Uncle Crispin went back for an adz. Tristan omitted these mishaps when he told Tom-tom, but he smiled nevertheless.

"I don't believe it," Tom-tom repeated. "Pinpin did that? Never!"

Come to think of it, he did not remember Grandpa being with them that morning in the woods.

He had to brake again, this time because Columbus Drive had become too narrow for ordinary caution. The houses almost as suddenly took on a bedraggled look. On his right, an abandoned one seemed to beg for a handout: its front porch had collapsed and it appeared to have fallen to its knees.

"Termites," Tom-tom said quickly and returned to the offensive. "Your grandpa never told me anything like that and he told me everything!"

He sat back in his seat and dared Tristan to contradict him.

Tristan did not want to. Maybe Grandpa hadn't believed in any rituals whatsoever.

Tom-tom smacked himself on the forehead, like an old-time movie comedian. "I got ya wrong, Tris. I apologize. When I'm wrong I apologize." He reached over and patted his leg. "We feel the same way about this thing, you and me. I see that now. What an idiot—it's your folks."

Should he demur again?

Tom-tom held up one hand as if to stop him, as if he knew what Tristan might say if he gave him the chance. "Don't worry, boy. We'll figure it out. I got an idea. We won't give it another thought. Let's just enjoy ourselves. I didn't mean that—how can I enjoy myself with Pinpin gone?" He patted Tristan's leg again. "I mean let us not worry."

Tristan was willing. It was only a while ago, back at the airport, that he had first met Tom-tom, but he knew that he was not to be taken at face value. (Not to be trusted?) And then again he didn't have the right to think that: he did not really know. It might still be a cultural difference, like this funeral business, possibly explained by their being deists and still hung up on the afterlife.

Was he being euphemistic? Was he calling stupidity—reactionary stupidity, at that—a cultural difference? There were limits to anthropological cool.

He sighed. He had a list of things to do down here. He just had to concentrate on that.

"Don't worry," Tom-tom said.

He was not worrying: he knew he would, in time, reason it out and smooth it over.

"Don't look around like that," Tom-tom said. "You ain't gonna see a sign says Ybor City and it ain't gonna get much worse, if that's what you're thinking."

Tristan nodded; he didn't know what else to do.

"In fact, this is Tampa Heights. See that—"

A church built of dirty cake-icing? Solidified lava?

"—That's the old Episcopal church! Fancy. Junior League and all that. Usta be. No more. Ho-ho. Now they got this young priest he's always talking homeless. I don't think he lets you in if you ain't down and out."

"Good guy, huh?" Tristan said.

Tom-tom laughed. "You're like Pinpin," he said. "You got a sense of humor, stands to reason."

Tristan relaxed. He heard a funny noise and looked over and saw Tom-tom was crying. He sopped up his tears with his hands and wiped them on his stretch pants and stopped up a nostril at a time with his stubby right forefinger and drew in the mucus with loud inhalations and spat it out towards the sidewalk. A stoned derelict on a broken bench looked up a moment but could not focus, so closed his eyes.

"And see that, that's where he went to junior high school. Your grandpa."

An old red-brick building boarded up, its cement yard broken up and unswept: it was crying for help.

"George Washington Junior High. Or Thomas Jefferson. Or Benjamin Franklin. One of those guys. You can bet it wasn't José Martí."

He grabbed Tristan's elbow. "Don't hurry. You heard of José Martí. You know who he is? Or did I ask you that before?"

Tristan shook his head, then nodded, started to explain, but Tom-tom was not listening.

"That is one historical personage I make sure they know about, even Junior. You know my Junior? He's a little mentally retarded—but never mind about that. José Martí, that's who. Every last nephew and niece, I make sure they know about him. I ask them every time I see them—who is José Martí? A historical personage, that's what Grandpa called him, you can't call him a politician. That's a dirty word. I tell them about him because of Grandpa. My grandpa and Pinpin's too. Wait."

Tristan slowed down. "I heard about him," he said and sneaked a look at his watch while Tom-tom spat out more mucus. It wasn't quite an hour since he had landed—he could not believe it.

"And my old man, Papa Leandro, too. He loved Martí—and Fidel. Papa Leandro, he came from Artemisa. God almighty, he used to play Radio Havana in 1959 so loud the whole block had to listen to Fidel. Shush, shush." He ducked, then quickly sat up again. "What's the matter with me! Let them hear, fuck them. Fidel, Fidel, Fidel, he usta yell like the crowds listening to him. What was I saying?"

"Martí," Tristan said.

Tom-tom banged on Tristan's arm again. "You ever heard a politician writing a poem? Guantanamera, *aiee, aiee.*" He sang, "*Yo soy un hombre sincero* . . . And so on. Like that Peter Seeger sang. Papa Leandro used to make them listen. He used to say, You heard of Truman writing a poem? How do you like that? Truman writing a poem. Reagan writing a poem. They can't even fart good."

Tristan liked that, and Tom-tom slapped him approvingly.

"OK, you crossed Nebraska," Tom-tom said. "You're in Ybor City."

This is not New England. That was the only way he could describe it, and he realized that he was looking at everything with a view to telling Nanao. No style. Yes, maybe. Wooden clapboard houses (twenty-five feet wide?) on top of each other, often with no more than three or four feet between them, set back another three or four feet from the narrow, cracked-cement sidewalk; each with a front porch, again three or four feet deep, a door set in the middle and a window on each side of it. Some houses were clean and painted and wore iron grilles on the windows like black-lace bras, others had entered the terminal stage and would soon also come to their knees. A flimsy kind of poverty. Unlike the spread-out blight the poor in Maine extravagantly disported. Here the poor did not acquire enough goods to create any substantial litter, and anyway, there was no space in which to put it all on view. And the motley crowd of houses lacked the bravado of the Maine natives' stance: no rich people from away were forced to take Columbus Drive to and from home and each time be affronted by these indigents' indifference to neatness and propriety. This sunny slum threatened no one.

"It was nice when we were kids," Tom-tom said, as if provoked.

Tristan did not believe it.

He must suspend judgment. After all, Grandpa came from right around here.

"See that fire station?" The only building in several blocks not made of clapboard. "Aunt Mama and our grandpa once went to vote there for a politician. They never voted before, but this politician had promised—never mind that. They found out when they got there that they had already voted. Not only in that election but for years."

"What did they do?"

"They went home."

"Didn't they report it?"

"You crazy?"

"I guess democracy never worked much at the local level in the South," Tristan said.

Tom-tom nodded sagely.

"I tell ya something else. That politician never gave me a job, not even a part-time job. I couldn't even get to see him. It turned me sour as sour milk and I was only twenty-two years old. You know how many votes I got him in our family alone?"

"I suppose Tampa didn't have a branch of the ACLU then, did it?"

"It didn't have a branch of anything."

"Or the League of Women Voters?"

"What's that?"

"What's that?" Tristan echoed, but he meant the tower of a red-brick building ahead. "And that?" Another red-brick school building, stripped of everything—down to the window sashes—surrounded by sandy aggrieved grounds of which even the weeds despaired. They grew in beleaguered clumps and no longer expected their share of moisture and air: they were not long for this world.

"Oh, oh, oh!" Tom-tom said joyously. "Now we're there! You gonna turn left on the next corner. See, it's got a traffic light—it didn't usta when we were kids. This is it. This is our neighborhood. God almighty. I get a thrill outa showing it to you. That's the Ybor City Grammar School. That's where your grandpa went."

Tristan took another look. God.

"And that ahead is the Clock, the biggest cigar factory Ybor City ever had. I think. There's a lotta arguments about that. Or usta be. All the old-timers are dead."

This time, it was Tom-tom who sighed. "A year ago, would ya believe it, we got drunk together, your grandpa and me. Well, a little tipsy—we weren't well enough to get drunk. And he said, Tom-tom, someday they gonna put up a sign on that building that I went to school there. Whaddya think of that?"

Tristan nodded, but he did not really believe it.

"You know, you know that, all right," Tom-tom continued. "You read his books, so you know he was a great author. Right?"

Tristan hesitated a moment and it was long enough to get him off the hook.

Tom-tom added, "Now that he has passed away, I may get a chance to read them too."

Poor Grandpa, Tristan thought, but did not laugh.

"And see that? That's Cuscaden Park."

Two blocks wide, six blocks long. A swimming pool, basketball courts, a baseball field, bleachers. Worn and gray, but still functioning.

"Old man Cuscaden gave his whole place to the city for a park. His house was on Columbus Drive, and behind it, all the way to Twenty-first Avenue, was orange trees, grapefruit, tangerines. He was the only American living in Ybor City and he usta keep a beebee gun on his porch. He saw anybody climb the fence or hear his dogs bark, the old son of a bitch, and he shoots at us. And now, lookit, even black kids are playing on his property."

"Hey, that's all right," Tristan said.

Tom-tom winked at him. "I like that too, Tris. I ain't got any prejudices against anybody. Listen. Slow down, I want to tell you something before we get there." He put a hand on Tristan's arm, winked again and said in a whisper, "In the old days—in the Depression—when I was in New York, I was practically a communist. Like your grandpa. How do you like that?"

"That's very interesting," Tristan said. "I'd like to ask you some questions about that."

"You bet, we got a lot to talk about," Tom-tom agreed. "Whaddya want to know?"

"Well, not now," Tristan said. "Don't I turn again at the next corner and I'm there?" He looked to his right at an empty side street, past a row of houses leaning on each other like cards, and saw another old red-brick building. "Is that a cigar factory too?"

"Was," Tom-tom said. "Perfecto Garcia and Sons."

"And do I turn now for Grandpa's house?"

"Yeah. Slow down. Wait." He pulled on Tristan's arm anxiously. "I gotta tell you something. Stop."

Tristan let the car slow down but did not stop. He checked the side and rearview mirrors. Just as there were no people in the streets, there were no cars coming or going.

"What's that you said about the local level?" He narrowed his eyes astutely. "You meant something about the family, didn't you, right?"

"Oh no," Tristan hurried to reply. "I was just talking about democracy in general."

"Well, whatever," Tom-tom said. "You understand, I don't wanta put my family down. It's your family too. But . . . ." He inhaled deeply and then exhaled explosively. "That's no reason for trusting them, you understand?"

Tom-tom held him with an unblinking stare and waited for an answer.

Tristan nodded, but he hoped it was noncommittal.

"OK, we gonna go there now and whatever any one of them bastards proposes to you, you check it out with me." Tom-tom relented: he smiled and patted Tristan's arm. "OK?"

Tristan nodded and was afraid he was promising something he might not . . . well.

"OK, you turn now. It's the next house after the corner. You can't miss it. The others are a mess."

Tom-tom was right. For one thing, the house was grander than most they had passed, its porch circled it on three sides, there was enough yard for a driveway and carport and lawn and azalea bushes and one palm tree, and there were a half-dozen cars parked as close as they could get to the house. Unlike the streets Tristan had driven, this block was peopled: on all sides of the porch of the house, on the sidewalk in front, and across the street, some of the people talking to neighbors on other porches, some standing on the porch on the lookout but talking all the while. There was stir and life here. As he brought the car to a stop, wondering where he could park, Tristan saw and felt and heard them all freeze and become silent.

The fat lady of the airport—sweet Aunt Clem—moved to the top of the cement steps that led to the porch. He looked upon her as an old friend now, and she called out in a high voice, “There he is, God love him!” She smiled and shook her fat body and threw out her arms unashamedly and reached for her highest note. “Welcome home, Tristán!”

Four

TRISTAN MAKES A TV APPEARANCE

Tristan could not take it all in at once. He stepped out of the car feeling the kind of intense shyness he thought he had conquered at prep school. And yet he was eager too. He looked at Aunt Clem on the porch and raised a hand and smiled and saw that everyone there had come in from the sides and crowded round her. Smiling like her too. Some of the cousins from the airport leaned over the veranda and waved as if he were far away. Somebody slapped him on the back. Everyone was happy with him.

A young man stood on the sidewalk waving him to a halt. He did not look like a cousin. He did not even look as if he belonged in Tampa at all. But he must be in charge and

Tristan obediently stopped. What could it be? Some cultural ritual? He would play it by ear.

The fellow called out for everyone to hear, "Aunt Clem, everybody, that was real good. Now, once more for the cameras."

Aunt Clem began, "There he is, God bless him—" but the fellow stopped her with a wave of his hand.

Aunt Clem said, "You want me to say it in Spanish?"

The fellow paused to consider it, then shook his head and quickly turned and snapped his fingers at Tristan. "You go back and stand by the door of the car, leave it open and walk straight up to the house and right up the steps to your aunt Clem. And clinch. Or whatever comes naturally. We want this to look like the real thing."

A TV newscaster! Tristan recognized the type from those few days in New Haven when the local news teams had paid attention to their demonstrations on campus. He saw the van now, parked just beyond the house. *You're in Luck,* it announced in big letters, *It's Channel Seven!* A pony-tailed fellow stood on the sidewalk holding a camera on his shoulder. No question about it, a news team. Why?

"I'm Joe Sorrento," the newscaster said to Tristan. "I'll ask you a couple questions later, on the porch and in the house if the light in there doesn't give us too much trouble. Look at the camera and call me Joe when we're taping. OK?"

The cameraman said to Joe Sorrento, "Maybe he should get back into the car, and we'll take it from there."

Tom-tom caught up with Tristan, and immediately threw an arm around his shoulder. Out of the side of his mouth he asked, "What the hell is this?"

"I don't know," Tristan said. "TV people, I think."

"I mean you, Jack," Tom-tom said.

Tristan saw then that Jack, the engineer with the Water Department, stood on the other side of him. He was happy and smiling at the cameraman and the newscaster. It must be he who had slapped him on the back just now. A congratulatory slap. Why?

Because of these TV people?

Jack said, "I was trying to tell you at the airport—these boys from Channel Seven are friends of mine. Right, Joe? Ran into him at the Tampa Club last night."

Jack tried to place an arm on Tristan's shoulder, but Tom-tom would not move his own off.

Jack winked at Tristan. "Tom-tom didn't give me a chance at the airport and he won't now either. OK, Joe, you tell us when you're ready for us, hear?"

"I know all about them too," Tom-tom said. "They're here because of Pinpin, don't you forget."

"Sorry, guys," Joe Sorrento said. "I want him walking up to the porch alone. Maybe at a half-run, Tristan, and looking eager. OK?"

Tom-tom looked to Tristan with pleading eyes. "You want me with you, Tris, right?"

Whatever it was they wanted, Tristan decided he would have to think about his part in it. He would not participate in—he could not even finish the thought now. "I'm sorry," he said to Joe Sorrento. "I don't know what this is all about, I can't talk to you now."

But Joe Sorrento stood in his way and kept talking. "I only wanted to catch your arrival on tape first, lifelike, and then I was going to explain. You got it? You won't step back to your car?" He raised one hand and motioned to the cameraman to start filming. His voice took on a deeper, more formal ring. "Would you tell the viewers of the West Florida area what the death of your grandfather, the famous Hispanic writer Juan Granada—"

"You got his name wrong," Tristan said, looking straight at the camera and talking fast, having learned in New Haven that was the best way of not getting edited and getting your own message across. "Have you read his books?"

"Christ!" Joe Sorrento said and snapped his fingers at the cameraman.

The whir of the camera stopped, and there followed the silence of universal disappointment.

"Hey, mister!" called a youngster standing on the veranda railing and waving his arms at Joe Sorrento. "What if I stand here like this first and I look out like this and you take a picture of me saying, I think I see him now! Wow! Then Aunt Clem says—"

Tom-tom roared, "Eloisa, get that idiot off there. Get him off!" He was angry, he didn't quite know at whom. "Clem, where do you get off welcoming anybody?"

"Listen," Joe Sorrento appealed, still blocking Tristan's way. "This is Channel Seven Evening News. We go on just before the national news. The whole west coast listens—up to Apalachicola. We do this right and we get a chance for the closing human-interest spot. A whole segment to ourselves. Like Charles Kuralt."

"Excuse me," Tristan said, and walked round him.

Joe Sorrento turned to the cameraman. "The hell with it, just shoot. We'll go with it and see what we get."

Tom-tom pulled at Tristan's elbow. "Think about it. I'll help you talk about Pinpin."

"It's a great break," Jack said.

"Do it for the family," Tom-tom said. "They loved Pinpin and want the best for him."

In a generous voice, Jack said, "Tom-tom's right. His books are out of print and . . ."

Joe Sorrento called up to the porch for help. "Hey, Professor, what do you say?" He tapped Tristan on the shoulder. "Talk to the professor—he's not media."

Tristan headed for the porch. The crowd there made way for a man who was coming out the door. He wore a sports jacket, a plaid tie, a judicious look; he was a professor, all right.

"Professor Wallingford!" Tom-tom yelled. "I called him, I called him! Wasn't it me who called you?"

Wallingford nodded but managed to look neutral. Tristan envied professors this ability.

"And the professor called me," Joe Sorrento said to Tristan. "He's an expert on your grandfather. He's read every word he ever wrote."

Tom-tom pushed Jack onto the lawn. "So much for you, buster. Get lost."

A gray-haired, neatly dressed old lady showed up at Tristan's side. She took his hand; hers was dry and light. She said, looking up into his face, "I'm Marina," and then she kissed him on the cheek. It felt like a cool breath of air.

Everyone on the porch and the street became quiet again.

She sighed, then continued, "I am so sorry about all this, Tristan. They're acting like riffraff. I have not let anyone inside, only the professor and the ones who brought food."

Tristan said, "Hello."

"Now, don't you feel bad," she said. "He led a full life."

He nodded: he had not thought of that. Maybe that was what was troubling him. Was he feeling sad? If not, why not?

"He didn't suffer," she added.

He looked at her a moment to check again what she was like and she was looking up at him doing the same with him. She reminded him of those sweet, unshy old women he ran into at the general store in Maine.

"Why didn't they take me?" Aunt Clem called down from the top of the steps. "I'm of no use to anybody."

"You say that at every funeral," Marina said. "One of these days somebody's going to hear you."

She turned to Tom-tom. "Let go of this boy, Tom-tom. He's not going to fly off. And you go around and get rid of this riffraff. Today's not the wake. They're here because they got nothing better to do."

Tom-tom removed his heavy arm and protested. "I can't

do that, Marina," he insisted, but his voice was weak. "That's what family is supposed to do when a loved one dies."

"You know better than that," she said. "Some of them never even saw Pinpin when he was alive."

She pressed lightly on Tristan's arm to apologize for bringing up his grandfather's death in this contentious way. He did not press back because he thought that might appear presumptuous. Or did he mean inapt? Anyway, he simply paused, which is what life seemed to call for most of the time.

She led him up the steps to the professor. "Professor Wallingford," she said. "This is my cousin's grandson."

The cameraman showed up alongside the professor with the camera whirring on his shoulder. He pushed back against some children to pan from Tristan to the professor. There was an outcry, but no one moved.

Aunt Clem said, "Get outa the way, kids." She moved behind the professor and smiled at the camera.

The boy who had stood on the veranda whispered loudly, "Wave so they'll see ya, Aunt Clem."

The professor cleared his throat. "I think I should explain. I called the TV station because I thought they should carry some notice of the death of the most important writer Tampa has produced—not to help them harass you."

Joe Sorrento's voice rang out behind Tristan, "I can't use that, professor! Say something for the viewers."

"Show some respect for a university professor, young man," Marina said.

Tristan kept his head down. He didn't much care for professors, except some.

The boy who had stood on the veranda whispered to the people on the lawn, "She was a libarian!"

Aunt Clem giggled. It set off ripples of titters and strangled but irrepressible laughter.

Joe Sorrento protested. "Lady, we're just trying to get the

news. And to pay tribute, like the professor said. I mean, you know, some people would be glad—"

Tristan nodded to Wallingford and said, "Excuse me," and started for the door of the house. He did feel harassed. This was not the way he had expected to walk into Grandpa's childhood home. He had hoped to be alone, to take it in little by little, and to pause as often as he wanted. He would do that as soon as he got inside.

Joe Sorrento called out to him with urgency, "Just tell us what you thought of your grandfather."

He hesitated and thought of turning around and saying something to honor Grandpa.

Joe Sorrento said, "Just a few words."

He was ashamed to tell the camera he had not read any of Grandpa's books, only an article in an anthology of ethnic literature. And the rest about Grandpa was too personal. You didn't go around talking on TV about what was personal. He shook his head and did not turn around.

But he did turn when Tom-tom roared a second time.

This time it was a prolonged leonine roar, there was no other way to describe it. There he stood, arms out, calling for attention, as if he had been wounded and was desperate for help and the damn world was going by looking the other way.

"Ask me, ask me!" he yelled. "I'll tell you, I am the oldest in the family. I know and I want the whole world to know. He was the greatest man ever come outa Ybor City! Out of Tampa too. The greatest. Everybody wants to get outa Ybor City and forget it. Not him. Not my cousin-brother. He didn't forget us. He wrote books, big books—you oughta read them—all about this place. About us Latins. He knew, he was brought up on this street and he played ball on the corner and right there on that porch he read every book that was ever written. They're never gonna make them any smarter than him. He coulda lived anywhere in the world, but he come home to live in Ybor City!"

He stopped, gulped, looked around, at a loss. He drew one fat hand over his face to keep from crying.

"You got that?" Joe Sorrento said to the cameraman and the cameraman nodded and kept his camera aimed at Tom-tom.

"Uncle Tom-tom," Tristan called and motioned him to come inside with him. He decided he really appreciated Tom-tom.

"Coming, Tris," Tom-tom said happily. "Just one more thing." He stopped on the steps to wave at the camera. "All you idiots up there on the porch, just remember there's never gonna be another great man in our family. Lightning don't hit the same place twice. Be proud of him and of Ybor City. Act right, don't make a fool of yourselves."

Halfway up the steps he had another thought but he did not direct it at the camera. He told Tristan, "I left out Dwight Gooden. Maybe I shoulda mentioned him?"

Inside, everything went black, then returned in deep shadows. He held out a hand, instinctively, to keep from bumping into things—there seemed to be a lot of them in the small space of the living room and in the smaller one of the dining room beyond: chairs, ottomans, sofas, coffee tables, dining sets, a breakfront and a sideboard touching elbows. People he did not know looked up at him in the gloom, and half rose to shake his hand.

Santo, the old man from the airport, said, "I share your loss," as if he had not said it earlier. "I shall never forget your grandmother, never." This time no one told him Aunt Mama was Tristan's great-grandmother.

Tristan blinked and blinked.

"There, there," Marina said in a consoling tone.

"It's only natural," Tom-tom explained.

The people on the two sofas and various chairs did not speak up like Santo but watched Tristan with pitying looks.

The sun, of course. Proof how incredibly bright the Tampa sun was. "I'm OK," he said.

"Sure, sure," Marina said.

"The sun," Tristan explained.

"It's a shock," Marina said.

"Coming to the old house, where you and your dad really come from and all. I mean, the real origin, Ybor City and all," Tom-tom said. "You remember it?"

Tristan shook his head.

"You don't remember running around the porch outside holding my hand?" Tom-tom said.

He did not remember.

From sofa to sofa to chairs the news traveled that the boy could not remember his other visit.

Santo had to be skipped. He only repeated, "I'll never forget his grandmother."

Tom-tom persisted. "When Aunt Mama died?"

"Tom-tom, go out there and tell them to be quiet," Marina said. "Better—tell them to go home for now."

"You go and do it," Tom-tom said, rebelling. "You was the libarian. I want to make Tris a good cup of *café con leche.* Right, Tris?"

Marina said, "Librarian has two r's. I'll take care of Tristan and food."

The screen door creaked. A man holding a large flat paper bag, held out in both hands like an offering, pushed the door open with his hips. "God," he said, "what a mob scene."

"Tony, what's that?" Marina said.

"Sandwiches from La Guajira," Tony said. "Alice ordered them, I only picked them up. Where do I put them?"

Marina threw up her hands. "What am I going to do with all the food!"

"You ever had a Cuban mixed sandwich?" Tom-tom asked Tristan. "You haven't lived." He nudged him towards the kitchen, himself leading the way. "That's Tony, he only married into the family, so he don't count. Ha-ha! God knows how he makes a living, probably illegal. Right, Tony?"

The screen door creaked open again and Tristan decided to stay with Marina.

Marina exclaimed, "Don't tell me you brought food too, Cookie! What am I going to do?"

Cookie was not an old woman but that was as close as Tristan could come to her age. It had to take her hours and hours to make up her face. Green and blue and black and pink and places where they merged. Was that beauty mark on her right cheek originally a mole or did she paint it on from scratch each time?

Cookie spoke shyly, almost timidly. "I had all this meatball sauce in the freezer, Aunt Marina."

"And what's that?" Marina pointed to her other hand.

"Ziti and linguine and penne," Cookie said. "I didn't have any of the flat noodles for lasagna, so I just grabbed these." She looked at Tristan shyly. "Hello."

Cookie stepped inside, but the screen door behind her did not slam to. Joe Sorrento held it open and stood in the doorway smiling expectantly, several cousins around and behind him.

"Give him some of my black beans, Marina," a woman there suggested. "You think he likes black beans?"

"I am definitely not going to make rice now," Marina replied. "Later. You keep the children out on the porch, Manuela. You said I could count on you."

"Yes, yes," Manuela said quickly, waved at Tristan, and disappeared from the doorway. Another took her place.

This one said, "Cookie, you got to find another fella to do your cooking for!"

"Oh, Aunt Dolores," Cookie said and held her head down, she was so embarrassed.

Dolores waved at Tristan. "I'm your Aunt Dolores. Dewey's mother. Also Delio's. Did you meet Derby—they're my three D's."

Marina sighed. She turned to Tristan. "You have to have some lunch."

Tony turned around in the doorway to the kitchen. "There's two dozen sandwiches in here. He better start in on them now."

"Yeah," Tom-tom said. "Warm up the sandwiches."

Dewey pushed his way in past Joe Sorrento. "You get any of the crab croquettes, Tony?" He tapped Tristan lightly. "Hi, remember me, Dewey? Charlene had to go back to work."

Tony shook his head. "Those croquettes ain't had any crab in them for years."

"Fish, that's all it is," the boy who stood on the veranda said. "Any old kinda fish."

Dewey said, "Everybody knows that, but it gives a feel of seafood to them."

"Well, I didn't get them," Tony said and passed on into the kitchen. He yelled from there, "Marina, where do I put them? My God, looka this!"

"Wait, wait," Marina answered. She left Tristan in the living room and hurried through the tiny dining room holding her hands up to her head. "My goodness, oh my goodness!"

Dewey sneaked in after her. "Let me help," he said and he made it to the kitchen without anyone objecting.

Tristan finally got to look around. There were photographs on the walls. Old ones of people he did not know. A large oil painting of a distinguished man standing in a foyer somewhere about a hundred years ago. An oval portrait of a woman in profile. That was all he got a chance to see, for the crowd from the porch, with Aunt Clem in the lead, moved in, carrying Joe Sorrento with them into the living room.

Aunt Clem went straight to Tristan. "I didn't bring anything today, honey," she said, taking his arm and sticking close. "I got a couple pounds white beans soaking and I'm gonna make you a *favada.* I learned that from my Asturian mother-in-law. You'll love it. It's got Spanish sausages—"

"Make way there, Clem," Tom-tom called from the dining room. "Let Maggie through. What you got, Maggie?"

"Pote," a woman with very black hair said. Her voice was strong and husky. "I saw Jack outside taking off in his car like it was *Miami Vice*. What's with him?"

Tom-tom shrugged his shoulders like a winning fighter in the ring. "*Pote,* huh?"

She held the large pot with no trouble and looked at Tristan with large, sad eyes. "Is this him?"

"Yes, ma'am," Tristan said. He was using ma'am for the first time, but it seemed natural here. "And you are—?"

"Maggie Aleman." She handed the pot to Tom-tom and placed a hand—it was still warm from the pot—on his face. "I'm a granddaughter of Reinaldo, he was a brother of Aunt Mama and she was your daddy's—no, your grandpa's mother. And besides that, my mama married a nephew of Reinaldo on his sister's side. That makes us God knows what. Family twice over, I guess. And you better like *pote* 'cause I brought a lot."

"Don't hold him up," Tom-tom said. "He hasn't had any lunch yet, what with all these people."

Aunt Clem said, "Did you make that *pote* with garbanzos?"

"That's what you make *pote* with," said Maggie. Her low-pitched suggestive voice took on a hard edge. "Why'd you bring it up for?"

"Garbanzos is chick-peas, honey," Aunt Clem said to Tristan. "Some people don't like chick-peas. Skin's too thick."

Maggie pulled Tristan away from her. "Tom-tom, I'd like to hold him up, all right. But I think I'll save him for my youngest daughter!"

Aunt Clem let go a peal of laughter.

Tom-tom commanded, "All the children out on the porch. Out." He handed Maggie's pot to a tame husband waiting to shake Tristan's hand. "Go on, take it to Marina."

"I'm Duran, Dolores's husband," the man said and left for the kitchen.

"Or maybe I'll take this one," Maggie said, looking up and down at Joe Sorrento. "What funeral I seen you at?"

Aunt Clem slapped the person nearest her. "That's the TV man, Maggie! Oh God, oh God!"

"Channel Seven, Channel Seven!" the boy who had stood on the veranda called out.

The other children took it up. "Channel Seven, Channel Seven! Joe Sorrento, Sorrento, Sorrento!"

"Oh my God," Maggie said. "How do I look?"

Tristan tried to edge away towards the kitchen, but Maggie's arm held him back.

"We got lights in the van," Joe Sorrento said to Tristan. "We can shoot inside with them."

Maggie said, "Naw, it's bright enough in the kitchen."

Tristan shook his head and said, "Excuse me," to Maggie, who still held him back.

She looked confused.

Aunt Clem whispered, "He don't want to," and nodded towards Tristan.

"Oh yeah," Maggie said and left Joe Sorrento. "It's not nice, not now."

In the dining room, she asked Tristan, "What he want to make movies for? Is he family and I don't know it?"

Tom-tom was disgusted. "You don't know Pinpin is a famous writer? Was."

"I forgot," she said apologetically. She nudged Tristan. "I'm dumb, you know. Everybody knows that. I never read a book. Now you take my daughter Shana, she's—" Maggie interrupted herself and gripped Tristan with all her strength. "You mean he wants to put us on television? Jesus, I never been on television, never."

Tom-tom said, "What's the matter, Maggie, you looking for publicity?"

"Oh, oh, big shot," she said.

"You ain't got any class," Tom-tom said. "Tristan doesn't go for that kinda thing and he's right."

"Whyn't you say so—Tony!" Again she interrupted herself when she stepped into the kitchen and saw Tony and Marina unpacking the sandwiches. "I want one of those—the hell with my *pote!* Heat them in the oven."

"Maggie," Marina said quietly.

"Aunt Marina, I know I'm behaving outa line," she said. "I only got to look at you and I know it. Hey, Cookie, what did ya bring? Don't tell me it's *pasta e fagioli,* I'll have to eat some." She turned to Tristan and whispered. "She was married to an Italian and learned all these great Italian dishes." In full voice, she said, "You know what great cooks there are in this family? Right, Cookie?"

Cookie said in her timid voice, "Too hot for *pasta e fagioli.*"

"Then what about my *pote!*" Maggie said. "That'd be too hot too. Ya putting it down?"

"I'm sorry, Aunt Maggie," Cookie said. "I didn't mean anything. I love your *pote.*"

"I don't like you calling me aunt," Maggie said, "when we're practically the same age."

"You're one minute in the place," Tom-tom said, "and you're already insulted. What're ya yelling at Cookie for with her sweet temper?"

"That's all right, Uncle Tom-tom," Cookie said. "I don't mind. Aunt Maggie is—I mean, Maggie is very good to me."

"I got a right to be upset," Maggie said. "You all forget I lost my mama." She sat down abruptly on a chair at the head of the kitchen table, and cried while she talked. "She was your sister or your first cousin at least, but I'm the one who remembers. Poor Mama!" She lifted her head and bawled. "It's only right, it's my duty, I'm her only daughter!"

Marina said, "Right now, only your mother's cousins are here but—"

"No, no, I'm here," Aunt Clem called from the doorway. "My sister Adelaida. Who can forget?"

Aunt Clem stepped forward and hugged Maggie's head to her broad belly, and they cried together.

"Oh, don't make me cry, don't make me cry," Cookie said. She was ashamed to say her makeup would run, so she turned and looked out the window. She held her eyes wide open to allow her welling tears to soak back in.

Maggie called out to her, "Oh, Cookie, I'm sorry, I'm sorry, but I can't forget my mama."

Aunt Clem said, "Adelaida never forgot anybody. There wasn't a wake she didn't bring chicken with lemon and oregano. Remember?"

"I remember!" Maggie cried.

"For crissakes, that was five, eight years ago," Tom-tom said. "She was my sister too, but we're not holding a wake for her—it's Pinpin who died. Adelaida had her wake."

Marina waved Tristan to her end of the kitchen, near the stove and the back porch. He walked over, picking his way past chairs and counters filled with covered pots and casseroles and stands with tiered chocolate cakes and coconut and white cakes, and flat one-layer coffee cakes and long-sleeved paper bags with Cuban bread. Who was going to eat it all? Windows above the stove and sink and work counters let in bright sunlight and he got a glimpse as he went by of shiny green citrus leaves on a tree by a fence and red hibiscus flowers.

"I'm sorry," Maggie called out to him. "Of course I know the real wake will be at the funeral parlor, but I couldn't help myself."

God. They wanted him to do it all over again.

"In the old days, the wake was at the house. I remember—it was still that way when I was a little girl. Not so long ago as Cookie thinks. Joke. But in the old days they used to lay out the body in the house too. So of course people stayed up. To keep it company. That's why they called it a wake. God, the smell of flowers. I remember old Gumersindo on Sanchez Street they had to put a lot of them on the porch. He had been very active at the Centro Español. What a smell of flowers."

"And cognac, I bet," Dewey said.

Aunt Clem giggled.

Tristan looked around. Many of them had been at the airport, like Aunt Clem, when he told them Grandpa would be cremated and there would not be any funeral. Of course, he had not said anything about a wake and maybe that's why they all seemed to go along with this talk about a wake. It had not occurred to him to say anything about a wake. It was logical he would not think of it: wakes happened in literature, among the Irish.

There was an espresso pot on the stove and his heart was gladdened by it: the first evidence of Grandpa's presence in the house.

Marina saw him looking at it. "I made coffee and now I'll heat the milk. *Café con leche,* right?"

He nodded. He more or less knew what it was.

He felt her soft, dry tap on his shoulder. She said, "You sit here at the head. The old house is yours now."

He had to look away to think about that. After all, he was here to sell it. Everyone in the kitchen fell silent. Because he was a property owner?

"I got six sandwiches in the oven warming up," Marina said. "Somebody, bring Santo, he'll get lost out there with those wild savages. How about you, Tony? You staying?"

Tony shook his head and held out a hand to Tristan. "But I want to say hello. And condolences and all that." He leaned over and slapped him on the shoulder. "I won't even tell you my name now. Maybe tonight or tomorrow. 'Cause, man, you got cousins! Ask Tom-tom, he's the official score-keeper."

Tristan took his hand and said thank you. Then he smiled. He was getting the hang of it.

"See, he's feeling better," Tom-tom said.

"Lookit him, he is great!" Maggie agreed. "Hi, I'm a big

nuisance. You hear, Marina? I apologize. I'm sorry, I really am." She laughed. "I'm having one of those sandwiches."

Marina placed a hand over her heart. "Oh my goodness—the professor! Where is he?"

"What professor?" Maggie said.

Aunt Clem said, "I'll get him. I left him on the porch."

"Not you," Marina said and looked around but found no one suitable. "I'll get him—watch the sandwiches."

As soon as she left, Maggie leaned across the table and grimaced at Tristan. "Don't tell me she's going around with a professor!"

Even Tristan was tempted to laugh.

"Well, you can't tell about a libarian," said Duran, Dewey's father, who had said nothing until now.

"Libarian has two R's," Aunt Clem said and laughed louder than anyone.

Tom-tom laughed but recovered fast. He sat down next to Tristan. He said, "You can't talk to anyone in this family about serious things. Especially the women. Except for Aunt Mama. Professor Wallingford usta spend a lot of time with Pinpin, talking about books and Ybor City. The professor wanted Pinpin to talk into a tape recorder. You ever seen one of those little things?"

Tristan nodded.

Tom-tom lowered his voice. "You wanta hear something—the professor hinted around he wanted me to do it too!"

"Did he?" Tristan said.

"Did who what?" Tom-tom said.

"Did Grandpa?"

Cookie and Maggie and Aunt Clem jostled one another and the men, and laughed while setting the table, opening the oven and exclaiming and slamming it closed after conferring. They argued about the cups and saucers. All three decided that they should after all have a bite themselves.

Aunt Clem tapped Tristan on the shoulder and announced, "I'm going on a diet Monday. Ha-ha!" They were partying while Marina was out of the kitchen.

Tom-tom edged closer to Tristan. "He wants to talk to you about that. He told me on the phone. Maybe he wants to put you on the tape recorder?"

Tom-tom peered into Tristan's face.

Tristan thought: am I going to be the subject of an anthropological study?

Finally, Tristan said, "OK," for want of anything to say.

Tom-tom confided in a judicious voice, "Of course, he's a professor and all that." He paused and looked closely at Tristan. "But you oughta be on the lookout, anyway. You never can tell what people have up their sleeve."

Marina came in with Professor Wallingford and Old Santo. Joe Sorrento followed. Probably uninvited. Tristan frowned without meaning to.

Joe Sorrento said, "I couldn't resist a Cuban sandwich." He looked over at Tristan. "No camera, no interview."

The women all chuckled at this. They made him sit. In a faintingly shy voice Cookie asked, "You like Cuban coffee too?"

Marina took care of Wallingford. "You sit on that side of Tristan, Professor. And Santo, you next to him."

"Hi, Professor," Tom-tom said. "Here's my boy right here, ready to talk to you."

Marina frowned at Tom-tom, but he did not move away.

"Why am I sitting here?" old Santo asked.

Aunt Clem called, "For a Cuban sandwich."

"Oh, all right," Santo said. "I shall never forget Aunt Mama."

Tristan thought of the list in his notebook. He could not remember a single item.

"Tom-tom, you're going to have to go to Seventh Avenue for more coffee," Marina said. "There's only a pound left."

Tom-tom said, "Did Tony leave yet? He's good at errands."

Aunt Clem replied, "I think he's out there getting pointers from the camera fellow."

Tom-tom said, "And there's Dewey here too. Let him go."

Dewey gripped the table.

Marina gave up. "Tell Tony, Clemencia," she said.

Aunt Clem raised her voice to a piercing shriek. "Tony! Tony! Go to La Naviera and get two pounds of coffee." She paused only an instant. "Tony! Tony! Go get—"

Marina waved at her and she stopped. "I could have yelled too. Go out there and tell him."

Aunt Clem said, "Dewey's just sitting here doing nothing."

Dewey did not get angry. He said, "I've been doing a lot of driving."

Aunt Clem said, "OK, but save a seat for me here," and went out. She returned with several more persons. Tristan could not tell how many: they did not all fit into the kitchen. Some merely stuck their heads in at the doorway.

Marina said, "Oh my goodness."

"When these sad duties are over," Wallingford said, "I want to talk to you about your grandfather's papers."

Aunt Clem said to the cousins who had followed her back, "There's a TV room over there—some of you can go in there. I'll pass you a sandwich."

"Clemencia," Marina admonished.

Aunt Clem was confused. She explained, "They can't fit in here."

Marina shook her head and refused to reply.

Maggie said, "Put in another dozen sandwiches in the oven."

She did not see the look Marina gave her, but Aunt Clem did.

Aunt Clem said, "Don't worry, Marina, they'll take theirs with soda. You don't have to make *café con leche* for them."

Marina pursed her lips this time.

Aunt Clem knew that pursed lips meant danger and quickly said, "I'll help, I'll help."

Cookie hesitantly stepped over to Marina. She carried a tray. "Aunt Marina, you tell me what to do," she said timidly, an eye on Joe Sorrento. "You're so good, Aunt Marina."

Marina sighed. "Take out the ones in the oven and put in another bunch."

There followed a noisy grateful exhalation and busy movement through the kitchen to and from the TV room. Marina could not subdue the cheerful, light-hearted, festive murmur let loose in the rooms.

The boy who had stood on the veranda said, "I love a wake!"

Marina said, "Clemencia!"

Aunt Clem said, "Out, Buddy, out of here!"

Jack made it into the kitchen with a large bakery box, calling, "Let me through, let me through."

"So that's what you were going for?" Maggie said. "I thought it was the water works had broken down."

"Guava pastries," Jack said. "I figured Tristan never had guava pastries. These are still warm."

Aunt Clem said, "Quick, let's eat the sandwiches."

Maggie laughed.

Aunt Clem explained with a show of reason, "The pastries get soggy if they stand around."

Tom-tom said, "Everything gets soggy if it stands around. You know what I mean."

Maggie said, "Uncle Tom-tom, I always loved your sense of humor."

Jack opened the huge box and placed it under Tristan's nose. "Isn't that a great smell? You ever had guava pastries up there?"

"I'm not sure," Tristan said.

Scarcely able to look at him yet, Cookie ventured, "I understand there are a lot of Cuban refugee restaurants in New York."

Tristan nodded.

"Those bums are everywhere," Tom-tom said.

"Oh," Jack said, "they're not all bad."

"Pinpin hated them," Tom-tom said. "And take the pastries away. Marina is serving the sandwiches now."

Jack asked, "Who brought the sandwiches?"

Cookie looked at Jack and said, "Tony," and blinked her heavy eyelashes at him and smiled, the only one in the kitchen to welcome him.

Jack looked around for a place to set his box.

Marina said, "Hold it in your hands until I serve these sandwiches. And the *café con leche*. I'm going crazy."

"But, Aunt Marina," he whispered intensely, "I want a sandwich too."

Cookie pointed to the top of the refrigerator, and Jack set it there.

"Hey, everybody, look," Maggie called out. "Tristan is gonna take his first bite of a Cuban mixed sandwich from Seventh Avenue in Ybor City, Tampa, Florida!"

Tristan had already picked up the sandwich and now was forced to bite into it while they watched. It was much lighter than he expected. Not like a hero. It must be the bread, weightless, doughless. He had thought his taste buds could not be operating under all this personal scrutiny—even from the TV room they were watching him eat—but a wonderful mixture of tastes filled his mouth. He nodded as he chewed and there was a collective whistle of rejoicing. He wished he could hum as he ate, as he had done as a boy whenever he was enjoying the food.

"He loves it!" Aunt Clem announced.

Tristan nodded, chewed some more, then asked, "What's in it?"

Tom-tom raised a hand to keep anyone from replying: this was his job. "First of all, ham," he said. "But ironed with a little sugar."

"Ironed?" Tristan said.

"Glazed," Joe Sorrento said.

"Hey, Joe," Jack said. "You still here? And Tristan did the interview. You see!"

Joe Sorrento shook his head.

"Let's not interrupt here, Tristan wants to know," Tom-tom said. "And fresh pork. *Perniz*—what's that, Maggie?"

"It's the hip," Maggie said, and smacked her side.

Very shyly, Cookie whispered, "The rump."

"Fresh ham, for goodness sakes," Marina said.

"Oh?" Tom-tom said. "And thin, thin slices of sausage, Spanish sausage. And thin slices of pickle."

Tristan took another bite. It was all true. He said, "And mustard?"

"On one slice of the bread," Maggie said. "I think the upper side. On the other, a mixture of mayonnaise and—something, I don't know what."

"Yeah," Aunt Clem said, holding hers open. "It's not regular mayonnaise. I don't know, I don't think these are warm enough."

Marina said, "They are warm enough."

"*Hmnnn, hmnnn,*" Tom-tom concurred.

"Great stuff, huh?" Jack said, trying to get Tristan's attention. "You know I don't know where people get the idea it's unusual for people to come back to Tampa—there are some four thousand new people moving into the Tampa area each month."

Aunt Clem said, "And all of them using the bathroom."

"Whaddya know?" Tom-tom said. "They don't serve no Cuban mixed sandwiches at that Tampa Club you and the politicians go to. When was the last time you ate one?"

"You're eating this one 'cause it's free," Jack said.

"That's the end of that," Marina warned.

"Hey, Joe, you oughta do a story—like on us eating Cuban sandwiches," Maggie said.

Cookie put down her sandwich and covered her face with both hands. Lightly, so as not to smear her makeup. She laughed quietly behind her hands. "Oh, Aunt Maggie," she said.

"Yeah, get a picture of us all eating the deluxe ones," Aunt Clem said.

"Oh, Aunt Clem," Cookie said.

"How do you like me," Maggie said, "calling him Joe already." She elbowed him. "This is not your first time, eh?"

Tom-tom said, "This is not Maggie's first time for anything."

Everyone laughed, even Marina. Not Tristan, however.

"Hey, I could get mad at that," Maggie said.

Another outburst of laughter.

"Hey," Maggie repeated. Then she noticed Tristan. "You're a gentleman, little cousin. You know some things are serious, not ha-ha stuff." She winked at him. "I gotta introduce you to my daughter Shana."

Aunt Clem said, "She's too old."

Maggie slapped the table. "Now I'm really mad!"

Marina held out a sandwich on a paper plate. "Where's Eloisa? She's been here all morning."

"She is out on the porch with Manuela," Aunt Clem said.

"What are they doing there?" Marina asked.

"How should I know?" Aunt Clem said.

"You always know about everything important," Marina said.

Maggie laughed.

"Well, if you want to know," Aunt Clem volunteered, "they're hurt."

"They're hurt!"

"Tom-tom yelled at Eloisa about Buddy," Aunt Clem said. "And you told Manuela yourself to go out and take care of the kids like she was a kindergardening teacher."

Maggie said, "You're their lawyer or something?"

"Eloisa's sensitive," Aunt Clem said. "They always been the poorest in the family, and even her own brother won't give her an apartment in his building like he did someone else."

Tom-tom did not bother to swallow before he yelled, "What? What building?"

Marina remained calm. "Go out and tell them to come in and eat," she said.

Aunt Clem looked distressed.

"No one is going to steal your sandwich," Marina insisted.

"They gonna say no," Aunt Clem said.

Marina said, "Give them a chance to say no."

Aunt Clem left, but she took her own sandwich with her.

Maggie looked up at the ceiling and somehow that got everyone's attention. "I hate people who say no when you know they damn well want to say yes. I guess you got taught that old Spanish courtesy business, Tristan. You say no three times and then you say yes, thank you. It's a waste of time."

Tom-tom said, "You got a lot to learn about manners."

"Uncle Tom-tom, let's call it a draw," Maggie said. "You and me are evenly matched." She shifted her attention to Wallingford. "Well, Professor, you aren't keeping up with your sandwich."

"Mind your manners," Tom-tom said.

Dewey said, "You can't eat a sandwich with your glasses on, Professor. You can, but they get in the way. Take them off and you can chew better."

The professor liked that.

"It's a crazy family, isn't it, Professor?" Maggie slapped the table lightly. "But I guess you know that already."

Marina said, "Maggie."

Cookie hid her face with both hands and tittered.

Tom-tom growled.

"Aunt Marina," Dewey said, "have you got more coffee?"

"I mean, the professor knew Uncle Pinpin," Maggie explained.

"Don't slap the table," Dewey said. "It spills my coffee."

Maggie slapped the table. "I mean, Uncle Pinpin was as crazy as the rest of us."

"Maggie!" Marina said.

Maggie waved a hand at Tristan, asking for understanding.

She said, "I came by a month ago, I was driving up Twenty-second anyway to the cemetery and I stopped by. Like I do every month. Might as well, I say to myself every time. My good deed for the month and I might learn something. But he wasn't in a good mood this time and he didn't have a murder mystery or a science fiction I could borrow. Nothing I could read. And he told me I was a disgrace to my ancestors and lots more because I don't read the right kind of literature. I tell ya, he was a character."

"And he was right!" Tom-tom said.

"He told you too?" Maggie said.

Everyone in the kitchen laughed.

Maggie looked at Joe Sorrento and Wallingford. "He was important, huh?"

Joe Sorrento bit into his sandwich so he would not have to confess he had never heard of Antonio Granados until that morning.

The professor nodded. "He was."

Everyone waited for him to say more. Some watched Tristan. Tristan also hoped the professor would say more. He expected he would. That's the way professors are.

"He was and he is," Wallingford said. "He was the best Hispanic writer in America, and he left an account of Ybor City life that is not likely to be surpassed."

"Ybor City?" Maggie said.

"Ybor City was an extraordinary community," Wallingford said. He lay down his sandwich. "I am a professor of American Studies, and I would hazard that our country produced no other community so democratically organized on such farseeing principles, one that cared for the whole man. The trade unions, the fraternal societies with their wonderful buildings, the hospitals, the medical services, the cash compensation for illness."

The cousins in the TV room and the living room came to the doorways to listen. Tristan felt an unexpected elation: college studies and family history had wed.

"Take the readers in the factories," Wallingford said, raising his voice slightly. "Two hours a day of journalism and news. Two more of novels or nonfiction books that the cigar-makers elected to have read! Paid for by themselves! It was better than Plato's Republic."

"You can say that again," Tom-tom said.

"I don't want to take anything away from you, professor," Dewey said. "But they made very good cigars too, they weren't just having a good time." He nodded fast to Tristan until he got his attention. "You know what my old man says, he says Alfonso the Thirteenth used to order his cigars from Ybor City!"

"Corona-coronas," Aunt Clem said, returning with Manuela and Eloisa. "The best."

"From Sanchez y Haya, I think," Dewey said. "Or Perfecto Garcia around the corner here, was it?"

"Corral," Tom-tom said definitively. "Corral."

Marina interrupted to introduce Eloisa and Manuela to Tristan. They made their way, heads down, across the kitchen to him. By the time they were halfway, Eloisa was crying.

"He's the image, the very image," Manuela said. She placed a hand on each of his shoulders, bent down and kissed his forehead and straightened, all in one motion, a kind of exercise. "The image."

"Of who, for crissakes?" Tom-tom said.

Manuela looked around for help.

"Aunt Mama," Eloisa managed to say and then her crying

turned to sobs. She held out a hand towards Tristan, unable to contain herself enough to embrace him, and Tristan got up and took her hand and shook it.

"That's your great-grandmother," Aunt Clem said. She suddenly laughed and stopped herself. "I don't mean Eloisa. Aunt Mama."

"Oh, Aunt Clem," Cookie said and hid her face again.

Manuela squared her shoulders and with a stern, unswayable look said, "Aunt Mama was a saint."

"No, she wasn't," Maggie said. "She was a great cook and that's much better."

Marina said, "Maggie!" and Tom-tom boomed, "What a mouth she has!" and the others fell silent as if something terrible was bound to follow such blasphemy. Aunt Mama! No one looked at Tristan, but he laughed out loud, the first time since they had met him. They could not believe it; they had to look.

Maggie winked.

Tom-tom said, "I gotta admit, Pinpin didn't go much for saints and religion." He sneaked a look at Tristan. "That don't mean he didn't have a lotta respect for some things."

"OK, Professor, tell me something," Maggie asked. "If Uncle Pinpin was the numero uno Hispanic writer, who was numero two?"

Wallingford smiled.

"Gotcha," Maggie said. "Who?"

Wallingford had to think it over, and in the interval Aunt Clem complained, "Maggie, you ain't very polite."

Wallingford cleared his throat. "Literature is not my field. American Studies is."

"In that case, you oughta know Uncle Pinpin was not, I repeat not, very pro-American," she said and looked around for someone to argue with. "In fact, he was a red-hot communist, if you ask me."

"Well, now, just a moment," Jack said, but Tom-tom would not let him be arbiter.

Tom-tom raised his voice louder than anyone and pointed a fat finger at Maggie. "He was as good as any American! You wanta insult us 'cause you went and married some cracker, you go ahead. But get outa here and take your *pote* with you."

"What're you getting hot under the collar for?" Maggie said. No one, she could see, was on her side, and she wavered a moment. "I'm just telling the truth."

Tom-tom pointed to the older women in turn. "Marina, Clem, Eloisa, Manuela—you too, Cookie—see what you women can do with her. It's your responsibility. Her mother isn't around to wash out her mouth and her husband's too dumb to call the police and put her in the booby hatch."

Eloisa moaned and tried to get to the TV room, but there were too many cousins in the way.

Cookie managed to get her head under the table.

"I know what I am talking about, you old bull," Maggie insisted, but she looked around for support. "I'm the one who knows Uncle Pinpin. I go to the Centro Asturiano cemetery twice a month, sometimes three, and before I go through North Tampa and all those colored housing developments—God help me—I always stop over here and talk to him. He wanted me to, and he went on and on about the capitalists and religion and the bourgeoisie ways. Why, he wouldn't even let me criticize the blacks. I kinda liked it."

Marina said, "Everyone in this family always talked that way. It's not for us to say they were right or wrong."

"Yes," Tom-tom said. "What was good for them is good enough."

"Tristan is right here. Let's ask him, he oughta know his own grandpa," Maggie said. "What do you say, Tristan? Aren't I right about your grandpa being practically a Red?"

A relaxed chuckling went the rounds. Of course, whatever Pinpin had done was OK. Maggie didn't mean anything with her talk, but they looked at Tristan anyway.

Nevertheless, Tristan took a moment to think it over, and

they waited for him. He could hear the soap opera going on in the TV room. My God, it was already afternoon.

Maggie had cleared the air of piety. He liked her. This was the time to get the problem of cremation out of the way, once and for all. She would back him up and it would all blow over and he could be friends with his many new cousins despite what he had come to Tampa to do, and he would take out his notebook after they ate the guava pastries and check the list for what he had to do next.

"I'm not sure about Grandpa's political orientation," he began. "Maybe Maggie is right. You all probably know better and I want to hear all about it."

Dewey said, "Leave it to Maggie and Uncle Tom-tom. They'll tell ya."

Tristan decided to get right to the point. "I do know he was not religious—"

"I'll pray for him," Aunt Clem said.

"He was not, not at all," he continued.

Maggie nodded emphatically and winked. "He didn't want any prayers."

"My folks all know that too. That's why there's not going to be any interment or any funeral or any ceremony."

Maggie said, "What'd you say?"

Tristan nodded. "I'm going to have him cremated."

"What!" Maggie turned and looked at each person. Some, like Aunt Clem and Marina and Jack, nodded yes, they knew. Others, like Eloisa and Manuela, began to moan and look about them for a place to faint.

"Did ya see where they give this American woman the cremains in a Baggie with just a twistum to hold them in?" Aunt Clem said into the dead silence. "You could see the stuff and there was little pieces of bone and what all. And it was her mother!"

Manuela emitted a keening moan like a tea kettle's.

"She's suing!" Aunt Clem said. "You better believe it!"

"Shut up," Maggie said. "Tom-tom, you knew about this?"

But she did not wait for a reply. "And you're letting it go on and—and lookit me bringing the *pote!* You son of a bitch!"

"Now, listen," Jack said.

Maggie threw out her arms to the sides and screamed. She did not want any interference and she was clearing her throat for battle.

Without looking at him, she addressed Tristan. "You little fucker, you think you can come down here and do that? You think you can rob this family of its rights. I'm not going to let you, you hear! I'll kidnap Uncle Pinpin first."

"Please," Tristan said and he did not know what he meant.

She tried to get to his end of the table, but they held her back. She flung her arms around. "You Tom-tom, you Jack, you pig Dewey—you got no balls, tear him limb from limb. He's not gonna hold any inquisition and burn up my Uncle Pinpin!"

She made a last effort with a lunge of her body, but she and Jack lost their balance and fell on the kitchen table.

Dewey groaned. "Oh God, oh God, lookit, she squashed the guava pastries!"

Five

TRISTAN ENCOUNTERS GRANDPA

There was no reconciliation. Maggie walked out before Tristan could think of what he should say to her. He waited for her to pause, and half raised an arm to call her back, but she did not look his way as she tramped out of the kitchen and she did not return. Silence fell on them all, even on the children in the TV room. They stuck their heads in, looking like imps, hoping for more action. Did he hear Maggie's car screech away? She was not like Tom-tom and the cousins at the airport: they had stuck to him even after they heard the worst. She was more like a non-Hispanic.

Marina said, "Maggie isn't happy if things do not end up in a fight."

Aunt Clem said, "At least she didn't take the *pote*."

But no one's spirits were lifted by this talk. Not even by Dewey's finding a guava pastry that was not entirely squashed. Things did not go back to their happy normal. Jack and Dewey differed about whether the intact pastry should be put away until Tristan felt like eating it or whether it should be eaten now while still warm.

"It will get stale," Dewey insisted.

It was a quiet dispute. Jack mostly looked up towards the ceiling with exasperation. Finally he whispered angrily, "Go on, eat it."

Tristan was aware of this, but mostly he was aware that people were slipping out of the kitchen and TV room. Why hadn't he spoken to Maggie in time? He got up in a daze and drifted to the dining room, where he could see to the front porch, and noticed some persons leaving without saying goodbye. He was not sure he had been introduced to them all. Each raised a hand tentatively and weakly waved. When they moved away and unblocked the view, he saw Maggie on the sidewalk, as in a movie long-shot, talking to the cameraman.

To the camera, more likely.

She turned and walked towards her car and out of the frame.

Should he go after her? And say what?

Before he could decide, Joe Sorrento stood in front of him. He had been out on the sidewalk, but Tristan did not recall when he had left the kitchen table. Unlike himself, he had finished the Cuban sandwich and the *café con leche*, and now held a half-eaten guava pastry in one hand—the one Dewey retrieved or had a second one survived Maggie's thrashing? With his free hand, Joe Sorrento lightly held him back.

"Look, let me explain," Joe Sorrento said in a tone that was confidential and also acknowledged that he and Tristan were not part of this Southern scene. Indeed, that they were smarter. "We got the people on the street and your cousins on the porch, we got your uncle, we got you saying nothing and walking into the house. I don't know what else DJ got on his own, but I was in the kitchen and heard everything and now we got your cousin Maggie spelling it out loud and clear. All that. It makes quite a nice little story. Maybe not such a nice story, but a story."

He lifted his shoulder, took a bite of the guava pastry, and waited, as if for an offer.

He added, "DJ is my cameraman."

Tristan saw more cousins heading out. Whereas he had only a while ago wanted them to leave—yearned for it, in fact—he was now sad at their going. He had failed. He did not know quite at what, but he had failed and he was sad.

Joe Sorrento was forced to ask, "You want it that way?"

Tristan heard Tom-tom panting in his ear, eager to join in.

"You're saying I can influence you to change your story?" Tristan said.

"Aw, come on," Joe Sorrento said.

Tom-tom blurted, "You gonna let Maggie talk for the family? It'll be a scandal. She's only gotta open her mouth anyway and it's a scandal, but you heard the way—"

"What do you want me to do?" Tristan asked Joe Sorrento.

Tom-tom said, "You gotta leave her out, Joe. Just me and Tris or the deal is off."

Joe Sorrento said, "What deal? I got no deal."

The cousins in the porch and kitchen started to come closer, and Joe Sorrento held up a hand to keep them at a distance.

"Get back there," Tom-tom said to them.

Jack did not go back, but he did not come forward either. He stopped halfway, keeping up his courage with a smile.

Joe Sorrento repeated, "What deal?" This time pointing to Tristan. "I got a deal?"

Tristan shrugged. Did he dare suggest this was censorship? He decided to say it. "That's censorship."

"That's right, thank God," Tom-tom said. "You can't let idiots go shooting their mouths off."

Joe Sorrento threw one arm up, then the other, surrendering. He shook his head. He smiled. "What censorship? You do me a favor," he said. "I do you a favor."

Tristan took a deep breath. "What favor?"

"Talk to the camera about your grandfather," Joe Sorrento said and finished the pastry. "OK?"

"And no Maggie?" Tom-tom said.

Joe Sorrento nodded.

That was not the end of the negotiations. Tristan had learned a lot at Yale. Not just with the apartheid issue but also later on when he was involved in the union demands of the maintenance workers. Everything must be spelled out, a stance easy for Tristan to adopt in any situation.

Joe Sorrento made the mistake—in order to prove his sincerity—of volunteering that Channel Seven was only interested in happy local news. No Dwight Gooden run-ins, no controversies, no exposés. "I'm not an investigative reporter," he boasted. "A word from you about your grandpa, something nice that'll make everyone feel good that they're living here in God's country. And that's it. OK?"

"And?" Tristan said.

Joe Sorrento promised no family quarrels would surface.

"How do I know?" Tristan said.

Joe Sorrento gave him his word. Tristan hesitated. Joe Sorrento called DJ inside. He informed DJ in their presence of his promise to Tristan and asked him to go along with it. "Sure," DJ said. He looked at Joe Sorrento to see if he had given the right answer, and then he and Joe Sorrento looked at Tristan for some sign.

Tom-tom said, "I'm sold. Just keep Maggie out of it."

DJ and Joe Sorrento waited for Tristan to respond.

"Well?" Joe Sorrento finally said.

"I'm not happy with this censorship," Tristan said.

"What censorship?" DJ said and looked to Joe Sorrento for guidance.

Tristan explained, "It has to be your decision and because you want to do it."

"I want to do it," Joe Sorrento said. "I told you, we don't like to rock the boat on the local news."

DJ opened his mouth to speak but stopped when Joe Sorrento put out a hand to stop him. They waited.

Tristan took a deep breath and exhaled. He said, "Now, about your questions."

"What questions?" Joe Sorrento said. "All I asked is, will you do it."

Tristan blinked but kept his voice level. "The questions you plan to ask for the camera."

That took another round of negotiations. When it was done, Joe Sorrento said, "Jesus, you're tough. It's going to sound like an interview with Chairman Mao."

"Good, huh," Tom-tom said. "You can count on it. Tris is studying up there at that Yale, you know."

"I know," Joe Sorrento said. "And he's going from there straight to the State Department."

"Tris, Tris, whyn't you tell me!" Tom-tom said.

Joe Sorrento added, "The State Department can't wait to send him to Geneva for those continuing disarmament meetings. He is perfect for them."

"What?" Tom-tom said, but Tristan knew he had won. It did not make him feel good.

DJ did not want to film the interview in the house: he'd have to get lights from the van. He preferred the porch where there would be enough light but not too much as on the sidewalk.

Tristan said he could not do it now. He had too many things to attend to. They could come later, perhaps in the evening. Or tomorrow morning.

"I don't believe this," Joe Sorrento said. "This is gotta be on the six o'clock news and I want to get back to the studio to edit it myself and sell it to the anchorman—"

"When?" Tom-tom said.

Joe Sorrento answered him, but he meant it for Tristan's ears. "Six o'clock news, that's when."

Tom-tom turned toward the kitchen shaking with excitement. He yelled, "It's gonna be on the six o'clock news!"

Aunt Clem shrieked first, then repeated it for the others. She grabbed for the phone just inside the doorway. "I gotta let them know!"

Tom-tom hissed at her. "Call my home first."

Aunt Clem protested. "Lila is deaf and Olivia can't—"

"Call them!" Tom-tom insisted.

Dewey stole the phone from her and began dialing. "I'm calling Charlene at the office. She'll call everybody."

The fog of disappointment cleared from the house. Tristan became less confused; he saw his duty clear. He went right out to the porch to say his piece.

"I am here for the immediate family to make all the necessary arrangements," he said to the camera head-on. Then he went totally blank.

Joe Sorrento said, "The immediate family?"

"For reasons of illness, my father can't come," he said, remembered that he had not yet phoned him, and went blank again. Joe Sorrento nodded encouragingly. "And my uncle is in the Pacific, beyond reach." He had a happy thought: "But of course my grandfather has a lot of family in Ybor City—many, many cousins who remember him. Yes."

"And they are all here with you, aren't they?"

"Oh yes, yes," Tristan said and smiled.

Joe Sorrento was very pleased with this last unnegotiated response. He ventured into another area: he asked, "And will your grandfather's remains stay in Tampa?"

Tristan went blank.

"The funeral?" Joe Sorrento said.

"Oh, arrangements have not been completed," he said and nodded and regained his grave look. He went blank once more. This time for good.

Funny, going blank in front of the TV camera was different from hesitating or mulling over what to say. He really did go blank; not a thought showed up in his mind. God. It was scary.

Still, he was glad he had gone through with it. That was a feeling that came to him without thinking; he did not reason himself into it. He had done right. It was not a capitulation, as he had guiltily felt when he negotiated with Joe Sorrento. Nor was he censoring a newscast. He saw he had done right in the faces of everybody around the camera, neighbors who came over and shook hands and said, "I accompany you in your sorrow." He said thank you to each without hesitation this time.

Tom-tom looked down on him from the porch like a trainer in his corner and nodded approvingly.

He got his reward immediately—he felt this on the spot, *spontaneously*, he said to himself. It followed so quickly on the interview it seemed right to believe it was a reward for good behavior. There was a special quiet, an auguring lull, and a woman came up and said, "I am Rosita." She was dark, a polished, even olive; her eyes were black and lively like the eyes of those women in the movies about Latin America and Southern Italy. Her face was unwrinkled, her black hair had only a few strands of gray, and she wore it tight, pulled back severely to a small, trim bun. She wore a cotton housedress, starched and crisp, and she exuded coolness though he knew, as both her hands clasped his, that her flesh was warm.

"We are chaff, you know, chaff," she said. "Worthless, worthless as those withered leaves I am always sweeping up in front of the house."

Why was everyone quiet?

"I have been living on this block all my life. Aunt Mama

used to yell at me like my own mother. If the truth be told, she had more sense than my own mother."

She laughed a tinkling laugh.

As soon as Tristan smiled she looked away and smiled at the others.

"Hello, Rosita," Aunt Clem called from the porch.

Rosita, Rosita, Rosita, the others murmured.

"If you want to be strict about it, I can only claim that an uncle of mine married a cousin of Aunt Mama's and that's how I'm in the family. Besides having been born on this block. So was your grandfather, we were two old relics on the block," she said. "I was nine years old when he left Tampa and sixty when he returned. It was as if he had been gone only for a moment, during which I had learned to cook and not much else. But not him, not him. He knew about the whole world. I could never catch up." She smiled at him again. "I was a special friend. Now I have the block to myself and the muggers."

Clear, clear eyes. Not a tear.

"You can think of me as a great-aunt," she said.

Tristan nodded. He hoped she could tell that he liked her. He nodded again.

She winked.

He noticed she wore no makeup, but that her eyebrows were carefully plucked. They arched lightly and made her eyes appear to be alertly open.

"I peeked in the window and saw him in bed. But he was not right. On his back across the bed, not head to foot. So I called Marina and waited on the porch. It was no time for doctors."

She waved to Tom-tom and he nodded but did not come down to them. She took Tristan's hand again.

"But not Tom-tom, though I like him very much and he is certainly devoted to Pinpin. Was. But—you understand?"

Tristan nodded.

"Too bossy," she said.

She closed her eyelids slightly. She was ashamed to have criticized Tom-tom.

"It's not true that I did not go in," she added and took her hand away. "I did." She looked at Tristan directly. "I wanted to kiss him."

Then she laughed—she surprised him all the time—and took his arm like a lady and turned him towards the house. "We old people get very foolish," she said. She looked at the diminished group on the porch and greeted them without speaking, like a public figure used to crowds. "Now, tell me, what can I do to help you?"

She attracted him like Nanao that first time they met. He had wanted to hear her talk and talk. It had not been sexual, he was almost sure. To Nanao he would have said libidinal and she would have laughed. Still, it embarrassed him to react any which way to an old woman (Nanao's locution, this time) and in order to cover up he looked at his watch. God, it was almost four!

"I've got a lot of things to do," he said. He took out the notebook and went down the list. "A lawyer. Do you know who Grandpa's lawyer was?"

She shook her head.

"Whaddya want?" Tom-tom said. The moment he saw Tristan consult his notebook he was on the alert. He crowded the other side of him, away from Rosita.

"Pinpin's lawyer?" she said.

"A lawyer!" Tom-tom said. "Pinpin didn't sue nobody—what he want a lawyer for?"

Both Rosita and Tom-tom were perplexed.

"I want to find out first of all if he left a will," Tristan explained. "And where his papers are."

"He didn't need no will," Tom-tom said. "Nobody gets anything. I won't let them cheat you outa nothing."

"Now I understand," Rosita said. "You must not have seen his office. Everything like that must be there. Did you see it?"

"What office?" Tom-tom said. "Whaddya mean an office?"

Tristan shook his head no at Rosita and did not listen to Tom-tom. For him now, Tom-tom was a thunderstorm in the background.

Rosita explained, "The second bedroom, Tom-tom. Aunt Mama's old bedroom."

She pulled ever so lightly on Tristan's arm for an answer.

"I didn't get to see anything," Tristan replied. "I was only in the kitchen." Then to be fair added, "I ate a delicious Cuban sandwich."

"Come," she said.

She cleared the way for him. She understood. She knew he needed to go about his business like any man and that even she might be in the way. She communicated this somehow to the cousins. She was not officious, she did not give orders. She did not manipulate anyone; she simply brought sense and lightness into the house and everyone did what they should and things fell into place. Even Marina was happy to see her. Tristan felt both manly and like a kid, and he quickly suppressed the feeling.

"Isn't he handsome?" she said to Marina.

Marina nodded, but said, "He's a good boy," as the proper response for now.

Rosita took her hand away from Tristan's arm as they arrived at the closed door of the second bedroom, and not only let him know this was where he was going but did it without speaking and yet all the while looking at Marina so that Marina felt she was in on it too. Rosita usurped nothing, supplanted no one.

Marina said, "Tristan, everything is how he left it. I closed the door yesterday and it has stayed that way since."

"Yes, yes," said Tom-tom impatiently and grabbed his elbow now that Rosita had let go.

"Tom-tom," Marina admonished.

"I'm only standing here," Tom-tom said, "so that they'll let him be in peace."

Rosita went on with Marina to the kitchen. Tom-tom watched them but stayed with Tristan to one side of the door.

"Later, later!" Tom-tom waved some people away and Tristan let him.

Tristan opened it—the door to Aunt Mama's old bedroom, a place that should have been sacred to her children and to her many nephews and nieces. A sweet old lady, she must have created a bower that Grandpa kept like a shrine. Here it was.

Bright, startling; black leather, white formica. Black formica too. Ceramic tiles on the floor. He closed the door behind him. The room was painted flat white and the black appeared darker in the brilliant Florida light. He touched the black formica on the long work surface. It was edged in oak, a wood that Tristan approved of, and ran along one entire wall and then curved and continued on the outer wall until it reached the windows to the side porch. The surface was not formica. It was that other stuff, impervious to everything, very expensive.

The floor was black and white also; large-sized tiles in the center diminishing towards the edges. On the wall across from the work surface, black and white files and above them discreet wall cupboards revealing nothing but a dull black finish on flat knobless doors. A leather chaise looking like an S lying on its side made a thin black silhouette from any angle. Italian design, he knew that much. Behind it, to one side of the door, a hi-fi set of NAD and Denon components, all black and gray. He looked for the speakers. On the ceiling corners of the far wall. The best. Maybe too powerful for this size room. The disks and cassettes must be hiding in the cupboards.

Near him at the work surface, one of those chairs you knelt in rather than sat; black leather seat and knee pads, white birch. In front of it, on the work surface, the room's real center: a Toshiba 3100 in its dark gray case. A little farther along, to this side of the windows, a Hewlett-Packard laser-jet printer, white and austere. Ah.

Tristan moved to the computer, touched it, and saw that in fact it was a Toshiba 3200. One up on Dad's 3100. Forty megabytes!

He looked around the room once more, with greater respect this time, and came back to the work surface and saw then the Baskin sculpture, one of his Dead Men. A ravaged body of an old man; one leg and two forearms missing, its face blurred by time and pain. A small figure, seven or eight inches, no more. Bronze, a shiny nose where it had been most handled. He picked it up in one hand and saw that it served as a paperweight for some sheets and a notebook on which it had lain. What a funny idea. What a crazy old man.

A black, slim phone with white numerals sat an arm's length away from the Toshiba. Behind it, a black answering machine. A shallow drawer, almost invisible, was built into the work surface at that spot. He pulled it out. Many pens, Mont Blancs and Watermans mostly, and a red leather telephone/address book, like a spill of blood in the black/white room. A Smythson, elegant with its wafer-thin blue paper.

He sat/knelt on the chair and as he did so remembered it was called the Balans chair. Mom would not let Dad buy one. He began leafing through the address book. Mom and Dad. Uncle Crispin in California. Marina. Rosita. Tom-tom. Maggie. Auto Mechanic. No one else in Tampa. A firm in Boston. And nobody else anywhere.

The Balans chair was great. You could not slump in it. He remembered that he had tried to ask Marina about a lawyer, but Tom-tom had not let him finish. The door to the room was closed, and he listened now for sounds of the others. How strange it all was from what he had imagined in New York. Most of the cousins had stayed after Maggie stomped out. Actually, they had not left, they had milled about in the street, momentarily embarrassed, that's all. It surprised him—as if he had learned something new about himself—that he was glad so many had stayed.

He leafed through the notebook again. This time he noticed that he was not listed. Why should I be? he asked himself. Grandpa was not in his address book. No one was. He owned no address book. God. If he died now, he would be just as hard to track down as Grandpa—no sign that he knew anybody, that he loved . . .

He picked up the Dead Man again and saw the notebook and the sheets of paper, saw them as evidence this time. The sheets were a print-out. Beautifully neat. Nothing like a laser-jet for clarity and definition. A letter to the editor. A Tampa newspaper, he suspected. A denunciation. Reminding them about a cigarmakers' strike in the 1930s and what finks they had been then and were now.

There were corrections in longhand. A firm, stylish script whose t's and h's and b's were much alike, as were the a's and o's, and also the m's and w's. But you knew the words they formed, the flow was so forceful and unvarying. Grandpa's handwriting, the first time he was seeing it. Across the bottom of the last page he had written, *Yuck, no use sending to that loathsome newspaper.*

The notebook bound in black leather was also a Smythson, also with fine light-blue paper. Grandpa had used it as a diary. The entries were all dated by him, and they were very short, several to each page.

An entry last month was only one sentence long: *When are the social democrats going to die out?*

The last one was—Tristan checked with his watch—only two days old, the day he died. It said: *Work. Drove to Clearwater to the old beach at Palm Pavilion. Ate formaldehyde shrimps at Pelican. Drank café on Rosita's porch. Flirted. Should have eaten at Tio Pepe's.*

That was the end. No farewells, no words of advice, no old

man's wisdom? Grandpa was certainly no professor, he didn't talk needlessly. But of course he hadn't known it would be his last entry. He opened the diary at another spot and did not let the date written in numerals sink in. *Work. Two whole pages. Celebrated with a mixed sandwich on 7th Ave. Tom-tom waiting on porch. Let him make café. Read Baroja outside until sundown.*

He saw an entry, written only one week ago, that was only one line: *Reread Plato. Maybe less reactionary now.*

He thought: Grandpa is like me, unsure of things, unsteady on his intellectual pins. He wished the phrase were his; it was Uncle Crispin's. Amusing if said in a beery drawl. Except Uncle Crispin drank only very fine wines.

What was he looking for? A lawyer's name. The diary had no place for vital statistics etcetera on its frontispiece. It began, with no warning, one day seven months ago. There must be others. He crossed the room to the cupboards and files. The cupboards were full of CD's. All the greats. No, there was no Bach, no Scarlatti. One shelf, three deep, of Beethoven. The same for Mozart and Schubert. A lot of Shostakovich.

He expected to find two or three more Smythson notebooks used as diaries. There was a whole shelf in one cupboard. At least twenty more. He picked one of the first ones. 1968. January. The entries were longer, but the script, the black ink, the blue paper the same. *Harvey called, proposed article on King and Poor Peoples Campaign. Thinking it over. Rockefeller Inter-American Inst. also called. Cooptation? Go, but don't kiss ass. Cora doesn't approve; Susie will, a swinger she.*

He crossed the room slowly and sat/knelt. He knew all the elements of this puzzle, but it would take him time to decipher it. He bit his lip and worked at it. He did not, he had to admit, really know that Rockefeller thing. Some right-wing something, it must've been. Wasn't Susie a close friend of Grandma's—why would she approve? He called her up in his memory: a lot of makeup and furs and much intrusive hugging.

Martin Luther King! Did Grandpa write the article? God. He looked at the phone. He ought to call Nanao right away and ask her. She would know. That Montgomery bourgeoisie knew everything there was to know about King. They had not missed a footnote. Nanao called him their patron saint. If Grandpa wrote the article, then he must have met him. He closed his eyes and tried to recall if Dad or Uncle Crispin had ever said anything about Grandpa and Reverend King.

A jumble of celebrities rushed into his mind. Movie stars, many of them. Several directors. Writers and writers, a traffic jam of them. One opera star. Several performers. The mayor of New York—Lindsay, not the present one, he was vulgar.

Why was he so excited about Martin Luther King?

Nanao, that was why.

He felt the beginnings of a blush, but there was no one in the room and it subsided.

Too much happening in one day, that's what it was. It was understandable. Imagine, learning that Grandpa was going to give him points with Nanao! What a find! Still, he must take time. He held Grandpa's diary in one hand and, to calm himself, slowly, thoughtfully raised and lowered it, hefting it like a bowling ball. Suddenly he felt he shouldn't know all this about Grandpa. And yet he wanted to know more, much more than these tantalizing bits. He would read the diaries later. Now, he must find the lawyer Grandpa used.

The will! Of course, he would find the lawyer in the will. The will was bound to say who had drawn it up, in fact would likely be witnessed by the lawyer and written on the firm's stationery. He looked around the room.

He went back to the cupboards. Go through them systematically, that is what he would do. He opened the one nearest the windows first. God. All 78s, the great jazz ones of the

Commodore label. Trios, sextets. Lots of Teddy Wilson. More Benny Goodman. The Duke. Mildred Bailey. Paul Robeson. Communist stuff. The International Brigades in Spain. Woody. *Spirituals to Swing.* The originals. Disks he had read about. The real thing! He took down the Lotte Lenya, cut on the West Coast in 1946, and removed it from its sleeve. Perfect, not a scratch. He turned to the hi-fi to play it and only then came to his senses.

What would the cousins think?

He returned the record to its cupboard and went on with his search. One cupboard of cassettes. He did not allow himself to remove a single one from the shelves. Another cupboard contained all the Library of America volumes of authors that Tristan meant to read someday. Grandpa did not seem to have done so before he went. One cupboard of stationery: two reams of paper for the printer, computer supplies and instruction books, three boxes of envelopes of different sizes, note pads, paper clips, a stapler and a sharpener. One empty cupboard.

There were still the files under the cupboards. On the shelf formed by their common top were books: Dickens, Balzac, Zola, Chekhov, William Dean Howells, Twain; and some Spaniards Tristan had not heard of, that fellow Baroja again, Clarin, Perez-Galdos. He touched none of these volumes.

Could the will be in the files?

Of course.

He squatted. Two drawers were filled with correspondence whose folders showed on their tags the year their letters were written. The tags of the folders in the next three files were blank. He looked in these. Stories, articles, reviews. The last of these files contained manuscript boxes: the originals of his books, corrected galleys too. Grandpa was an orderly man.

The last three filing cabinets were empty. On the inside edge of one of the shelves there was a small typed sign that said *No Baroque Shit.* A horselaugh. And that was that.

Tristan sat on the leather chaise, but he could not relax in it unless he lay back and that was inappropriate. So much beckoned to him in this room that was not the business at hand. He got up and sat/knelt at the chair, and it occurred to him that Grandpa might well have kept really personal papers in a dresser in his bedroom. No, it did not take him long to discard that idea.

There was a soft knock on the door.

It was almost a relief. "Yes?" he said.

Tom-tom looked in before he could have heard him. "You OK, Tris?" He looked about quickly, furtively, without moving his head, his eyes as loose as a broken doll's. "You found anything?"

"Am I needed?" Tristan asked.

"I'm taking care of things," he said. Obviously, he wanted to step inside, but Tristan made no gesture of encouragement. Tom-tom leaned forward as far as his stomach would allow him and whispered, "Jack's still here. Pay no attention to him."

"Does he want me?" Maybe Jack would know of a lawyer if—

Tom-tom hissed, "They all want ya, that's the trouble."

Tristan raised his eyebrows coolly and waited, encouraging him as little as possible.

"You know what," Tom-tom said, "that Joe Sorrento made a date with Cookie. He's smart. She's a good girl. She don't forget a friend. Every other Tuesday she brings Olivia a lasagna, and don't think Olivia don't know it."

Tristan was pleased (he was not sure why) but waited.

Tom-tom looked about the room again. This time with nostalgia. "Many's the time I saw your grandpa in front of that word presser. He would let me look at that crazy orange screen and see the letters running along like the dogs at the races."

Of course, Tristan said to himself, of course.

"He was gonna teach me," he said. "Me. Would ya believe it?"

That was Grandpa's real file—the Toshiba 3200 with all its forty megabytes of hard memory. God. Dense, dense, dense.

"You think I could learn, Tris?" Tom-tom said and placed one foot inside the room.

"Uncle Tom-tom, I can't—"

"Not now," Tom-tom said quickly and retrieved his foot. "I didn't mean now."

"Uncle Tom-tom, I'm very grateful to you," Tristan said. "I'll be with you in a little while, OK?"

"You're busy, huh?"

"For just a little while," Tristan said. "I'm looking for his lawyer's name."

"I told you, he don't have one," Tom-tom said. "He never sued anybody about anything."

"The will, remember?" Tristan said.

Tom-tom shook his head. "It's not a good idea to tell a lawyer what you own."

Tristan simply raised a hand and waved to get rid of him. He was too eager to get to the Toshiba to say any more.

Tom-tom gave up. "I'll stand out here. I won't let any of those pests in."

"Thanks, Uncle Tom-tom, thanks," he said as he pushed with his knees and turned the chair to face the Toshiba. He really was grateful for Tom-tom's having led him to the Toshiba, but he did not even hear the door close. Fleetingly, he felt real greed for the first time in his life, and was not ashamed. That Toshiba and its forty-megabyte hard drive was going to be his, nobody's but his.

At first he thought the computer was dead. Zonked.

So soon? The latest model?

He had to get down on his hands and knees to trace the

cord from the Toshiba and the laser-jet printer to a wall plug. They led, instead, to a surge protector which was neatly installed under the work surface on the far side of the drawer, its on/off switch comfortably to hand when one knelt/sat at the Toshiba. Neat. Grandpa was no dum-dum, everything in the room said so.

He opened the lid of the Toshiba. Two clicks, and the bright orange screen came to vivid light. It spoke to him. At its upper left-hand corner it blinked a message: *Tell it like it is, Pinpin.*

God.

The screen steadied, the message remained there for him to study if he so wished, and all forty microbytes of data it had room for waited for him too. Grandpa, that's who was there. Awesome. He could not tell why. Not unless he thought about it, and he did not have the time.

First, he tried Word Perfect, for he figured that Grandpa had no other use for the Toshiba than as a word processor. Bad command, it told him. He tried WordStar and it came on immediately—the most updated form of it, as he expected. Tristan was so pleased that he took time to think through Grandpa's using WordStar: he was true to old loves but preferred them refurbished and . . . He was a little afraid to take that generalization further, and anyway, the directory for WordStar was waiting for him. Grandpa had compiled it, left out DOS titles.

A group of names. Only given names. He recognized some cousins. There was Tom-tom's file. He called it up without thinking.

Let me say it immediately, the screen said. *He saved my life. Of course, he almost took it too, but that was earlier. Still, he did save my life, and now he squats on the dusty porch when I am in here and looks around for bones I may have carelessly dropped, varlet to the feudal lord he sometimes thinks I am. He's an old hound dog. Ugly. Full of fleas.*

But one loves him and gives him a good scratch occasionally.

I am not happy with this cliche. Let me try again.

Tristan looked to the door of the study and was ashamed to have participated in Grandpa's judgment. God, but what a thrill. Grandpa didn't spare Tom-tom. He went right to it; he was really something.

He decided he had better not read any more about Tom-tom, not because he was not interested but because he had to think about what he was doing. The rightness of it, that is.

He hit the key to abandon that file and found himself staring at his own name in the directory. Tristan. Had he looked for it? Why hadn't he noticed it earlier? He did not allow himself to answer that and quickly hit the key for calling up files. He was supposed to write his own name next and he as quickly ran out of spontaneity. His hands froze over the keys. *Document to open?* the bright Toshiba asked him. Document to open? Should he?

Maybe he should read someone else's file first?

But he had not resolved the moral problem of reading any of the files at all. Was it a moral problem or an ethical problem? Then why would he feel free to read his own file? Wasn't it as unethical? As snoopy, really. Unfair to Grandpa. Yes, he had written it all.

He remembered Grandpa urging him—against what he knew would be Mom's, even Dad's advice—to take a second chocolate-covered strawberry at Balducci's. He suddenly heard Grandpa's voice, its deep tones, its insinuating ring. "Let's finish the jelly beans before you get home," it said.

Wait, wait logic first. What was his goal? Why was he working the Toshiba? To find Grandpa's lawyer. Right. Logic always gets you back on track. Like *The Hitchhiker's Guide to the Galaxy*, the computer game he and Nanao were cooperatively doping out on an old Compaq with no hard drive. Yes, all a matter of logic getting around in the galaxy.

The lawyer would have the will and the will would name the literary executor and then it would be decided who could properly read Grandpa's private papers.

Inexplicably, he rapidly typed his name, hit the Enter key, and there was Grandpa's file on him.

In the woods, when it became too mysterious, he always reached up and took my hand. His was invariably sticky with sap. Each time we entered the Tristan Path he picked up a sharp-pointed twig at the falling-down cabin (as we called an old studio gone to ruin) where the path we made began and with the twig punctured the sacs of sap swelling the bark of the pine trees. The globules of clear liquid glittered so enticingly each time that he could not resist tapping, like any research scientist, this thick jewel-like syrup with his forefinger. Was it really liquid? It was. It spread to the other fingers somehow. What a mess. He stopped being a careful city boy in these tantalizing woods. What a grand, sharp piney smell too. It was worth coming home to a fuss with his mother. The glittering sap turned into black tacky spots on your hands, stiff sticky globs on your pants. He would throw away the stick to be rid of it all and the stick would sometimes not leave his hand, it stuck to his fingers. It made him laugh, and me too. In the woods, he laughed with an abandon I never heard him display (wrong word) elsewhere. No constriction in his throat, I think was the difference. His laughter rose up into the sunlight as part of the dappled, odorous scene: he could have been an unafraid red-fox pup gamboling on his well-traveled path. And when he took my hand because he sensed danger he was as unrestrained and right as when he laughed that trebled, mellifluous laugh. There had occurred the unexplained crackle of a twig, the moan of a tree branch, the whir of a car's tires strange to the ear so far from the road. I reached for his hand perhaps sooner than he did for mine. And then I laughed too. I was scared and very happy with Tristan.

Is this grandfather talk?

From whom comes this boy's sweetness? Not from what we call the world. Nor from Streets & Fields, that smug progressive vipers' nest. Certainly not from his dumb mother and father, too old to be genuine yuppies, too young to have been activists. Nor Cora's Wasp Bostonians, they have all curdled at their mothers' breasts. Maybe some Midwesterner filtered through the Ohio Valley migration from New England puritanism, mellowed by the Civil War, bypassed by ambition, or one of those mid-nineteenth-century German socialists unacknowledged by that big-city hustler, his mother.

Walking down Fifth Avenue he does not reach for my hand. Police cars, ambulances, fire engines, and at best he may look their way for a glance. Cursory, at that. No mysteries there. He is alert to other dramas. Serenity is his bag.

Once a fire engine inspired him to ask me, "Grandpa, have you ever been in a real fire?"

I loved him so much that it did not occur to me to invent an adventure to entertain him or to build myself up. Only the truth for that boy. I simply said, "No."

He nodded sagely at that. He said, "Very few people have been in a real fire. I don't know anybody."

I did not ask him what he meant by a real fire. Unlike one on TV, I suppose.

Later that night, when I had gone on home, I remembered that I had been in a real fire during the war. At the airbase in Norfolk. Two sailors ran out from the burning hangar after the explosions went off, their work shirts on fire. I tackled one to the ground and rolled him to stamp out the fire. It took him a while to feel the burns. I would never have told Tristan about that. Anyone else, yes, but not Tristan.

Let him find out about the world on his own. Not from me. Who the hell wants to teach his grandson about the world, who?

Tristan looked away from the screen. It slithered and blurred and he could not focus it by squinting: his eyes were full of tears. God. Poor Grandpa. He looked to the door to check that it was closed. He allowed himself to cry, thinking all the while that he was a phony. Wasn't this just guilt he was feeling? Not love for Grandpa? He had not given Grandpa a thought in years, he had never read his books—that's what he was crying about. The thought made him almost sob. Nobody in his family would approve of this behavior, this display. His tears stopped, only the tightness in his throat remained.

He looked at the door again. That did not apply to this family down here. If you could say they were family. They had already cried more for Grandpa than Mom and Dad ever would, more than if you threw in his brother Owen in Oxford and his sister Emily at Buxton and Uncle Crispin fucking somewhere. And who else up North? God, what a small little family his was. A minor epidemic could wipe it all out.

The orange screen waited for him. It was as patient as he, as tenacious as Tom-tom outside the door.

Tristan and I had an experience in the city that equaled—in time topped (in our memory of it)—our catching our first toad in the Maine woods. We were walking down Fifth Avenue again and we stopped to look at the excavation that had begun at the Twelfth Street Church entrance and at the fence along the avenue. The old crumbling soft granite edging had been dug up and a temporary wire fence put up. We looked through it at the small moat now formed and saw in the dank dark autumnal colors—a ground cover of ivy and pachysandra was poised sullenly above the moat—a small very clean white mouse making its way with care.

"Look, there's a white mouse!" I said in that disgusting tone we use when reading children their dumb-ass pretend-innocent books. "A white mouse in the city!"

"Yes," was all Tristan said, but he remained there quietly after we lost sight of the mouse among the pachysandra. He was thinking it over. "Where did it go?" he asked when it became clear it was not going to return and disport itself for our pleasure.

We did not see it on our way back from Soho. Tristan hardly paused as we passed the Twelfth Street Church. Better than I, he knew there would not be more white mice climbing the miniature moat. It had been an occasion. That was not the case with toads in Maine. Our moist woods were full of them and God only knows how often we went out with small plastic containers to catch a couple and bring them back to Tristan's plastic wading pond. We were always successful (I think) on such expeditions. But the scarcity of white mice in Presbyterian churchyards may have been the reason our experience that early Saturday afternoon came to appear so extraordinary. I had immediately believed it was something to be remarked (a Latin propensity) but Tristan never said another word about it. Until one year later. The new church walk and stone fence were up and Tristan slowed down as we went by and said, "Do you remember when we saw the white mouse?" and he looked up at me with shining eyes.

It was a thrilling hurting blow. I was afraid for Tristan. That is how art begins. In remembering and wonder. The world protect him from it. Burn that awe out of him.

God. What did he mean? He had to think about this. Later.

Let him, rather, be another of those inward-looking, self-indulgent middle-class sons of bitches. I'm feeling good, you're feeling good. I'm comfortable with that. No sweat, no strain. That grates. He has had all the proper schooling for it. Let him be that. Anything but dedicate himself to knowledge of the real world.

I saw him go off gradually on his own. In an emergency

his mother and father, who spent a large part of his malodorous Hollywood income on nannies and baby-sitters, would ask us to take over of an evening. I always read Tristan two stories. He listened and never commented, except when, as with the mouse, he would say something weeks later that showed it had all been digested. In time he began to be read full-length books. He understood Huckleberry Finn! That he was read this masterpiece is perhaps the only good thing I can say for his parents. I read him the chapter on Huck's going ashore by himself. A month later, after reading him a chapter of those faceless Hardy boys, he did not let me put the book back on its shelf by his bed. He said he was going to stay up a little longer and read to himself.

"Okay, fella," I said, but it was a wrench.

Then came the night when he said that he did not want me to read to him. "I can read more of it if I read to myself," he said, and then added a reasonable explanation that should have assuaged me but did not, "The eyes can move faster than the lips, Grandpa."

And so he moved away.

That was the end of his file. He looked up and a funny electric tingling spread out to the ends of his body. When it receded, he was tempted to scroll the screen up and read his file again. He wanted to solve the mystery of his feelings: why was he exhilarated when what Grandpa had written was so sad?

His whole body felt different for having cried. As if he had been through a workout and were now healthy-tired. A catharsis. Like Greek drama. He sat/knelt with his head slightly bowed; he did not want to be staring at the end of the file on himself. Without looking at the screen he hit the keys to return to the directory.

He searched among the names for one that might be the lawyer's. He decided to try Orlando.

The freeway with which they disemboweled Ybor City

takes you there in less than an hour. I did not know why I drove there, but I had only to run into a man masquerading as a Disney cartoon character (one of the abominable dwarfs, I think) to know without equivocation ("Hi!" he said right at me in a ghastly cheery way) that I had to get out. It was a physical reaction. I turned about on that cutie-pie street and with a great effort managed to hurry out without vomiting or punching a few retired idiots. I had the sense that people were watching me as I fled to the diagrammed fascist parking lot. How soothing to get back to this decaying neighborhood with its scaling paint and sandy plots. Decaying? Can it get worse? Can life get worse? Yes, it can always get worse.

That was all Grandpa wrote on Orlando. How did it get in this directory? It was not a person, like the other files.

This directory!

Of course, of course, of course, there had to be another directory. Maybe even more than one. This one did not even list the program files which ran the computer. He hit the keys to get out of WordStar. Back to the C command. He called for the basic directory and it immediately rolled before his eyes. There were the Elgins and Autoexecs and all his old friends. Those funny guys, Nanao called them. No lawyer, however, and no will.

That was that. Life was no murder mystery; there was nothing to track down in the word processor. He would ask Marina or Rosita or even Tom-tom—why not?—for a lawyer to advise him. Maybe that professor, if he was still here. He would certainly know. He was immediately a little ashamed of that thought—why should the professor know any better?

He opened the door and at the same moment Marina and Rosita came out of the kitchen together.

"There you are, Tristan," Marina said. "I'll bet you're thinking of a shower and change. That's the way Tampa is—"

"Hot," said Rosita.

"Have you ever been in hot weather before?" Marina continued.

"I wanted to ask you something," Tristan said.

"Not every room in this house is so cool as that one," Rosita said.

"I left it the way he left it," Marina said. "With the air-conditioning running at low."

His senses had not taken it in. He looked back as if he could check with his eyes. Yes, it had been cool as well as black and white. In there he had stopped sweating. How smart Grandpa had been.

He nodded to Rosita. "Maybe you can advise me too."

Tom-tom said, "What? What?"

"You too, Uncle Tom-tom," he paused to say.

But the women did not stop. Rosita took his arm and they led him the few steps to the front bedroom, and on the way a couple of men held out their hands to shake his. "I accompany you in your loss," each said, and then each added his version of being at his service.

"Thanks," Tristan said, doing his part. "I appreciate your coming."

"Those are Manuela's boys," Marina said as if they had sped by. "And here is Pinpin's bedroom. It used to be his sister Celia's."

"And her husband Cuco," Rosita added. "God bless him—if you knew the number of errands he ran for me!"

Manuela's boys did not mind being so briefly attended to. They went back to the sofa where with the professor they had been discussing the terrible record of the Phillies and the Cleveland Indians during spring training.

"I unpacked your . . . thing," Marina said.

He stopped himself from saying he did not expect to be babied.

"Boys," Rosita said. "They are the same everywhere."

Tristan figured this was what a Tampa bedroom looked

like. A dresser, a double bed, a wide mirror over the dresser, and both venetian blinds and filmy curtains plus drapes at the windows. Flowery covers on the bed and pillows.

Marina pulled a drawer open. "Here are your things," she said, and there, indeed, they were. Even the extra notebook and the Sting and Bruce cassettes lined up on one side of the drawer, two refolded brief shorts and socks on the other. "I'm ironing the shirts," Marina added to explain their absence, "and I hung a clean cotton bathrobe behind the door here. You're not superstitious, right? I'm not. You can use it and if you run out there's more underwear here." And she pulled open another drawer.

Grandpa's.

Rosita said, "Of course."

"But don't worry," Marina continued, "there's a washer-drier in the utility room and I'll be taking care of your—"

Rosita said, "Or I will."

Marina chuckled. "Or any other woman in the family. Even Maggie, you'll see, she'll be back soon. Anyway, there's no dearth of women in the family." She was proud of the phrase and repeated it, "No dearth of them."

Tom-tom stood in the doorway of the bedroom. "Don't worry, Tris, we'll take care of you."

Tristan was not thinking about it and yet the words came to him. Drove. Auto Mechanic. Words from Grandpa's diary and address book. They came to mind inconsequentially. He must own a car. He said, "Grandpa owned a car?"

"Of course," Marina said. "It's in the carport, the keys must be around here someplace." She opened another drawer and looked there for them.

"He mostly drove me to the shopping mall," Rosita said.

He figured Tom-tom would know for sure. "He drove?" he said to him.

Tom-tom nodded.

"You wanted to rent a car," Tom-tom reminded him.

Marina said, "You let him rent a car!"

"What a waste," Rosita agreed, but not too vehemently.

"Money thrown away," Marina said.

"He wanted to rent a car," Tom-tom said. "Would you deny the boy the pleasure?"

No one answered him.

"I've got the keys," Tom-tom said. He waited a moment, then added, "If you want to use it."

"You hang on to them for now, Uncle Tom-tom."

"You sure?" Marina asked.

Tristan shook his head. Then nodded. None of that bothered him. He simply wanted to clear his mind of the snag it had hit on with those words in Grandpa's papers. Papers! There were no papers anymore, in that old-fashioned way: there were electronic signals zinged out into the future.

God. Someone could have come along and erased them. Without knowing, of course. He sat down on the bed and all three watched him. Were there floppy disk copies?

"Does any one of you know about a good lawyer here?" he asked. "I want to call him."

"In Tampa?" Marina said.

"You know what your grandfather would have said?" Rosita said. "There are no good lawyers anywhere."

"You bet," Tom-tom said. "And he woulda been right."

Tristan said, "I need a lawyer to advise me about . . . various things."

"You got us," Tom-tom said, generously including the women. He stepped into the room.

It becamed crowded. Marina and Rosita had to sit on the bed with Tristan.

"Nobody in the family ever needed a lawyer when they died," Tom-tom said. "None."

Marina nodded.

"It was very simple," said Rosita, "we just called Puig and they arranged everything." She brought a hand to her mouth, remembering she had been told that Tristan did not mean to have Pinpin buried.

Marina said, "Now, Tristan, do you want to take a shower this moment or can we talk about the funeral instead?"

"There's not—"

She placed a hand on his. "You want to take the shower, of course—"

"Yes, yes," said Rosita.

"You want to think it over and not rush into anything," Marina concluded and patted his hand again.

He realized he was nodding, going along. He must stop that. He must not be a prevaricator. That was for bureaucrats. Or did he mean procrastinator?

"You will enjoy the shower," Rosita said.

"Yes, yes, Pinpin had a shower built in, tore out a piece of the porch for it," Tom-tom said. "Like that office, all black and white tiles and two shower heads. One down there. I never got a chance to use it and he said I was welcome."

"So let me just tell you about the figures," Marina said. "So you can think about them while you're taking the shower."

"Figures?" Tristan said.

"Yes, I got them from Puig's Funeral Home," Marina said.

"Puig!" Tom-tom said. "You know he's a Catalan."

"Maybe his grandfather was," Marina said. "He's just from West Tampa."

Rosita smiled at Tristan. "My grandmother was Catalan. From Sitges. That's by the sea."

"They're the Jews of Spain," Tom-tom said. "I know Puig well. With him you never can tell what he really gives you. It could be carboard."

"Tom-tom," Marina began, but did not go on. She simply tapped Tristan's hand to let him know he was not to give Tom-tom's objection any thought. "That's where Pinpin was taken."

"You shoulda gone to Inchastegui," Tom-tom said. "He did very well by Papa Leandro."

"A Basque," Marina said. "They really are the Jews of Spain, if you're so picky."

Rosita nodded.

Tristan thought he should, at this point, demur. He said, "Jews are like everybody else."

"Oh, absolutely, we all believe that," Rosita said. "But, of course, they're smarter."

"Now, Tristan, these are the statistics," Marina said. "It costs six hundred dollars for a plain cremation. No services with that—it's the absolute minimum. They pick up the body within twenty-five miles, refrigerate it for forty-eight hours—that time will soon be used up, I think—"

"Oh yes," Tom-tom said. "Day before yesterday in the morning."

Rosita said, "It was only yesterday," and sighed.

"And the cremation container is included. But it costs five dollars for each certified copy of the death certificate. On top of the six hundred dollars."

"And what have you got to show for it?" Tom-tom said.

"It's a thousand dollars if you want a service at the funeral chapel. They give you a book for people to sign and you get to keep that. They throw in the organist too, for the service."

"And they charge you a thousand dollars!" Tom-tom said.

"No, no," Marina said. "It is more like two thousand when you add it up for"—she counted off the items on her fingers for Tristan to note—"the cremation, the viewing of the body, the book for people to sign they were there, the rental of a casket, and the service."

Tom-tom said, "The casket don't get burned up?" He looked with wide-open eyes at each of them. He moaned.

Both women lowered their heads. Tristan was afraid they were crying. He knew he was on the verge and did not dare look at Tom-tom to see how he fared. Still, he had to stick with it. They were already talking about having a service and only after that the cremation. His parents had told him what to do. It did not too much matter what Mom thought, she was not Grandpa's daughter. But Dad had to be respected in this. Yes.

"Can I put it on American Express?" he asked.

Six

TRISTAN DRIVES THE VOLVO

It was in the shower that Tristan first thought of giving Tom-tom Grandpa's old car. He was pretty certain from the reluctant way in which Tom-tom had offered to turn over the keys that Tom-tom liked the car. Sure, he'd pass it on to him. Why not? Tristan could not give in on the Hertz car's insurance paying for repairs on Tom-tom's ancient one, nor agree to the funeral Tom-tom wanted for Grandpa, but this gift might make up for all Tom-tom's disappointments. He had escaped to the shower before Tom-tom and the women could come up with comparative statistics on burials, something Marina had also researched, and he must now think of reasons, the good reasons that ruled in his family, to convince them why funerals were primitive, irrational acts. And burials even worse. Why did he, instead, think of giving Tom-tom Grandpa's old car?

Because if you got Tom-tom on your side, he very likely could drag all the cousins along.

He was ashamed of that thought. Even more ashamed of being tempted to say that his family had not decided on cremation in order to save money and it was no use therefore to bring up statistics on costs. He had stopped himself in time. It would not have been courteous and they might not have believed it, for one thing. And if he had said it too cavalierly, they might have thought worse things. God.

He leaned back against the white-and-black tiled shower Grandpa had installed in the old house, and allowed all the shower heads to spray him at all levels. He closed his eyes and calmed down. Real privilege, Dad had once told him, consisted of never having known any but stall showers with strong sprays.

Dad. He must phone him, but he did not want to call him until he had accomplished something. Talked to a lawyer, at least, so that he could report what legally had to be done if no will was found. There must be one down here. The firm in the address book! Boston. Grandma. Joint will. Boston. Didn't Mom and Dad go there immediately after Grandma died? It returned like an irrepressible racial memory. Boston was the real family base. That firm must be the lawyers.

At home Tristan would have at most wrapped a towel around his middle on the way to the nearest phone, but here he got dressed entirely. Even a bathrobe did not seem proper enough, but he did carry his shoes in his hands on the way to the phone. He managed to reach Grandpa's studio without being introduced to anyone new. "Excuse me, excuse me," he kept repeating, and Tom-tom shooed off anyone who came close.

He found the Boston number in the address book, and the very tone of the greeting at the other end seemed worlds away. He made his explanations, stumbling only a little in identifying himself, and heard that he was speaking differently. More refined? Guiltily, he glanced at Tom-tom and noted that he was alert to it too. But Tom-tom was impressed—the same look of awe in his eyes as when Tristan took out the American Express card at the airport.

Mr. Peters sounded avuncular. He was not about to give him any information. He would talk to his father. *Only* your father, he said, and Tristan figured he was excluding Uncle Crispin with that too. "Your father is the executor," he explained and then coughed to cover up that he had, with this, revealed too much.

To himself Tristan said, that's what happens when you're a fucker like Uncle Crispin, you don't get to be the executor of a will.

To Mr. Peters he explained that he was in Tampa carrying out his father's instructions. At first he had only informed Mr. Peters that his grandfather was dead and that he needed to know if his firm kept a copy of his will. Tristan did not think he had to get sloppy and tell more. Even when Mr. Peters first offered his condolences in his pro forma way.

"When did you say Mr. Granados died?" Mr. Peters immediately asked after his condolences.

"Yesterday," Tristan replied.

"Your father should have been in touch with me."

Tristan remembered: "I will have a power of attorney to act for him in all this."

"Do you have it now?"

The question hung there for a moment. Should he lie?

He said nothing.

Mr. Peters coughed. "If I do not hear from your father, I shall call him in the morning. Meanwhile, I should appreciate it if you sent us a certified copy of the death certificate, to my attention."

Who the hell did he think he was. He was only a lawyer.

"I think you are wasting my time," Tristan said in a slightly louder voice, and it was in Tom-tom's eyes that he first saw that he sounded teed. "By tomorrow morning I shall have the power of attorney and I don't know that I shall want to deal with you in this bureaucratic way then."

"Young man, tell your father to call me," Mr. Peters said.

Tristan thought: the old geezer thinks this is some kind of fraternity joke. The idea silenced him.

Mr. Peters added, "It's late in the day," and hung up.

Tom-tom said, "You wasn't taking any shit, huh?"

Tristan nodded and kept his head down for a moment and tried to think it through. He won't cooperate, I'll do what I think is right. He thought of the car and looked up at Tom-tom.

"Keep the keys," he said. "I'm sure Grandpa would want you to have his old car."

Tom-tom pulled Tristan to him and hugged him. Hard. Tristan felt his feet leave the floor for a second. "Okay," he said, but Tom-tom was not done yet. He kissed him on one cheek, then on the other, wet kisses Tristan felt as cool spots when Tom-tom removed his lips, and once more lifted him off the floor, so hard this time his chest was compressed and he had to exhale. He tried to loosen Tom-tom's grip by thrashing his arms, but they were pinned to him and he had to look into Tom-tom's eyes to plead to let him go. He could not talk, but he heard in a rush of breath the cavernous sound of Tom-tom's voice. "God bless you, Tris, you're your grandpa's boy!"

His big meaty hands slapped him on the back. Tristan tried to speak, but each time Tom-tom's hands slapped the words out of him. They came out as a dry cough.

"You'll see, I'm gonna take Olivia out a lot now," Tom-tom said. "She likes to go out, but you gotta have a nice wide bucket seat like that, to strap her in. She's gonna love you for this, Tris. You gotta come and have dinner on us. Lila will cook. Olivia is a better cook, but you know how it is for now."

Tom-tom stepped back and looked at Tristan and threw his arms out to the sides as if he might charge forward and hug him once more. "Tris, my boy," he said several times, dropping his arms between each repetition, a flapping exercise that looked as if he wanted to take off.

"It's okay, it's okay," Tristan was finally able to say.

Tom-tom dropped his arms for the last time and his face became solemn. He whispered, "Don't tell anybody about this now. They're a jealous, greedy bunch of bastards."

Tristan said, "I like them, Uncle Tom-tom. They're very thoughtful. I think."

Tom-tom challenged him: "Maggie, too?"

Tristan nodded.

"You're a good kid," Tom-tom said and punched him playfully on his arm. He reached out a hand and it looked as if he were going to be hugged again, but Marina and Rosita came into the room and, instead, Tom-tom spoke to them. "I didn't say nothing to him yet. Did ya hear! He turned the Volvo over to me. He guessed what Pinpin wanted."

"What's that?" Marina said.

"The car," Rosita explained.

A Volvo? It must be the old station wagon they kept years ago in Maine for use in summer only.

Marina looked sadly at Tristan first, then said to Tom-tom, "Congratulations, I guess you got what you wanted."

Tristan decided he must give Marina whatever she wanted also. But not now, later. It did not seem nice to do it now.

Tristan was saved from the embarrassment of saying something by the phone's ringing. They all looked at it with puzzlement. Who had the right to answer? Marina and Tom-tom reached out for it simultaneously. Marina won out and said hello and looked surprised.

"Dad?" Tristan asked her.

She shook her head and spoke into the phone, "No, no, I'm his cousin. He passed away yesterday." She held the phone out to Rosita. "It's for you."

Out of the side of his mouth Tom-tom asked Marina, "Who's calling her here?"

Marina whispered her reply. "Her daughter-in-law."

"That one!" Tom-tom hissed.

Marina made a point of showing Tom-tom that she was not happy with him by turning away from him and saying to Tristan, "Do you expect your father to call?" But she was still curious about Rosita's call and kept an eye on her.

"Actually, I mean to call him," Tristan said.

"What's wrong?" Tom-tom said.

"Nothing, I just want to call him," Tristan said.

"Nothing wrong?" Tom-tom said. "Something I can do?"

"Tom-tom, control yourself," Marina said.

"But we gotta talk to him first," Tom-tom said. "Before he calls his father. Didn't we decide that?"

"Tom-tom," Marina said.

Rosita reached into their midst with one hand to get their attention and with the other held the phone against her breast. "I'm getting off in a second," she said. She looked worried. "Yes, yes," she said into the phone. "All right, very well, I'll try. Repeat what you just said."

"Rosita?" Marina said when she got off the phone.

Rosita shook her head, said, "Excuse me, I want to get a glass of water," and left.

Tom-tom immediately said in his normal voice, "That girl is the cause of all Rosita's troubles. She got him into all that business, I bet."

"How come she called here?" Marina said.

"She musta heard about Pinpin."

The phone call was important to them but not to Tristan. He picked up the phone and paused to recall the number at home.

"No, actually she was calling Pinpin," Marina said. "Did she know him?"

Rosita returned looking distracted but remembered to close the door behind her.

Tom-tom changed the subject. "I oughta go and see the car is locked," he said. "There's a lotta people around here loose today." He fanned out the fingers of one hand and rapidly closed them into a fist.

"Tom-tom, they're all family and so far they have brought things, not taken them," Marina said. She said no more because she heard the pinging of Tristan dialing this fancy black phone, but frowned to keep Tom-tom in line.

Tom-tom said, "Who're you calling?"

Tristan said, "Dad."

"We gotta talk to you first," Tom-tom said. "It's very important!"

Tristan said into the phone, "Dad, you're home?"

Dad said yes on a high note. "I'm wearing an air cast! Small, light, discreet, a miracle of plastic engineering, I can navigate superbly with your Boston great-grandfather's Malacca cane with the silver boar's head, but forget about that. What have you heard down there? The *Times* called to get information for their obit and one of their puff reporters wants to do a story. The *Book Review* called too—they thought I might want to write a short memoir of the old man for them. You know those features they do that have nothing to do with literature. Did the obit people call there? Your mom is surprised—ha-ha! She always underrated him, I fear. She never saw the beautiful side of his nature either. An essentially sweet man who loved people. That's the point I'll make. Why did you call?"

Dad did not sound like himself. Not at all laid-back. It surprised Tristan, but he kept his notebook open at the list and began with the lawyer. As soon as he said Peters, Dad interrupted, on the same high note.

"Forget about Peters," he said. "All they've got up there is their joint will. Trust funds etcetera. Tampa property, like that shotgun shack the old man inherited, came later. If you can call it property. That's all his and we can just dispose of it without referring to any will or to my brother Crispin." He paused. "Like small change." An impatient pause. "Listen, I've got to keep this line free. Public Radio is calling to do a phone interview for 'All Things Considered.' They want me to talk about the old man's Hispanic roots. It's now the news program with the largest audience in the country, did you know? It's all very exciting. I'll call you. Tonight or tomorrow."

No pause. He hung up.

The phone rang as soon as Tristan put it down. It was Dad.

"Listen, 'All Things Considered' is nationwide. You can hear it there—just ask anyone what station Public Radio is. I'll get back to you. Goodbye."

"What did he say?" Tom-tom said.

Once more Marina said with lips pursed, "Tom-tom."

Well, he did not quite know what Dad had said. Should he tell them that Dad had been asked by the *Book Review* to write about Grandpa? Instead, dutifully, he asked about the Public Radio station in Tampa.

"Public Radio?" Tom-tom said. "There is no such thing."

Marina shook her head, she did not know. It took Rosita, still in a daze from her phone call, a moment longer to say no.

"Whaddya mean, anyway?" Tom-tom said. "It's all free to the public—you just gotta buy the radio."

"It's just a name," Tristan explained.

"Stop getting so excited, Tom-tom," Marina said. "Now, do we want to talk to Tristan now or would it make you happier to go look at your inheritance?"

Tom-tom muttered, "There're no chairs here to sit down and talk."

"There's no empty chair in the whole house," Marina rebutted. "No peace and quiet to talk. I didn't know we had so many cousins."

Tom-tom said, "You wanta know how many?"

"No," Marina said with emphasis. "Rosita, you don't look right—anything happened?"

"I'm all right," Rosita said. She wet her lips and pressed

them together thoughtfully. "I want to talk to Tristan for a moment."

Marina touched her. "You're sure you're all right? I'll go get you some of that Domecq, it'll strengthen you."

At the door, Marina turned around and confirmed that Tom-tom stood there waiting for Rosita to begin. She beckoned to him.

This puzzled him. "What's the matter?" he said.

Marina said impatiently, "Tom-tom, go look at your new car."

Tom-tom eagerly jumped in place, then looked torn; he wanted to do both. "Tris, I'll be back in a minute, OK?"

Tristan nodded, trying to think of what he should be doing. What point was he at? Should he look at the notebook?

Before the door closed, he heard a man in the living room say, "They got him in there to themselves and don't let the rest of his family see him." Tom-tom closed the door and Tristan still heard him. "Who the hell you and Marina think you are, the bosses? I'm gonna bust in there."

Tristan waited; so did Rosita with a rueful smile. The man did not come in. They heard his diminished voice talking to Marina or Tom-tom as he followed one or the other away from the dining room outside.

"This is a terrible time to ask you for a favor," Rosita said. "I have to sit." She sat on the edge of the chaise and then looked up and smiled at him the way she had done on the sidewalk. "On the few occasions it was necessary Pinpin used to do this for me."

Tristan remembered he liked her, but he still had not composed his thoughts about what he must be doing. What came next? The lawyer seemed less of a necessity now, but there was still the question of the cremation. All these solicitous cousins were really in the way. If he could ask them to stay away for a day, he could get everything done.

Rosita was saying, "So I could tell you I needed to go to

the Tampa Mall and don't have a car and no one to take me. But that's not right."

He said, "I can't do that now."

She nodded.

"I'm waiting for my father to call," he said, remembering finally just what came next. "Maybe I can ask Tom-tom?"

She shook her head.

"When?" he said.

"I should be there in an hour," she said. "She asked me to take something to him. It must be money. My son—you know he has been hiding from the police for two years."

Without thinking he said, "He has!"

She nodded.

He saw that she could put a lot into a nod. He wanted to ask for details but did not think it was nice.

She said, "Drugs. Everybody knows, it was a big thing in the papers. By tonight somebody would have told you. They look at me and think, I'll bet she knows where he's hiding."

He really did not know what was the proper thing to say.

"Pinpin would drive me there, drop me at the Burdine entrance, and twenty minutes later pick me up at the Sears entrance," she said. "Then we would go to Seventh Avenue and have a Cuban sandwich and when we got home I took a lot of Mylanta tablets because I knew I was going to have acid stomach."

She laughed softly and that confused him at first. She was a tough lady. No wonder she was Grandpa's friend. Still, he had to think it over. God. He discovered he was actually holding one hand up to his head for it to rest on.

"I really don't want my father to call and not find me here," he said.

"Of course," she said. "Maybe I'll ask Tom-tom . . ."

He wavered. "Maybe he'll call before an hour."

She only nodded this time.

"Once he calls, I guess I can drive you," he said. He

sat/knelt at the work surface and turned the chair towards her, so that he appeared to be pleading with her.

There was so much on his mind, so much had been coming at him since he got off the plane. Every few minutes his thoughts needed sorting, like Dad's desk. He wanted a quiet moment to reason things out. A relatively quiet moment—that's all it could be, for he heard the noise of many conversations outside and they were not going to stop. Each time he saw his way clear, as in the shower, it became muddied by some new person or happening. Not that Rosita bothered him; she remained very quiet on her perch and simply waited. Okay, she was on hold. Now, for Dad—he had not taken this Tampa property very seriously. Peters and the joint will were all that mattered to him. So why was he going to call him back? What about? What was new since he had given him his instructions in the hospital? That he wanted him to hear him on "All Things Considered"? Dad could be very frivolous. He should be able to ask Dad, for example, about this favor Rosita had asked. Was it dangerous? Was it right? Whom was he abetting? But he could not. He sneaked a look at Rosita and saw that she had thoughtfully left him alone. He had not heard her go. It made it easier to breathe and think to have the room to himself—but he still had to answer all those questions and he had only himself to count on. It surprised him that this was not dismaying. In fact, it was an exhilarating thought.

He sat up. He had got a brilliant idea. Brilliant. He would ask Grandpa.

Two clicks, and the bright orange screen came on invitingly. He asked for the WordStar directory and looked for Rosita when it immediately came on. There she was. He called up her entry, looked at the door, and went back eagerly to the screen.

She makes very good coffee. It's all in the purity of the water (*bottled Spanish water, of course*) *and the absolute cleanliness of the pot, the strainer and, finally, the demitasse or glass in which you serve it. She says she learned this from my mother, but they all say that they learned this or the other from Aunt Mama. They are trying to get on the good side of me and there is no good side. Rosita doesn't need to. She acts as if she knows it. She is as self-assured with everyone else—friends, neighbors, deliverymen. There are people like that. They know in their bones that they are liked. This gives Rosita an air of sophistication as well. Not the manufactured kind which is what we mostly know. My idea of a sophisticated lady when I was a boy on this street: the movie star (Jean Harlow?) in the tight silk dress cut on the bias, one arm up flaunting a cigarette on a long holder, her pelvis's forward thrust framed by enticing hipbones. I studied that pose carefully and was misled by it. A fraud, like all Hollywood products. I believed that the valley between the hipbones was a dizzying vertiginous vortex and let my mind only fearfully approach its environs. It haunted me, as bad writers say. Imagine then my delight at discovering the caressable mons, not too much later. Which brings me back to Rosita. Her cousin from Key West up on one of her long visits sat talking with her on the porch and I sat with them for the sake of that coffee and for respite from my thoughts. (A throw-away hour for me whether Rosita has a visitor or not, but better anytime than TV news programs.) The conversation of old Latin women, in any case, is as soothing now as when I used to fall asleep to its sound. Very likely I was dozing with open eyes that dusk when I heard Rosita say with more brio than usual, "One promise I made when my poor Carlos died—I would never present my children with a stepfather and I would never sleep with a Negro. And I kept it." I laughed so hard and for so long that her cousin got up and went inside with a cowed look, and Rosita said, "What's the matter? She's going to think you're laughing at her." How I enjoyed that pronouncement of hers for the next few days. (I still do.) It lightened my mood, leavened my thoughts; I chuckled each time I thought of it. In three or four days, when the memory only made me smile, Rosita again called me over for coffee. Her cousin had returned to Key West. I discovered that even in old age I still don't get women right, not immediately. If I now believed, when I settled in my chair on Rosita's porch again, that she could be charmingly inconsequential too, I also gave her credit for a certain sophistication—scarce in Ybor City now and when I was growing up. I thought one could talk to her about sexual matters without joking or self-consciousness. I had finished the first demitasse, and in the natural expansiveness that comes with knowing one can have another as delicious, I said, "I don't think I have ever thanked you, Rosita, for having let me see when I was a boy exactly how girls are made." She was appalled, but again I did not notice immediately. "It was at a particularly important time for me. You saved me—" I took for granted that she was getting up to serve me more coffee and she did come towards me, but instead she kicked me hard without a caution for my diabetes and the months it takes for such a bruise to disappear from my poor old legs. It was so unexpected that I did not think to protect myself and she kicked me a second time. She breathed hard and she said not a word but kept her head down and concentrated on her aim. I jumped up. She aimed with her foot again, exhaled loudly like a karate fighter, and almost fell when I sidestepped her kick. I had to catch her, old lady that she is, and she did not thank me but kept up short kicks at close quarters. I had to leave. A worse rout than when the mounted police in New York used to chase us to the subway entrances at demonstrations for the Spanish Republic. I have never won at anything. I'm a true descendent of Ybor City cigarmakers: they never won a strike. The next day she came over and for the first time asked me to drive her to the mall where she meets her depraved son and hands over bundles of cash her redneck daughter-in-law brings her. The dear boy's allowance. And if they catch him, she will be the first one in court appealing for its mercy—Oh Your Honor judgea hesa gooda boy my son. My ass. He is probably living in Las Vegas in Mafia style and not a bruise to show for taking it on the lam. I have three bruises, a large one on the leg bone (what do you call that?) where the skin was scraped off and two more lower down on the little bit of flesh and muscle left me on my shins. What was I talking about? Why am I putting this down? These are refractions not reflections. Oh yes, sophistication—*

The door opened. Without looking, Tristan abandoned Rosita's file. Sometime, he must go through every one of them. Maybe tonight. Yes. Grandpa was really something.

The three of them were back. They looked in on him with conspiratorial unity: all solicitous, all smiling, even Rosita. A new pose for Tom-tom: his smile was fixed and unconvincing. Marina said, "Can we come in?"

Tristan stood. "Okay," he said to Rosita, staring at her with new eyes. "I'll drive you. No need to wait."

He looked at Tom-tom and Marina and began his explanations, "I'm going with her to—"

Rosita interrupted him. "I told them!"

Marina said, "I'll stay here and talk to your father if he calls."

Rosita said, "You're so good to do it, you're Pinpin's grandson, there's no doubt about that."

What's the matter with Dad, Tristan thought, calling this old house a shack?

Another unexpected thought: where was Grandpa's wallet?

"I just thought of something that might help me," Tristan said. "Grandpa's wallet."

Marina answered quickly. "I put it in his dresser drawer where the socks are and I forgot."

"You got his wallet!" Tom-tom said. "How much was in it?"

"I didn't look, of course," Marina said sharply.

Tom-tom made a gesture of impatience. "I didn't make no accusations," he said.

Tristan said, "I just want to take a look at it now before we go . . ."

As soon as he was out the door, an old man with a deep youthful chest grabbed and then hugged him. "I'm Anselmo," he said, "and if you can't tell, I'll inform you myself. I'm a Gallego."

The people on the couches laughed.

Tristan nodded although he did not know what the old man meant. He only took in his wide black eyebrows and his thick unruly gray hair.

"Anselmo, let him go by for now," Marina said.

Anselmo continued talking with one hand on Tristan's upper right arm strangling his biceps. "I'm a cousin of these characters, but my mother had the good sense to marry a man from Galicia, not Cuba or Asturias—and you, Rosita, where did your grandfather come from?"

"None of your business," Rosita said, but Anselmo liked her and laughed at her reply, his cheeks turning rosy in the process, and Rosita laughed also. "Oh, Anselmo," she added.

Marina placed a hand on Anselmo's chest and pushed.

"Listen, my boy, let me just say this," Anselmo said, removing his hand from his arm and holding it up like a traffic cop to keep Tristan's attention. "We've all got to die and there's no getting away from that." He backed away a little to let all of them get to the front bedroom. "I'll talk to you some more later. Meanwhile, watch out for these characters."

Anselmo slapped Tom-tom on the back as he went by. "I hear you're a big operator in real estate in West Tampa now," he said. "Why don't you enjoy your old age like me, huh?" He looked around at the people in the room. "There is nothing like doing nothing. Who's gonna get me some coffee? You cannot talk without good coffee."

Aunt Clem called out, "I will, Anselmo, I will."

In the front bedroom, Tom-tom said to Tristan and the women, "He's so vulgar."

They heard Anselmo clearly through the closed door: "He read too many books. That can hurry you to your grave."

Marina said, "That's what he did to poor Aunt Laura—hurried her."

Rosita shook her head, not in agreement but commiseration and forgiveness.

"Get him the wallet," Tom-tom said.

Anselmo again above the other voices: "That's just ignorant prejudice. Eat grapefruit, lots of them. It's not true they make you skinny."

Loud laughter outside.

Tristan did not see the wallet until it was in his hand. He knew it well: it was the same as his, his Dad's too. A family tradition, he learned only now.

Tom-tom leaned his head in to see what was in the wallet. Marina pulled at his shirt, but it was no use. Grandpa's wallet was also the burgundy three-fold back-pocket model. The Coach Store. There were two twenties, a couple of tens, and one fifty in the main compartment. In the smaller ones, a medicare card, another fifty folded four times, an American Express card, a Brooks Brothers card, an up-to-date membership card to the Museum of Modern Art. Grandpa's loyalty again? A sheet of paper, carefully folded several times, with a poem (he thought) in Spanish. In Grandpa's hand.

"What's that?" Tom-tom asked.

"I can't read it," Tristan said. "It says Cesar Vallejo at the bottom."

"I don't know him," Tom-tom said. "Do you know him, Marina? I don't remember any Vallejo in Ybor City."

Marina shook her head impatiently.

Rosita said, "I think he's a poet Pinpin likes."

Tom-tom said, "How come I never met him?"

Rosita said, "He was Peruvian, or from somewhere down there."

Tom-tom said, "But did they move to West Tampa or Ybor City?"

Tristan hefted the wallet. "I'm going to keep this," he said.

"Of course," Marina said.

Tristan refolded the poem and replaced it in the wallet. He noticed now how evenly aged and clean the wallet was. Grandpa was a neat man, and Tristan decided to encourage this side of his own personality. He slid the wallet into his left back-pocket, a companion to the one on the right.

"Well, let's go now," he said to Rosita.

"You're sure?" Rosita said.

"Tris, I'm really going with you and Rosita," Tom-tom said. "They say I should."

Tristan felt relieved—had he been scared?—but did not know if he should say thank you in front of Rosita.

"Ask them, they want me to go," Tom-tom insisted.

Marina said, "That way I can tell everybody out there that the three of you are going to the funeral home."

Tristan nodded; he ought to say something. "I'm going to call the funeral home when I get back," he said. "No, maybe now."

Marina reached out an arm to detain him. "You haven't heard what we want to tell you."

Rosita said, "It's time. I'll go ahead to my house. You pick me up there."

Marina continued, "You want to wait until your Dad calls, don't you?"

"I'm leaving," Rosita said.

Tom-tom said, "Let's get going."

Tristan was out of the room and pointed towards the porch before he could think of any reason to call the funeral home now rather than later.

In the living room Marina announced to the people who came forward, "Only those who haven't met him yet."

"Me! Me!" some kids yelled.

"Just say hello," Marina said. "They have to go now, but they'll be back."

Maybe it was because all the men wore short-sleeved summer shirts and the women light dresses but there was no solemnity about their convergence on him.

They said things like, "We're all so sad," and smiled.

And, "You gotta bring your brother and sister next time so we can meet them. Promise?"

And, "I save my vacation every two years for New York. Whatta place! You live right in the middle of it, huh?"

"Remember me?" said Delio and laughed at the notion that Tristan might not.

Who was he? A cousin, he supposed. He decided to give up on names and relationships. Maybe in time he'd absorb them naturally like rain.

The sexy girl he had met at the airport kissed him and put a hand at the small of his back and pushed his pelvis into hers. "Don't tell 'em I already met you," she whispered, "and don't worry. For serious stuff I got my own boyfriend."

"He's got to leave," Marina said pointedly.

There was a relaxation in the air that must mean they thought a regular funeral was in the offing.

"Let him go," Marina said with decision.

"Tom-tom, you going too?" Aunt Clem said.

Tom-tom stared at her angrily.

"I figured," Aunt Clem said lamely.

"Come," Tom-tom said and ostentatiously placed an arm proprietarily on Tristan's shoulder.

Tristan knew then the whole thing was a mistake. He was letting them think rites were going to take place, ceremonies acted out. God. He ought to speak out, but no one had addressed him yet.

In an urgent voice, Aunt Clem appealed to Tom-tom, "Don't let Puig sell you the one that's not waterproof. Don't let them do that."

Manuela said laughing, "Don't worry, they don't push the cheapest one."

Dewey said, "That Puig didn't get rich selling pine caskets."

Anselmo laughed a rich, deep laugh.

Old Santo said, "This is my last one, my very last one. The next one is for me."

Eloisa asked Manuela, "Is Rosita going with them? Is that why she ran out? Why is she going and not one of us?"

Manuela shook her head as if she did not care.

"Why not you?" Eloisa insisted.

Someone called out over all the others, "How do you like us Latins?"

A louder voice answered, "He's a Latin too!" It was Maggie. She was standing at the front door holding her arms out to Tristan.

"Oh Maggie, I knew you'd come back!" Aunt Clem said.

Manuela called to Aunt Clem, "She never keeps a grudge, good old Maggie. She's got a wonderful heart."

"Tristan, Tristan," Maggie said in her vibrant baritone.

"And a mouth like a loudspeaker," Tom-tom said.

"I'll get to you next," Maggie said to Tom-tom and tapped him as she went by. "Tristan, I want you to forgive me. Do you forgive me?"

She pushed Dewey aside and embraced Tristan hard. "Do you?" she repeated.

Tristan heard the notebook in his shirt pocket crackle, but he did not care. This letting them think he was on his way to buy a waterproof casket, this bothered him and kept him silent. Nevertheless, he nodded to Maggie at close quarters and felt the sharp points of her breasts on his rib cage. She did not embarrass him. He liked her and was glad she was back.

Maggie reached up and squeezed his face in her broad hand. "I love you," she said.

Eloisa told Manuela, "I like Maggie. She can handle Puig. Why isn't she going with them?"

It irked Manuela that Eloisa did not suggest her. She said, "Stop being so picky."

Eloisa only then dared to call aloud to Marina, "Why isn't Maggie going with them?"

Marina would not even look her way.

But Maggie heard and she half-turned and strenuously shook her head. "No, darling," she said. "It's too morbid." She moved away from Tristan in a semicrouch and began to cry. "I had to do it for my mama, oh my mama!"

"Maggie, Maggie!" Aunt Clem grabbed her and rocked her in the small space left open to her. "Maggie, forget it, it's no use remembering!"

Old Santo said, "It is really a wake now. Have they served anything to eat yet?"

Dewey threw up his arms and yelled at Maggie and Aunt Clem. "For crissakes, you did that already. We wanna talk to Tristan."

Cookie lightly caressed one of Santo's old bony hands which had found its way to her knee and thus removed it without any fuss. "Would you like some more *café con leche,* Santo?" she asked him.

He looked at her to check her reply. "Did I have *café con leche?*" he asked. "Did they already serve?"

Tristan looked at Dewey and the girl from the airport and others whose names he hoped sometime to absorb. "It is very kind of you," he said. It was his way of saying goodbye.

Wallingford appeared out of nowhere. "Not at all, not at all. I feel as if I am a member of the family too. I used to see your grandfather a lot, trying to convince him to let me tape him for oral history." He cleared his throat. "I should like to talk to you about his papers."

A couple of persons near Tristan stopped talking. At the same time, Maggie and Aunt Clem became too angry with

Dewey to continue keening. Tristan was thus able to clearly hear Eloisa say to Manuela, "I don't understand—has the boy given in on the wake yet?"

God.

Happy and unrestrained, Anselmo's baritone laugh soared over their heads. He headed off any comment from Tristan by volunteering, "I came with Arturo and Horacio, my grandsons—they're at your disposal, they can drive you, or do whatever you want. Go ahead, give them an order."

Aunt Clem said, "They're in the kitchen eating away, God bless them, they're beautiful boys."

The girl from the airport winked at Tristan and shook her head. He knew what she meant. She preferred him. If she wasn't careful he would blush.

Marina said with authority, "Tristan has to go. You'll see them later."

They were all going to be here later!

Tom-tom grabbed his elbow.

Dewey said, "I don't think there's going to be enough room for everybody to watch the six o'clock news in the TV room."

Aunt Clem said, "Why don't you get the portable one your brother has at the shop?"

Jack said, "Wait, everybody, I'm bringing one. I'm the one got Joe Sorrento interested, remember?"

Tom-tom paused to say, "You still trying to take credit?"

The phone rang.

"Go ahead," Marina quickly said to Tom-tom. "Go."

Tom-tom pulled at him.

But it might be Dad.

A young guy jumping in the doorway of the kitchen, receiver held up in one hand, called, "Hey, hey everybody, it's some fella named Puig wants to talk to somebody in charge."

Anselmo said, "That's Horacio, he always says hey before he says anything."

"Hey?" Horacio repeated.

"I'll take it," Marina said.

"Maybe," Tristan began. "Maybe I—"

Tom-tom yanked hard and said, "He'll get you embroiled."

Anselmo said, "He'll start with that 'Do you want a remembrance card with the Lord is my shepherd? Do you want a third limousine just to be sure?' "

Maggie said, "Just tell 'em they're on their way."

"Oh yes!" Marina said and waved to Tom-tom to take Tristan away now. "Go!"

"Hey, okay, if you want me to," Horacio said, but Marina took the phone from him and began speaking into it and continued to wave Tristan and Tom-tom away.

It was no use. He was out on the porch, and the sunlight again blinded him. He was caught in a bind: he could not talk to the funeral parlor man now or everyone would know there must be some other reason for their errand.

Across the street two houses down Rosita stood at the curb holding a small shopping bag. It was a good errand. A matter of honor—doing what Grandpa would have done.

"Hi!" the boy who had stood on the veranda said. He was on the veranda again. "Don't stay later than six o'clock. I'm sure as shit I'm gonna be in it too."

"Get off there," Tom-tom said. "Go talk like that someplace else. No education these kids."

"What did I say?" the boy asked Dewey's brothers.

"You, Delio," Tom-tom said to one of them. "Get your car outa the driveway."

"You taking it out!" Delio said. "That's some car, Uncle Tom-tom. I understand it's yours!"

"You understand nothing," Tom-tom said. "Just get your car out."

Delio ran down the porch to his Ford Escort, but the look of alarm and anger did not leave Tom-tom. He's worried, Tristan thought. Was this a dangerous errand, after all?

"Rosita wants to go in your grandpa's Volvo," Tom-tom said.

"Your Volvo," Tristan said and was glad he had thought to be, well, gracious.

Tom-tom still looked anxious. He nodded and looked at Tristan sideways. "You wanna drive it?" he offered. "Go on, drive it."

To please him, Tristan said yes.

Tom-tom half smiled but his eyes radiated anxiety. He pointed Tristan up the driveway to the carport and then looked down quickly, as if this moment was too much to bear.

There was the Volvo. The cause of Tom-tom's nervousness. A 240 GL. Deep blue; in perfect taste, unostentatious but rich, reassuring. He should have known that Grandpa would have steered clear of the 760: that was for the nouveaus of Long Island. What he had not known was that Grandpa's old car was, in fact, new. Brand new. Not the dusty, spotted six-year-old one Dad owned.

He controlled his reaction, but his thoughts kept on going: he decided he would never tell Dad about this Volvo.

He strode the few feet towards it in a daze of speculation, and saw as soon as he reached the back window that, of course, Grandpa had bought a bensi box with a CD player.

He heard his voice in some future time saying casually, lightly, with no emphasis of any kind, "Grandpa had an old rusty Ford Escort he used for going to the supermarket. I let Tom-tom have it." And, of course, Dad was very sophisticated about it. Not a word more was said about the whole thing.

Seven

TRISTAN TOURS TAMPA

For Tristan, scenery was vistas without houses. They made you breathe deeper, expanded your soul, reminded you of paintings in museums. Slums between New Haven and New York caused him to look inward, shrink from the world. Tampa was different: a cheerful sunlight bathed it all; the enemy seemed to be not poverty but bad taste. Until driving north out of Ybor City, a few blocks from Grandpa's home, he came upon a corner of North Tampa. Dwight Gooden country. The menacing look of low-cost housing. Blacks. Standing around, leaning against doorways, sweeping the dust out the front door. They followed you with their eyes, as if they had all the time in the world to weigh and gauge and project into the future the geometrically escalating distances that your new car would take you from them.

"I shoulda made you go back the way we came," Tom-tom said. He squatted forward in the backseat checking how Tristan handled his car. "I don't like it around here. They might throw a rock."

"This is the route Pinpin always took," Rosita said. She sat next to Tristan, the shopping bag held carefully between her knees. She looked at Tristan. "You inherited his profile."

"And his good heart," Tom-tom said. "Jesus, lookit them, I hope they don't throw a rock."

Tristan looked in the rearview mirror to see if Tom-tom meant it about his good heart. Tom-tom was checking the ashtrays and trying out the electrical window openers.

"Never mind a good heart," Rosita said. "Pinpin was a handsome man."

Nanao always kidded him about the narrow high bridge of his nose. He looked at it in the rearview mirror. Was it really Grandpa's?

Rosita sighed.

A police car came up on their left.

"Jesus, Joseph, and Mary," Rosita said.

The police car went on by.

"It's the only time I think of them," Rosita said.

"Who?" said Tom-tom.

"Jesus, Joseph, and Mary," Rosita said.

Tristan was not afraid of blacks. He did not turn back if he entered a block with only blacks in it. The few times he drove through Harlem he did not roll up the windows of the car. He knew all the jokes about whitey's fears. For the last three months he had also worked, as had practically all the anti-apartheid group, with the maintenance workers' union. Mostly blacks, and there was plenty of give and take. It suddenly occurred to him that many had been Hispanic. Not a one had ever spoken to him in Spanish. Had they been waiting for him to do that first? But he couldn't have, he did not speak Spanish.

He had to think about this.

Tom-tom tapped him on the shoulder. "You wanna put on the radio? I wanna test the loudspeaker back here."

"Tom-tom, it's not right," Rosita said. She half turned and shook her head, gently reminding him.

"There's nobody out here to see," Tom-tom said. "They won't know if we play the radio or—hey, what's that?" He threw an arm between the bucket seats and pointed to the CD player. "A cassette!"

"No, a CD," Tristan said. "But there's also a cassette."

"Oh, you gotta put it on," Tom-tom said. To Rosita: "That's hypocrisy, that you can't play music 'cause you're in mourning."

In the time it took Tristan to check if there was a disk in the player, he decided that if you weren't prejudiced about blacks you could not, definitely not, be prejudiced about Hispanics or be ashamed of Hispanics if you were Hispanic. Why was he thinking this?

"My God," said Tom-tom. "And there's two speakers too—stereo!"

There was a disk in the player. Bruce's *Tunnel of Love.* Wow.

"Stereo!" Tom-tom repeated. "And that CD thing and the cassette—is there a radio? I like a radio. Listen to the games, you know."

"I'll turn it on," Tristan said.

The bright insistent drive of baroque music filled the car from all sides. Vivaldi. Poor Grandpa.

"Oh, listen to that," Tom-tom said. "Wait till Olivia hears it. It's better than what Pinpin had in the house—"

Tristan checked on Tom-tom in the rearview mirror. He had covered his mouth and closed his eyes. Was he ashamed? Was he mourning?

"Now, can he turn it off?" Rosita said.

Tristan nodded and complied. Grandpa was really something. He remembered the records in his study; it stood to reason he'd have the latest Bruce in the car. Even his uncle Crispin was not that up on things. He did not want to call Grandpa a swinger. No, he wouldn't. So what was he? He could say Grandpa was not a snob, not a devotee of high culture. That's what Nanao would say. Those were her words. He would have to tell her about him.

He liked it that Grandpa had been a Red (how could they expect to hold a regular funeral for him?) instead of a liberal like everybody's uncle or a lovable old reactionary right-winger like Skitch's red-nosed grandfather. He liked it a lot that there had been so much vinegar in Grandpa. He must look up the difference between communist and social democrat. Get it exact, that is. He knew social democrats were more reformist than revolutionary. But he really did not know more than that. It was a big deal with Grandpa, so he should get it straight.

Floppy disks! Had he seen floppy disks in the study? He almost braked. He had not seen floppy disks. All that writing in the Toshiba was in danger of being erased. God. Thou shalt not leave a file without saving and without making a floppy-disk copy. It was one of the ten commandments of his generation.

"Something wrong?" Rosita said.

Tristan shook his head, his mind still trying to call up Grandpa's study and its contents.

"You must not worry about this thing," she said. "You let me out of the car at Burdine's and if I don't show up at the other end when I should, you just go on back to the house."

There was a surge protector. Grandpa had taken that precaution. Why wouldn't he have copied everything on floppy disks? Why would he take the chance of everything on the hard drive being erased? He could not answer that one way or the other. He was not reassured.

"You understand?" Rosita insisted.

"Nothing's gonna happen," Tom-tom said. "Stop talking about it, for crissakes."

"You are absolutely right, Tom-tom," Rosita said.

"I'm gonna go with you," Tom-tom said.

"With who?" Rosita said.

"You," Tom-tom said.

"It's not necessary," she said, but she was pleased.

"You women's lib or something?" Tom-tom said. "You're too old to be walking around the mall alone. It don't look right."

There was a red light ahead, an overpass for the freeway, and a lot more cars and trucks than on the streets of North Tampa, but of course the sidewalks were empty. "Where do I go?" Tristan asked.

"Don't take the freeway!" Tom-tom said. "I mean, just go straight. You head for West Tampa. I'll let you know when to turn."

The uniform clapboard houses had thinned out. One-story cinder-block buildings looking like skimpy old motels took their place. At the curb entrance to each were signs listing the names and specialties of the doctors who practiced there. It all seemed frivolous to Tristan. Could these doctors be as trustworthy as those whose offices occupied the ground floors of solid New York apartment buildings? He stopped himself from answering that at all. This is Florida, he said to himself, there's bound to be a cultural difference.

"You notice all the doctors?" Tom-tom said. "Everybody in Florida is old and sick."

Rosita sighed.

"When I was young and I used to go to the Cuban Club, everybody was young," Tom-tom said. "Right, Rosita?"

She did not reply.

"Now, everybody's old," he added.

When neither Rosita nor Tristan took up the conversation, he reached out and patted Tristan on the shoulder.

"Rosita, you used to go to the Cuban Club, right?" he asked.

She did not seem to have heard.

Tristan was glad he had given this super car to Tom-tom.

Tom-tom tried again. "Rosita, I got a confession to make. I'm still young in the head and a lotta times my legs gotta tell my head they can't climb the stepladder 'cause they're old. Does that happen to you?"

At last Rosita smiled.

"Don't worry about Sonny," Tom-tom said.

She half turned to look at Tom-tom. Tristan watched her out of the corner of one eye and saw tears welling in hers.

"I had him too late, Tom-tom," she said. "I was too old to bring him up right."

"Ah, Rosita," Tom-tom said. His voice was so gentle that Tristan looked in the rearview mirror. He was leaning forward nodding and patting Rosita's shoulder.

"I was forty-four—you think I meant to have him?" she said. "Pancho wanted me to, you know, abort him. We're too old, he said, and he was right."

"Ah, Rosita," Tom-tom repeated. "Don't say that."

"I asked Aunt Mama," she said. "And she said, You do what you want, Rosita. So I had him and then Pancho died and I was too old to bring him up right by myself. A boy needs a father, we all know that."

Once more Tom-tom said, "Ah, Rosita."

"I thought I didn't have to worry because he studied the bass and the drums every moment he wasn't eating," she said and this time included Tristan in her audience. "From the time he was a little boy he could drum out the beat of any music—with his hands, with two pieces of wood, anything."

"A born musician," Tom-tom said.

She nodded to show her pride. "And then that rock and roll had to come along. I used to tell him when he went out to play in those discos, stay away from drugs, stay away from all that. But I couldn't stop him from playing. It's my life, Mama, making music."

"A born musician," Tom-tom said.

"And then he stopped and he got married and opened the store and everything was all right. He dressed properly even—and bang! that was when he really got into trouble. If only he had stayed a musician, even in that rock and roll."

Tristan said, "Rock and roll is very good music."

"Thank you, my dear," Rosita said.

What do you say to that? He decided to say, "I mean it, it's as good as jazz."

This time she only looked at him and said nothing.

"Listen to Tris," Tom-tom said to her. "You know he goes to college at that Yale, don't you?"

"Thank you," Rosita repeated.

They drove a block in silence. More cinder-block buildings, painted dull green, with more doctors' signs out front. Then Tom-tom said, "Sonny never was in no trouble when he was a musician. Only when he went into that business selling carpets."

"Rugs and blinds," Rosita said. "I told him last time it was a relief to me when he stopped traveling around from disco to disco and became a respectable merchant. And he said, Mama, the rugs and blinds was just a front."

"Listen, Rosita, I gotta tell you," Tom-tom said. "I always suspected something. An apartment on Bayshore, a house right on the beach at Sarasota. That Cadillac."

Rosita said, "I worried he was taking drugs when he was playing the rock and roll, not that he was selling them."

They both sighed.

Unlike the other streets Tristan had been on, this one kept filling with traffic. He did not have time to think about Sonny now: he had to figure out whether the lane he was on would, at the end of the block, turn out to be a right turn or left turn only. He suppressed the thought that there was something amateurish, intellectually low-grade—indeed, third world—about this city of Tampa because of these dumb turn-only lanes. He was no elitist and was on guard always about any signs of it.

Tom-tom burst out nervously, "I'll tell ya, that's how I worried about Junior. Olivia worried too. She made herself sick. You think she isn't the way she is now from worrying years ago about Junior?" He turned to Tristan and touched him to explain. "Junior was a little backward since he was a little boy, he didn't learn well—I'll confess it, he could not read or write or add dimes and nickles. So we worried he would get into trouble. You know how we worried, Rosita, I don't have to tell you."

Rosita nodded.

Tristan wished he could stop and listen to Tom-tom. A retarded son, poor guy.

"But look how well he turned out," Rosita said.

"I thank God for that girl. The last thing Olivia said before she stopped talking regular was, I thank God for that girl," Tom-tom said. "He's happy with her, but I keep my fingers crossed. The other four all started off so good and then they took advantage of him."

Tom-tom hit himself on the forehead. "This is the way I could talk to Pinpin. Only to Pinpin! I can't talk to Olivia until she gets better and no one talks like this anymore. Who can talk to my sisters? Rosita, remember how the old folks used to talk on the porch? Now my sisters watch TV and talk like the people in the commercials."

Rosita made a demurring, apologetic sound.

"No, they ain't got no sense," Tom-tom said. "Look at Lila—she's got an eye out for that cracker across the street now."

"Maybe he's a good man," Rosita said.

"It is not like the old days," Tom-tom said. "You had all those friends in the factory. You could talk to them."

"But you never worked in the cigar factories," Rosita said.

"Oh, I'm talking about my father and my uncles. They had friends at the factory and at the Cuban Club or the Spanish Club. Just like the women, they sat on the porch and talked things over, politics and everything."

They were quiet a moment.

Rosita smiled a wan smile and reached out and placed a hand on Tristan's arm lightly.

"This is a good boy, Tom-tom," she said.

"The best," Tom-tom said.

What did one say to that?

Rosita sighed. Then said, "I suppose Sonny couldn't make a living from rugs and blinds."

Tristan leaned down to the steering wheel in order to look up through the windshield at the tall building on the corner.

"St. Joseph's Hospital," Tom-tom said. He lowered his voice and warned, "One and a half blocks and we're there."

"Right or left?" Tristan asked.

"Left," Tom-tom said. "You can't miss it."

Rosita sat up and gathered the handles of the shopping bag in one hand.

Tristan knew they were nervous, because he was also.

A sea of cars surrounding a long building; it went on for three blocks and the parking lanes radiating from it went farther. Tristan had never seen anything like it, not because he was deprived but because he was privileged. He had done all his shopping at Brooks Brothers on Madison Avenue and (only lately) at Bloomingdale's on Lexington. (He did not think he would ever go to J. Press in New Haven: he was no robot.) Actually, if he got back to New York in time, Nanao had scheduled a foray into lower Broadway. Not that he would ever go punk, except for a hand-painted tee shirt or two.

Would he get back to New York in time? When would he next see Nanao?

He was nervous, all right.

At the entrance to Burdine's, Rosita told him in her soothing voice, smiling all the while, that beyond Sears there was parking just like this and he could drive there now and sit in the car and wait for them. "Tom-tom and I will look for you when we come out," she added.

Tristan could see Tom-tom anxiously looking over her shoulder. He was pale, particularly around the lips. He shook his head, then nodded, then shook his head again. His jowls quivered and his voice came out thin and faltering. "No, no, no, Rosita. Tristan, you wait for us with the motor running where people come out of Sears." He gulped. "At the curb in front of Sears."

"Will they let me stand there for long?" Tristan said.

"Son of a bitch," Tom-tom said. "I guess you better park and look out for us when we come out."

Tristan watched him hurry to catch up with Rosita. He saw that Tom-tom was not only squat but also bow-legged, so that when he hurried away, as he did now, there was something funny in the sight.

Tom-tom turned one last time while he still was within shouting distance. "Don't forget, look for us," he called.

No doubt about it, Tom-tom was scared.

I'm driving the getaway car, he thought. God.

He put the Volvo in gear and set off for the other end of the mall. Wouldn't you know Grandpa did not buy a car with automatic transmission. Or fake leather. Or anything but state-of-the-art stereo.

Rosita was probably carrying cash in that shopping bag. Or worse. God. It was only she who was in danger now if that was so. But of course it was so. What else would she be taking him? Tom-tom was in danger, too. But not himself—they would cover up for him, never say he had brought them there. He knew nothing could happen to him. No more than at Yale with the maintenance workers' union. It was very frustrating.

At the Sears end, he kept circling until there was an empty slot right across from the entrance to the store. He could see the wide doors merely by raising his eyes to the rearview mirror. He noticed now an empty police car parked at the curb. He did not like that. It seemed an omen.

Should he do something about it? He remained in the car and tried to think of something else. He looked at the car's insides, checked on all the extras Grandpa had bought, and then watched the people come and go at Sears. They were not like New Yorkers. He turned on the CD and listened to Bruce. It was a good stereo, the best he had heard in a car. Better than the little Sony bookshelf set he had taken over to Nanao's when he cleared out of the dorm—when? God, only two days ago. No, yesterday morning. He had lived a whole life since then.

He turned off Bruce. He had to admit that these *Tunnel of Love* songs were too down.

He looked up and saw the cops come out the Sears entrance. There was a young guy between them. Dark. Latin. One cop held the guy's arms behind his back. The other took out his keys to the police car and walked a couple of steps ahead.

As Tristan turned round in his seat to watch them directly, he heard a woman scream. He was sure it was Rosita, even before he saw her in the store's doorway. She held one arm up and screamed again.

Tristan got out of the car.

"It's my son! My son!" Rosita ran, swinging the shopping bag for impetus. "Stop, please, stop!"

The cop with the keys in his hand got between her and the other two. She tried to push his arm aside and he roughly flung her to one side. "Please, please, he's a good boy," she said. "Please!"

Tristan ran towards them but a moving car got in the way, and he jumped silently up and down. When the car passed, the cop yelled, "Freeze!" and he took that stance they were always doing on TV and pointed his gun at Tristan. "Freeze!"

Tristan stopped.

"Oooh! Oooh!" Rosita moaned. "Oh my God, it's not Sonny!"

For good measure, Tristan raised both arms over his head, sure that the cop meant him to do so.

"Right," the cop said. "Now, walk slowly to me. Slowly."

"Oh Tristan, I made a mistake," Rosita said. "Oh, mister, please put that gun away, I made a mistake. That is my nephew. I don't know that fellow."

Rosita pointed to the young man the other cop had handcuffed and was now pushing into the backseat of the police car. She said, "I don't know him."

The cop did not put his gun away. With his free hand, he whacked Tristan's buttocks, then pushed the hand up hard all the way between his legs. Tristan jumped slightly.

The cop said, "Now, what the hell's all this?"

His partner came over and waited for Rosita to answer.

Rosita still panted with fright, but she managed to say in her low, sweet voice, "He looked like my son. My eyesight—"

The second cop said, "You don't recognize me?"

Rosita stared and shook her head.

Tristan decided to lower his arms.

The second cop smiled. "Rosita Arenas, what're ya doing getting mixed up with the law?"

She was surprised, but she still did not know who he was.

The second cop said, "Julian Acosta is my grandfather."

The first cop put away his gun and went back to their patrol car, but on his way he yelled back, "She was obstructing even if she didn't know this guy."

"Oh please!" Rosita called to him.

"Listen to me, not him," Julian Acosta's grandson said,

then paused long enough to get Rosita to listen calmly. "Someone whose name I won't mention is inside."

"Someone?" Rosita said.

"He's looking the way he used to look," he said. "You know who I mean?"

Rosita touched her head with both hands. "Him?"

The cop said, "I don't know him myself," but he nodded and also winked.

"God bless you," Rosita said.

The cop turned to Tristan. "Now, who are you? You are not, definitely not, her nephew."

Rosita explained.

The cop put out his hand and said, "I accompany you in your sentiments." He looked over Tristan's head at the people on the sidewalk still watching and said to them, "Go on about your business now." He sighed, winked at Rosita, and to Tristan said, "I'm sorry," and left.

Rosita followed him with her eyes and explained to Tristan, "His grandfather Julian taught me to roll cigars. I was practically the last apprentice at Perfecto Garcia."

She pointed Tristan back to the Volvo and herself headed for the mall before he could ask any questions.

On his way to the car, his legs still somewhat unsteady, Tristan asked himself, Why didn't he arrest Sonny? Or Rosita? Or me? The answer was both a revelation and a relief: they were all family. God. But the cop had pointed the gun at him and he did yell freeze! Even if he was Julian Acosta's grandson. Or was it the other one?

He went over the scene in his mind several times before he again saw Rosita in the rearview mirror. She was smiling, but he could tell she was still edgy, not her serene self. He got out of the car.

Some blond kid in an early punk haircut standing behind her said something to her and pointed to him.

Where was Tom-tom?

Rosita smiled again. She crossed without looking for cars. The young guy followed. He was carrying the shopping bag. He must be Sonny.

Tristan looked around. Should he still worry about the cops?

Sonny reached him first, a hand out to shake his. His hair was dyed. You could see the black roots. Funky. He wore a gold earring. His tee shirt was skintight. It said *Me.* He said, "Hey man."

Rosita was breathless but said, "Tristan, this is Sonny."

Tristan then realized he had expected him to be much older, closer in age to his own dad.

Sonny swallowed and nodded. They shook hands, and Sonny lifted his eyebrows and lowered them and opened his mouth and shut it. Neither said anything. Tristan understood that.

Finally, Tristan said, "Everything all right?"

Sonny nodded again. His hair stood out from his head like a lion's mane and it nodded with him. Rosita must not have told him about the cops.

Rosita said, "Sonny, tell him why you came out with me."

Sonny looked down. "I'm very sorry about the old man," he said. "Pinpin, I mean." He looked at Rosita for help. He could not remember the formula. "You know."

Rosita smiled back at him but said nothing.

"He was a good guy," he added. He lifted his brows. He nodded. He brought up a hand but it remained in midair. "I wanted to come out and tell you. He brought my mama over here to see me. Whenever she asked. Every time."

Tristan said, "That's okay," as if he were speaking for Grandpa.

Sonny nodded rapidly this time. "You know what—the last time he came inside with her and read me the riot act." Sonny lifted his eyebrows again and ran a hand through his mane.

Tristan almost laughed at the thought of vinegary Grandpa.

Sonny winked. "He was right too. I'm all fucked up." He grimaced. "So, you come down, huh?"

Tristan nodded.

"Hey, listen, I got to thank you for bringing my mama over." Sonny put out his free arm and hugged Tristan to him.

Behind Sonny's back, Rosita brought one finger up to her lips and smiled.

Tristan tentatively placed an arm around Sonny too. Sonny wore perfume: another cultural difference.

Sonny kept his arm on him after the hug was done. "You going to college, huh?"

"First year," Tristan said.

"That's what I'm going to do," Sonny said resolutely. "Boy, do I need an education!"

Sonny had very white teeth and the same lips as Rosita. He was as pretty as a girl.

"When I get out of this," Sonny said and stopped smiling. "I been an asshole."

Tristan saw beyond Sonny's shoulder a new police car go slowly by. Sonny winked at him and did not turn around. Tristan knew that he knew. The car continued in slow motion and as it moved past the Sears entrance Tristan was able to see Tom-tom on the sidewalk standing with his eyes closed. Tom-tom held out something in his hands—Tristan could not tell what—like a homeless person in New York asking for loose change. Tristan figured he was pleading for the police car to go on out of sight.

"I want to talk to you about college," Sonny said. "You know what Pinpin, your grandpa, said? He said, play music, that's more important than college!"

Tristan smiled. Just like Grandpa.

"Sonny," Rosita said.

"That's okay, Mama," Sonny said. He turned back to

Tristan and grabbed his shoulder, just like Tom-tom. He had thought of the proper thing to say. "I want to come over to the house and extend my condolences. When's the wake?"

This time it was Tristan who looked down. "It hasn't been set yet," he said.

"Sonny, don't make promises if you cannot keep them," Rosita said.

Tom-tom stood by her now. He was holding a baked potato with cheese topping in one hand and a plastic fork in the other. "These potatoes are wonderful," he said, his mouth full of them. "I was gonna bring you one, but I'm very nervous. Did ya see that police car?"

"Tom-tom, there's all that food at the house," Rosita said.

"I can get that every day," Tom-tom said.

"I'll look in the paper," Sonny said. "Nothing's going to keep me away. We're like family. I'm old enough to remember Aunt Mama."

"That's right," Rosita said.

Tristan said, "Thank you."

"You got it backward," Sonny said. "I thank you."

"It's all right if you can't come," Tristan said.

"Oh no, no, I'm coming," Sonny said. "I gotta be there. Tomorrow night?"

It was not easy not to answer him, but Tristan remained silent.

"Sonny?" Rosita said, beginning to worry about the danger.

Sonny lifted the shopping bag. "See this? It's going to fix things up. There's nothing you can't fix with money. So they say, anyway. I'm learning about the world, man. Oh-oh!" He smiled and again his teeth gleamed. "I don't know if I want to know that much."

"You better go, Sonny," Tom-tom said.

Sonny nodded, looked over his shoulder at Rosita and Tom-tom, and nodded again to each, and, finally, to

Tristan. "Yep," he said. "But it's been so good, so good to talk to you!"

He turned and walked back to Sears.

"Sonny," Rosita called. She really had nothing to say, Tristan could tell. She simply wanted to take another look.

He called back over his shoulder, "See you at the wake!"

Rosita waved.

They watched him disappear into the building.

How could he say no to the wake now? He had said no many, many times, it seemed to him, but he suspected none had taken.

"Rosita, I like him, he's a good boy," Tom-tom said. He opened the back door of the Volvo and as they got in added, "These baked potatoes are delicious. You gotta hand it to the Americans. I think they're better than yellow rice. Maybe."

The rental check for the fall. It was crazy he should think of it now, but he had not only forgotten to tell Dad to send it, he had also forgotten to add it to his list in the notebook and that was why he had not thought of it. But he did not get too excited about this bit of forgetfulness, he had two more chances to get the check off today: when Dad called (if he called today) or when he talked to Nanao. About the other things on his list, however, today was a bust. He could not call a lawyer when he got back, it was too late; and he would have to lock himself up in Grandpa's study to tell the funeral parlor person to go ahead with the cremation, for that's what everyone at the house thought he was out doing now with Tom-tom and Rosita. That is, making arrangements with the funeral parlor. Maybe he should wait until he was alone in the house to do any phoning?

When would that be?

Never.

He enjoyed that bit of exasperated exaggeration. It was vinegary. Like Grandpa.

"You see, Rosita," Tom-tom said even before Tristan started the Volvo, "there was no need to worry. Sonny is in no danger. I could see that, I kept my eyes open when we were in there."

"Thank you, Tom-tom," Rosita said.

"He didn't have to put on no disguise," Tom-tom said. "The hair and all that."

"Oh no, don't you remember?—that's the way he looked before he opened the rugs and blinds store," Rosita said. "I suppose you have to look like that when you're in that rock and roll."

Tristan was glad—happy, in fact—that he had come to the mall and met Sonny. Even that crazy encounter with cops, you could say was exciting. But it had been a close call—how would he have explained it to Dad if he had gotten arrested instead of getting Grandpa cremated? Actually, Sonny had taken a greater risk, no matter what he said, in coming out to the parking area.

And after all, he had not lost too much time really. Tomorrow morning, after talking to Dad, he could get everything done—the lawyer, the funeral parlor, the real estate agent to put the house on the market, second-hand furniture dealers to clear out the furnishings. He got a wonderful idea: in the evening he could invite all the cousins to the house again and make it up to them with food and drink for the loss of the wake and the funeral. Sonny could come then, and it wouldn't be too much of a risk. It would be as good as a wake. As soon as he got back he would discuss this with Marina. He should be able to have it all catered. He had never done any entertaining, as Mom might say, except to invite Nanao out to dinner.

He got another wonderful idea. Instead of calling in a used-furniture dealer or Goodwill or the Salvation Army, he would ask each of the cousins to pick out what he or she wanted from Grandpa's house—they could have the things as mementoes of Grandpa, their Pinpin. Or of that Aunt

Mama, his great-grandmother. God. The cousins would like that. It was *better* than a wake. You could even say it was sensible. He'd tell them to take anything and everything and the house would be cleaned out and there would be no expenses for moving things out for the new owners. Mom and Dad were not interested in any of that stuff and they were right. They didn't need it. Only Grandpa's papers and his most personal things were what they would want, what they should want. And he too wanted them, he reasoned. For posterity, he said to himself.

He immediately saw the Toshiba 3200 sitting on the long white-formica work surface—so neat and ready to please—and he had to admit he wanted it for himself. He wanted it just as it was, with all of Grandpa's writings of the last few years in its hard drive. It should, in fact, be kept like that forever. (He must, underline must, immediately buy floppy disks if Grandpa hadn't made copies of his entries, and he must make several copies, to be safe.) Even if in his lifetime Grandpa had not won any genius or national book awards, any Pulitzer or Nobel prizes, it did not mean that someday everything he wrote would not be read avidly by everybody and pored over by scholars, and all the things in that study in Ybor City prized and treasured. He brought his thoughts to a halt as fast as he could. His mind was close to careening like a skidding car and that would be sloppy.

Still, he was pleased he had had these thoughts, gone off on that side road. Grandpa would have given him the go-ahead too. He suspected Grandpa knew he was important and hoped at least his family also knew. Else, why did he keep on writing? And with a Toshiba too. But why had he not made floppy disk copies? Why did he take the chance that it would all be erased by some human error or a thunderstorm, surge protector or no surge protector. Grandpa was hard to figure out. He wished he were here to help him reason about this wake and funeral and how to please his cousins.

Did Dad and Mom and Uncle Crispin know that in Tampa they called Grandpa Pinpin? Did Owen and Emily? He thought not. He was the first to know.

Rosita tapped him on the knee. "I see you are smiling about it all," she said. "I am glad."

He had not known he was smiling.

Tom-tom made him leave the mall at the Sears end. He explained to Rosita that he wanted Tristan to get a look at Tampa Stadium. "It is famous up North, you know," he added, for she had only nodded and not enthusiastically agreed.

"You heard of it, right?" he said to Tristan.

"Yes, I think so," Tristan said slowly.

"What did I tell you," Tom-tom said. "Lookit."

Tom-tom tapped Tristan's shoulder and made him look across the road to where the cement walkways rose up at the rear of the stadium.

"And to think this was all scrub when your grandpa and me went up North to look for jobs," Tom-tom continued. "You could buy it all for nothing in those days and nothing is just what I had. And Pinpin, too. I'll tell ya a story, about old Santori whose grandson married the granddaughter Lindabelle of my sister's sister-in-law—you know them, Rosita, from Sanchez Street. Well, old Santori was one of those crazy old Sicilians and he had this broken-down dairy and you know where it was?"

Tristan nodded.

"You guessed it!" Tom-tom hurried to say. "Right here! He had all these skinny old cows and his kids used to want to move right into Ybor City and work in the cigar factories instead of in all that cow shit. Well, you know what his dumb old dairy got to be worth? Take a guess."

Tristan waited a moment, but Tom-tom outwaited him. "Millions?" Tristan said.

That gave Tom-tom pause, but he recovered. "You bet," he said. "And to top it all off, old Santori was just as stubborn and crazy as ever and he kept the house and two acres around it for himself. He wouldn't sell for love or money. And you know what that became?"

Tom-tom banged him hard on the shoulder to show him he should turn left out of the mall. He then shouted, "Half of the mall!"

There was quiet in the car until Tom-tom tapped his shoulder again and pointed him onto Columbus Drive, the street they had taken from the airport.

"Half of the mall!" Tom-tom sighed and his saliva moisted Tristan's neck and one ear. "Pinpin used to love that story."

In a moment, it occurred to Tristan that Tom-tom had led him away from North Tampa, that he would not be driving past the black housing developments. They were on Columbus Drive at a point not far from Tom-tom's home. He must not, he told himself, go back there. Tom-tom said, "Pinpin used to say, Tom-tom, tell me about old Santori." He sighed, and Tristan waited for the mist to wet him but it didn't fall this time. "And I used to tell it to him, of course. Who could say no to Pinpin?"

When they passed the bridge over the Hillsborough River and saw the house with the collapsed front porch, Tristan knew he was safe. No going back to Tom-tom's. He also realized that everything about Columbus Drive now seemed unremarkable. It was not tacky, it was not run-down, it was just a place he knew. It was understandable. Back in New York, he no longer noticed the visiting kids from Queens and New Jersey punking out in the Village—green, orange, shaved, Rastafarian heads went by him as unnoticed as the overflowing trash cans on every corner.

"Did you ever notice that Pinpin was not one to take over the conversation?" Rosita said. "He encouraged others to talk. I think he must have learned that up North."

"Oh, he was a born gentleman," Tom-tom said, not taking the hint. "He didn't have to learn that nowhere."

"Yes, he was, a real gentleman," Rosita said. "Especially

with the ladies. He never said an objectionable word in front of a lady. I know, he sat on my porch and drank coffee many a time and never a word out of him that was an offense."

"And that is a fact," Tom-tom said.

Rosita sighed.

With deliberation Tom-tom said, "He never fought with anyone. He was always so agreeable. Yes, Tom-tom, yes, of course, Tom-tom. That's what he'd say, not just to me but to everybody, right?"

Rosita sighed for an answer, but Tristan suspected Tom-tom meant him especially to listen. To answer yes, Tom-tom, of course.

"Never a mean word, never," Tom-tom continued. "Never hard, you know what I mean. Always a kind response."

In a tone more concerned with truth than reverence, Rosita said, "I wouldn't go so far—"

"Oh, the bourgeoisie!" Tom-tom said. "You're talking about the bourgeoisie. He hated them. And the capitalists."

"And a few others," Rosita said.

"Fools, you mean fools," Tom-tom said. "All fools. And he was right, right?"

Rosita half turned to look at both him and Tristan. She said, "I didn't say he was wrong. He was never wrong."

Tom-tom exhaled moist breath again. "Oh, Rosita, you and me, we understood him, we sure did."

Rosita smiled at that but said, "Anyway, I am not intelligent enough to tell if he was wrong."

"You don't have to be intelligent," Tom-tom said. "No sir, you knew he was right whenever he talked."

Rosita sighed. "Look how we're talking, Tom-tom," she said and touched Tristan's arm lightly. "Without thought for this boy, making him sad."

Tristan shook his head. "Oh, that isn't so. I'm not sad. I'm really very glad that you're talking about Grandpa. I've been busy going to school and all that and I haven't been in touch with—I had not been in touch with him for a long while. There's so much I don't know about him and so I'm really glad, you know, to hear you talk about him. Please."

Embarrassing to have talked so much. He never spoke that long and in such a vein to Mom and Dad. With them he could never do it. But these Latin cousins allowed him to brazen out the momentary strain of what he'd done, and he looked quickly at Rosita first and then at Tom-tom, and smiled. They smiled back at him and he could see that for them too this was an event, this moment of community, this baring of their hearts about Grandpa. A quietness, too precious to break, hung in the car.

Later, Tristan was to recall this moment as one suspended in the eye of a mounting storm.

Finally, Rosita sighed.

Tom-tom placed a hand lovingly on Tristan's shoulder. "Oh, you will hear so many stories at the wake!"

Tristan heard the slight pause before the word 'wake.' Less of a pause than a catch in Tom-tom's voice. It said, *Will Tristan say something? Will he object?*

There was another pause when Tom-tom finished the sentence, a long one, and then he hurried to fill up the void: "Isn't that so, Rosita, isn't that what it's like?"

Tristan waited for her to speak, but when she did not—he could almost hear her silence and Tom-tom's suspense—he knew he had to speak up about the wake, once more and definitively. "About the wake," Tristan began.

"Oh, you'll hear more stories and more stories, you can bet on that," Tom-tom said hurriedly. "The memories they gonna have about Pinpin—"

"Uncle Tom-tom," Tristan said.

Tom-tom did not stop for breath. "Of course, I don't know if you can trust them all. But don't you worry about that. I'm gonna be there and Rosita too, we can tell you which are true—"

"Uncle Tom-tom, there's not going to be any wake," Tristan said. "Dad sent me down to have Grandpa cremated. That's what he wants."

"I'm not talking about your father," Tom-tom said. "Rosita, did I say anything about his father? I'm talking to you. You're in charge."

"Yes, but—" Tristan had to stop: his shoulder was pinned back against his seat by Tom-tom's hand.

"Just a minute," Tom-tom said. "Hear me out. That's all I ask. And let Rosita speak too. She has something to say and she should not be denied the right."

Tristan said in a low voice, "It's no use."

"You gonna hear me out?" Tom-tom said. "All his life your grandpa been my favorite—you gonna listen to me?"

Tristan nodded slightly. It was somewhat ridiculous the way Tom-tom carried on, but he was used to it now. A cultural difference, that's all. He could not dismiss him or every one of his arguments because of it.

"All right?" Tom-tom said.

Tristan nodded with more definition this time.

"What was I gonna say? You made me forget, I'm so upset. I never been so upset!" Tom-tom threw up his arms and Tristan heard his hands banging against the roof of the car. "Oh yes, I remember now."

Tom-tom leaned forward, and before he spoke, Tristan could feel his warm breath on his neck. "Now, you tell me," he whispered, "is it the money? Tris, is it the money? You can open your heart to me, you're like my own son now. I swear, you're as good as my very own son Junior. Isn't that so, Rosita? You tell him."

She caught Tristan's eye and said, "We have discussed that a little. Marina too. It's a big family, everybody's working—"

"Yeah, it's not like the Depression," Tom-tom said.

"So we can all contribute," Rosita said. "That's what Tom-tom means."

"We can pass the hat around," Tom-tom said. "Anybody don't give, I'll talk to 'em."

He patted Tristan's shoulder. Tristan thought he had been shaking his head no, but he was not certain. Tom-tom chuckled in a low confidential tone. Tristan decided he had better shake his head again.

"Yes sir, I'll talk to 'em," Tom-tom repeated.

Tristan shook his head determinedly. "It's not that," he said. "I'm sorry."

Rosita's hand reached towards him and her eyes looked bigger with pleading. "Maybe Tom-tom did not express it right," she said. Her touch on his arm was so nice and her voice so soothing. "He did not mean that your father and mother are trying to save money. He meant that we could all share in the cost, since it means so much to us to accompany him until the end and to have our friends come and pay him a last tribute too."

She kept her eyes on him.

"Uh-huh," Tristan said. "I mean, I understand. But it's a matter of principle with my family. Not to have religious rituals, that is."

"What religious what!" Tom-tom said. "Who said religion? Did I say religion, Rosita? Who mentioned a priest? I didn't mention a priest."

"I'm sorry," Tristan said.

"Don't tell me you're sorry," Tom-tom said. He was yelling now. "I hate people who tell me they're sorry when they ain't sorry at all. If you're sorry, then let me have the wake."

"It's not for me to say, it's my family," Tristan said and wished he could take it back.

"Your family!" Tom-tom said. "We're your family and we're a helluva lot more, you know. Not just a measly two or three people who don't even bother to come down when Pinpin dies. My cousin brother Pinpin! They don't love Pinpin enough to come down, they don't have any say in the whole thing."

Rosita said, "He doesn't mean you, Tristan."

"I'm sorry," Tristan repeated, and felt like a fool.

"Stop, stop!" Tom-tom said. "I can't think in a moving car." He opened a window. "Are you gonna stop?"

Tristan slowed down and stopped the car at the corner. He knew that on Columbus Drive he would not be stopping traffic.

"Okay, okay," Tom-tom said.

"Uncle Tom-tom," Tristan began, half turning to talk to him in the backseat.

"Wait a minute, wait a minute," Tom-tom said. "I don't have my thoughts together yet."

Tristan waited.

"Okay, Rosita, you tell him," Tom-tom said. "Rosita will tell you what we decided. I'll listen."

Rosita smiled. She reached out to touch Tristan but remembered she had done that before. "Tristan, we were talking about all this," she said. "Tom-tom and Marina and some of the other cousins—"

"Never mind them," Tom-tom said. "They don't matter, just you and Marina and me."

"We respect you and your father's wishes," Rosita said. "We don't want you to go against anyone. You understand that, don't you?"

She waited, so he had to nod yes.

"And this is what we would like to propose to you. You call Puig and tell him to go ahead and prepare for a wake tomorrow night—"

"They don't even call it a wake," Tom-tom said. "All it says in the papers is the family will be receiving friends on such and such, at such and such. No mention of a wake, get it?"

Tristan remembered his great idea.

"I forgot to tell you something," he said, and the excitement in his voice got him their attention. "I want to have a gathering like that at the house. Tomorrow night. All the family, everybody. I'll have someone cater it and it will be even better because we'll all be at the house."

Rosita said, "As in the old days? There hasn't been a wake like that in many, many years."

Tom-tom said to her, "You think Puig will bring the coffin to the house and all that?"

Tristan said no, only no. He meant no coffin but could not bring himself to say coffin. He shook his head for emphasis, then nodded, then shook his head, then nodded. Finally, he stopped, said no again, and looked down at the floor of the car stubbornly.

"No coffin! No Pinpin!" Tom-tom said. "You mean you just gonna send out for food? Who the hell needs that in our family? We bring the food."

Rosita said, "Let me finish."

"What for?" Tom-tom said.

"Let me explain, there can be a wake at Puig's without it going against your father's beliefs," she said. "Or yours."

"Oh, yeah," Tom-tom said.

Tristan wished he could interrupt and say he had no beliefs about that. He had never thought about death.

Rosita continued. "All of Pinpin's family can be with him one last night and all the friends can come and extend condolences. And then Puig can go ahead the next day and do whatever you want him to do with the body."

Rosita stopped. The word "body" had caught in her throat. She swallowed and then said to Tom-tom, "Is that it, Tom-tom? Did I say it all?"

Tom-tom had calmed down while she talked, and he now replied softly, almost in a whisper, "Only one thing bothers me about it. When you do something like this they rent you the coffin. Now, is that right? Do we want Pinpin in a rented coffin?"

Tom-tom's hand returned to Tristan's shoulder, patting him like a father. "What do you think, Tris?" he asked. "Shall we get him a new one?"

Tristan shook his head no.

"Okay," Tom-tom said. "I guess I'm being too sensitive about little details."

"No," Tristan said. "It can't be. I could not explain it to my parents. They'd have to know."

When had he separated himself from Mom and Dad's wishes? Did he no longer think it was barbaric?

"But don't you see the beauty of our plan?" Tom-tom said. "You don't have to tell 'em. They don't even have to know."

"Lie to them?" Tristan blurted out.

They did not reply to him and he could not catch either's eye. He shook his head one last time and turned on the ignition. "I can't lie to my Dad."

This time Tom-tom screamed. "You think you're Georgie Washington! You haven't learned to wipe your ass and you talking like that to us!"

Rosita said in a faint voice, "Tom-tom."

"Stop, I'm getting out. Your father—I don't care if I broke two legs I don't leave my father to be burned like a cigar!" Tom-tom tried to open the door, but it was locked from up front. "Open it! Open it!"

"Uncle Tom-tom," Tristan said weakly, but he did what Tom-tom said.

Tom-tom threw open the door and with both hands gripping the doorjambs propelled himself out of the car. He leaned down and yelled through the door, "You can keep the keys when you get there—I don't want this car, you can have it and stick it up your ass!"

Rosita turned fully in her seat and reached an arm out the back door to pull him back in. "Tom-tom," she said.

"I'm gonna walk," Tom-tom said.

"Please," Rosita said.

"I can't do that to Pinpin," he said to her. "How could I face him—how could I take his car and let them burn him without even a wake!"

They were at Fourteenth Street and Tom-tom crossed it to

the corner of the grammar school that Grandpa had attended. It took Tristan a moment to start after him. He was stunned by the sight of Tom-tom, squat, fat, waddling, in the foreground of the waste of the old red-brick building and its blasted yard. On the other side of Columbus Drive began Cuscaden Park where Grandpa and Tom-tom had tried when they were kids to steal oranges and grapefruits from the old cracker.

Tom-tom walked with both hands grabbing his head, talking to himself.

Tristan drove alongside him and waved and called, but Tom-tom would not look his way. Tristan opened the window on Rosita's side and called again, louder. At the corner of Fifteenth Street, he was supposed to turn left. Tom-tom too. Tristan saw that his face had turned a purplish brown, that his jowls twitched, that perspiration—or was it tears?—ran down the gullies of his face.

"Uncle Tom-tom," he called. "Please get in."

Tom-tom spoke only to Rosita. "I am walking back to that house where we were all once so happy, Rosita, but I am not going inside. My very own car is there, if Dewey did not destroy it, and I shall go home to Olivia and never come back. Poor Pinpin, that it should come to this!"

Rosita held her arm out the window.

Tristan got out of the car. He did not dare walk over to Tom-tom on the sidewalk. He called to him over the roof of the car.

"Out of my sight!" Tom-tom yelled.

Tristan said, "Uncle Tom-tom, we'll have a wake at the funeral parlor. Come back, please. I won't tell my folks."

"Oh Rosita, Rosita," Tom-tom said. "I told you this boy was a saint!"

Eight

MAYOR FREEDMAN CALLS TRISTAN

Again Aunt Clem was out on the porch with her arms out welcoming Tristan, and he was glad, glad to see her. His face flushed, his body tingling, he was carried these last four blocks on the high tide of new emotions publicly displayed. He had never so quickly yielded without reasoning, never fought and made up, never forgiven and been forgiven, so passionately, so generously. He was awash with feelings he had not yet begun to get under control, and the sight of Aunt Clem waving at him from the porch and the kids making way for the Volvo in the driveway made him feel sloppily happy and very close to tears.

The moment he was out of the car Aunt Clem began.

"Tristan, oh Tristan honey, you won't believe it. Marina was cooking and her hands were wet and I got to the phone first and who do you think was calling? Maggie will never forgive me for getting to the phone first—she's so jealous, everybody is, even Marina but she won't admit it."

"Shut up," Tom-tom said. "I got news."

"Tom-tom, just behave for once, I'm not afraid of you," Aunt Clem said. "I got news for Tristan. Oh Tristan, who do you think it was? I give you a guess. Go on, guess."

"What happened?" Rosita asked.

"Aunt Clem, don't drag it out," Maggie called from the door. "It's not the Academy Awards."

Tom-tom looked about him furious and expectant, but no one asked him for his news. "Pay no attention," he muttered to Tristan. "She's grandstanding."

"They're jealous, I'd be jealous too," Aunt Clem said and ran to the center steps and panted as she went down them the sooner to meet him. "Don't anybody tell him. It's my story. I was the one picked up the phone. Oh Tristan honey!"

She grabbed his face with both hands, then as at the airport threw herself against him. This time it felt natural.

"My God, what a family," Maggie said from the porch. "We just go on too much about everything."

At very close quarters, Aunt Clem told him. "The mayor! It was the mayor calling! I still can't believe it. That and the television coverage. What a wonderful day!"

"Oh," Tristan said. "The mayor of the city?"

"And who do you think the call was for?" Aunt Clem said. "One guess."

Maggie laughed. "Here we go again."

Tom-tom called to Jack on the porch. "Why you letting the women answer the phone?"

Aunt Clem led Tristan up the front steps. "The little green monster's got Maggie 'cause I answered the phone."

Maggie said, "Tristan knows that, he knows I'm mean and no-good, and if you don't give him the message, I will. You haven't got the exclusive on it, Aunt Clem, I can tell it too."

"Don't you dare!" Aunt Clem said.

"Was he calling me?" Tristan said.

Aunt Clem laughed her shrieking laugh. "He don't know! He don't know!"

Maggie said, "The mayor's a woman."

"Mrs. Freedman!" Aunt Clem said and shrieked again. "Freedman! Didja hear me?"

Tristan looked at her and then at Maggie. What was the problem?

Anselmo opened the front door. "What's going on here? Oh, Tristan, you're back. Everything okay? Tom-tom? Did that Puig squeeze you dry?"

"Wait, wait," Aunt Clem said. "I haven't finished yet. Everybody horns in. They're jealous they didn't get the call—"

Dewey called from the door, "The mayor wants to go to the wake—that's the message."

Aunt Clem screamed, "Dewey!"

Dewey covered his mouth with one hand, raised his eyebrows exaggeratedly, and retreated into the house. Aunt Clem pulled Tristan into the living room after her, saying, "I'll tell you inside, that's not the way it was," and when she saw Dewey there, she reached out and hit him on the head, shoulders, chest, wherever she could get at him. "You ruined it!" she screamed. He placed his hands over his head and doubled up defensively, but she could hear him laughing and she hit him three or more times with diminishing vigor and giggling herself.

To those still on the porch, Tom-tom announced, "The wake will be at Puig's tomorrow night." Tristan heard him and the loud happy outcry that followed. Tom-tom came in and went on past them towards the kitchen. "Marina, the wake is tomorrow night," he called before he reached it.

Maggie burst in from the porch. "Rosita says Tom-tom

isn't just bullshitting," she said. She grabbed Tristan. "Is it true?" She did not give him time to reply. She hugged him and squeezed his cheek with hers. "You forgive me for my tantrum? Say you forgive me."

Tristan nodded.

She kissed him and laughed the deep, throaty laugh he liked.

Anselmo clapped him on the back. "I told them they were wrong," he said. "I only had one look at you, but I knew you wouldn't do that to your grandfather. That boy is a Granados, I said."

From his place at the corner of the sofa, old Santos spoke up. "It will be my last wake. I am sorry it is not mine instead of Aunt Mama—"

"No, no," one of the kids yelled in his ear. "It's her son."

"Forget it," Manuela said.

Her sister Eloisa added, "He'll never get it straight."

If only he, Tristan, could get their names straight.

The two of them got up and stood in line to hug Tristan. It was the thing to do, he saw. The men slapped his back when they embraced him, and the women kissed him. Except Cookie; she didn't want to smear any of her makeup on him.

How wonderful it was that everything was resolved, that there was no holding back, that no one—including himself—had any reservations! That they were not sparring. He thought this as Eloisa—was she the shy one?—kissed him, and for the first time he kissed back. There was a little outcry about it, and he too laughed.

As each person had his turn, he or she would turn to Rosita and say, "Rosita, ah Rosita!"

Eloisa and Manuela took turns echoing, "Ah Rosita."

They thought she had done it. They were also saying that they hoped everything was all right with Sonny. He had thought they didn't know about their going to see Sonny, but they knew it, he saw that now. Nothing was actually said, but he had learned to hear them better. They didn't have to be English majors to know how to express themselves fully to those who really listened.

He also saw that they had been conniving. He saw it so clearly that it made him feel smart. There need be no more of that. They had got their wake. His too: he wanted the wake. Everything was openness and he rejoiced.

"Oooh, oooh," Aunt Clem cooed. "Whyn't you tell me. Oh Tristan, I'm so happy!"

Jack cleared his throat loudly. "Do you want me to call the mayor's office for you?" he said and nodded to encourage Tristan to agree.

"Wait, wait," Aunt Clem said. "Wait till I tell you the whole thing that happened."

Maggie said, "Hey Jack, you a friend of the mayor?"

"Well, as a matter of fact," Jack said. "I've met her."

One of the kids ran out to the porch yelling, "Uncle Jack is a friend of Mayor Freedman!"

"It's not polite to interrupt," Aunt Clem said. She held out her arms to signal everyone that she was resuming her story. "You listen, Tristan honey. This is the way it went. I picked up the phone and I heard 'em say Mayor Freedman calling Mrs. Granados about Mr. Granados passing away. And I said, Oh Mayor, I'm his cousin—I didn't want to take any credit wasn't mine—and I didn't faint. I just hung on to that phone for dear life. Didn't I, Eloisa? I said there was no Mrs. Granados—" Aunt Clem interrupted herself to shriek. "I mean she is dead, but Mr. Granados's son was here to take care of the funeral—I mean, things. And I said son 'cause I thought that sounded better. Don't you, Tristan honey?"

Anselmo laughed a deep laugh and it jarred Aunt Clem.

"Let her tell her story," Maggie said.

"Thank you, Maggie," Aunt Clem said.

Maggie added, "So she can finish and we can all go on with our lives."

Anselmo laughed again.

"And what did the mayor want?" Tristan asked.

"She wants to come to the wake!" Aunt Clem said. "She wants to pay her respects to Tampa's most important arthur. That's what she said, Tampa's most important arthur. Only you know what? I was so excited that I didn't realize it wasn't Mrs. Freedman in person, it was her secretary. And what she actually said was, This is the mayor's office calling, but I didn't hear that right 'cause I was so excited, can you blame me, I'm the first in the family to even talk to a mayor. I didn't know that meant it was the secretary and I guess I heard it wrong and what's more—"

Aunt Clem broke off to relieve herself with a shriek of the irrepressible waves of laughter that shook her generous bosom. "Oh, Tristan honey, oh Tristan honey! The secretary was a he, not a she! I was just too excited to hear right. I know what you're thinking, Anselmo, but he was not that way, I tell you. Oh, what a day!"

There, that was a good reason for having the wake. In case it came out and he had to confess to Dad and Mom that he had said okay. He was glad. You had to allow Grandpa's hometown to pay him homage. It wasn't just a matter of giving in to Uncle Tom-tom and the cousins.

He must not say Uncle Tom-tom in Mom's or Dad's presence. Or call Aunt Clem Aunt Clem. They would probably laugh at him. Certainly Mom would. It chilled him to think that. God. He did not want to think about what this funny crawling feeling meant, but he must. Later. Call Nanao and reason out his emotions with her. Why be ashamed to call Tom-tom uncle?

"Didja ever hear of a man secretary?" Aunt Clem said.

Maggie said, "Aunt Clem, your story is over."

He had better get the funeral parlor's number from Marina and give them the go-ahead, but he remembered that he should not say this to the cousins as an excuse for leaving them. They were all keeping up the pretense that he had been at the funeral parlor. Instead, he said he had to see

Marina. And they all followed him to the kitchen; all that could get in, that is.

Marina stood at the stove and Tom-tom was speaking into her ear. She put down the cooking spoon and said to Tristan with a kindly look, "I think you did the right thing, Tristan. Not that I don't believe your folks weren't being sensible to start with. Nowadays, all this to-do is more trouble than it's worth."

Jack answered her from the door. "I don't go along with that, Aunt Marina. It's too radical. I'm calling the mayor's office for you, Tristan, and I'm saying we'll see her at Puig's."

Tom-tom threw up his arms. He gave up. "I'm not voting for you for councilman," he called out to Jack, but Jack was gone. "If he can find some fools to put him on the ballot," he added.

Aunt Marina did not look at Jack specifically. She said, "What are you all doing here? You're in the way. This boy has many things to do and discuss. Out."

Aunt Clem retreated into the living room and with her went some of the kids. The boy who had stood on the veranda (Tristan never did hear his name) called back for Marina's benefit, "When do we eat?"

The audience in the TV room came to the doorway of the kitchen, thinking food was being served.

Marina said, "Get back in there or out in the street." To Tristan she explained, "I used to be a librarian, I know how to handle them."

"It's getting to be time for Joe Sorrento," Maggie said. She rushed into the TV room. "What station's that?"

Tom-tom said, "Jesus Christ," and hurried there.

Now that he was practically alone with Marina, Tristan turned his back on the rest of the kitchen and asked her for the phone number. "I'm going to call them now and let them know. Tomorrow night around when?"

He stifled a sigh: he too had become a conniver. Here he was, keeping up the pretense that he had driven to the funeral parlor with Rosita and Tom-tom. Was he like everyone else? Was everybody in the world a conniver?

He could hear Tom-tom in the TV room saying, "Naw, that's the shit comes before the news."

Maggie burst out of the TV room. "Too many damn kids! Jack set up a portable in the living room!"

Marina wiped her hands on a kitchen towel and touched Tristan to get his attention. She was calm; so was Rosita, who went on putting away the clean dishes, undistracted and serene. Marina looked directly into his eyes, and he felt sure she never was a conniver. Marina was one of those who get things done that need to be done, and nothing more.

"You don't have to worry about all that, Tristan," she said. "I took care of it. You had enough to do. I called Puig and it is all arranged for tomorrow. Seven to nine. That's enough time, Puig and I agreed. You can come home early, and we'll discourage as many as we can from coming back here and sitting up all night with you."

"Sitting up all night?" Tristan said.

But what he really meant was, You knew all along that there would be a wake. You counted on me folding.

Had she talked it over with Rosita and Tom-tom? Of course. Did Tom-tom mean that fit he threw? Would he really have given up the Volvo?

"The idea is to keep you company," Rosita said. She had been listening although she had seemed busy at the cupboards. "To sit up with you. To console one another that way."

God. Rosita was in on the plot too, he was sure.

Everyone was.

He could not look at Rosita. Nor at Marina and Tom-tom. And he certainly did not want to face any of the other cousins. Cousins! Mom and Dad were right to laugh at him.

Looking down, he said in a small voice, "I have to make some calls," and he turned away and left the kitchen.

Anselmo passed him in the doorway. He did not try to

stop Tristan—the boy did not look right—but went on into the kitchen and in his booming voice asked the trio at the stove, "What about the funeral? Is it still set for the next morning?"

Marina brought a finger to her lips to shush him.

Anselmo did not see the gesture. "At the Centro Asturiano Cemetery?" he continued.

Tristan hesitated long enough in the dining room to also hear Anselmo complain, "Why aren't you telling me? You can't keep me out, you know," the old man said. "I can't be kept out of anything—I got nothing else to do but butt my head into things!"

Cookie had to press hard on his arm to get Tristan's attention. Her face with all its makeup intact looked at him like a tragic gargoyle exuding sympathy. She said, "Don't feel sad, don't." Then herself looked down, ashamed of her audacity.

Tristan stepped quickly into the study and closed the door behind him. He did not want to hear any more of their talk. He did not need to hear any more. In less than a minute he had become wise. Wised up, rather.

There was Jack. He did not notice him until he closed the door. Jack was squatting to one side of the door examining the audio components. He sprang to his feet with a hurriedly composed smile.

"I called the mayor's office on the phone here," Jack said. "I told them, Puig's at seven P.M."

Tristan nodded and turned away from him. So he too knew the time and place of the wake. He sat at the Toshiba and hoped Jack would go away. The stoop of his shoulders proclaimed his wish.

"They asked me your name," Jack said. He paused. "They're very efficient. So Mayor Freedman can come up to you and know your name."

Tristan remained silent.

Jack cleared his throat. "I'd like to ask you something," he said. "Is it all right?"

Tristan turned to him reluctantly. He kept his head down. He could not lift it, it felt like the large immovable boulders in Maine. He looked at Jack's funny white shoes and waited.

"I don't want to—you know, it may not be the right moment," Jack said, "but I don't know if I'll ever get another chance—you see how our cousins don't leave you alone."

Tristan nodded. It was the best he could do.

"I'll tell you right out," Jack said. "I want a memento of Cousin Pinpin. Something to remember him by. Unless, of course, you're moving everything up North. I don't suppose anybody in your family's going to move into this place."

Tristan shook his head.

"That's what I thought," Jack said with a lift in his voice. Then he stopped and stared at the audio components. He broke off and studied the built-in cabinets.

To his own surprise, Tristan said in a clear, audible voice, "Everything in this room is going up to New York."

"Oh," Jack said. "I wasn't—"

"Or Maine, I don't know which yet," Tristan lied, now that he was a conniver too.

Jack hurried. "Last time I dropped by to visit, the nigger boy was using a neat lawn mower—"

Tristan flinched. "No!" he exclaimed.

"Then how about that Japanese television set in the TV room?"

Tristan shook his head, then nodded. "I didn't mean no. You can have whichever one you want."

"Whichever?"

How had it happened that he began to give Grandpa's things away? Without consulting his folks. Or Uncle Crispin. After all Uncle Crispin was a son too, even if he was out in the South Pacific playing. Screw them all, he, Tristan, was here and he would give everything away if he wanted to.

And he wanted to. His chest was tight and he had to wait a moment to speak.

"Excuse me, I forgot your name," he said.

"Jack, I'm your cousin Jack," Jack said. "My grandmother and your grandfather Pinpin were first cousins. Close cousins. First cousins, not by marriage or anything else." He decided to come right out with it. "Look, I'll take the lawn mower. I got enough television sets."

Tristan nodded just to get on to what he wanted to ask.

Jack exclaimed, "Thanks a million!"

Tristan said, "Listen, if you don't mind telling me—are they planning a funeral?"

"They?" Jack said hesitantly.

"Marina and Uncle Tom-tom," Tristan said.

"Just them?" Jack said.

"And Rosita helping," Tristan said. "Are they setting it all up like the wake and expecting somehow to get me to agree to let them go ahead?"

It was awful to watch conflicting emotions, dizzying speculations, dead-end ideas have their way with Jack's facial muscles. Twice they came to a total halt, a kind of spasm caused, Tristan figured, by the fear of losing the lawn mower. God. Or of losing the chance of a tie-in to the mayor?

The best in Jack won out. "Of course, they want a funeral for Uncle Pinpin, it's only natural. We are old-fashioned down here. Sorry, Tristan. That's only my own opinion but . . . you see?"

Jack tried to leave it at that, but Tristan still looked at him, waiting for more of an answer. Jack added with a laugh, a sure sign that he was going to lie, "But there's no plotting going on." He laughed again, less strained this time. "For one thing, Tom-tom isn't smart enough to put anything over on anyone."

Jack was saved by a sudden welling of the steady din outside. The door opened without warning. It was Tom-tom.

He glared at Jack but addressed only Tristan. "Tris, Tris, the TV news, hurry!"

Jack turned and ran as if he had been caught stealing.

Tristan wanted to hole up in Grandpa's study, that's what he wanted to do, and he got his way.

He heard Tom-tom explain it to Maggie on the other side of the closed door. "He's had a lot of shocks today and he's gotta think it over. He's like Pinpin too, hardheaded and won't be budged—let's go!" And they scurried away to a television set.

But Tom-tom came back by himself. He did not knock anymore. He walked in and said he was giving up the commercials, the best things on TV. "I'm worried about you," he said.

Tristan had decided to call Nanao and he kept one hand on the phone as a strong hint to Tom-tom.

Tom-tom winked, grimaced, said, "How's about it," tried chuckling, grimaced again. "You're just sitting here, anyway," he said. He held the door behind him half-open, on the alert for the changing sounds of the news program. "Come on, it'll cheer you up. You're going to that Yale, but you can't fool me—I can tell you're sad, my boy."

"No, I'm all right," Tristan said. "I just want to make a phone call and this is a good time."

Tom-tom closed the door and stepped into the study. "Listen, don't call until after tomorrow night. No reason to let your father know. He's not interested one way or the other."

"I'm not calling him," Tristan said.

"Who?" Tom-tom took a step to the door and opened it and stayed there, ready to go. "Who you calling?"

"A friend," Tristan said.

Tom-tom narrowed his eyes and smiled confidentially. "A girlfriend, huh?" he said. "You got a girlfriend."

Tristan did not want to talk about that.

"I can tell, I can tell," Tom-tom said. "Nothing like it when you're young. Go ahead, I'll keep them away, I'll tell you whatever that dumb Sorrento says."

He stopped at the door and came back to Tristan. He whispered, "You two living together like the yuppies on TV?" He laughed in his forced whisper, spraying Tristan with a fine mist. "I like you, Tris. You're old-fashioned, you don't talk about such things. It's nobody's business. You're a real gent."

Someone yelled from outside, "Tom-tom!"

Tom-tom stopped himself from running out, and said in a tone that Tristan had not heard from him before, a sage, fatherly tone, "I hope you living with her. It's better for your health."

Tom-tom was gone from the study before Tristan understood what he meant. He did not mean two square meals a day served by a nice obliging girl. That was not what he meant, though he meant that too. Oh no. What a funny way of looking at things, it almost jolted him out of his . . . what was it he was feeling?

"The blues," Nanao said when he reached her. "That's what old blacks say when they're in the dumps. Got those St. Louis blues, just as blue as I can be."

He sighed. He wished he could segue into song like her.

"Come on," she said. "Sing me your blues."

He was quiet.

She was quiet, but he could hear her breathe. He inhaled deeply so she would hear him.

"My grandfather had a Bruce CD in his car stereo," he said after a while. *Tunnel of Love.*"

"Oh-oooh," she said, surprise, approval, sorrow, joy intermingled.

A moment later, she said, "Maybe it wasn't his."

"The CD?"

"Maybe he loaned the car to someone and it was left there."

He shook his head, then remembered he was on the phone. "He has all the others here."

"Here?"

"In his study."

"That's where you're calling?"

He nodded and she seemed to know he had. She said, "He collected Bruce?"

"And the Grateful Dead and Sting—"

"That's not so good."

"You never said that before."

"Pablum."

He asked, "Roy Orbison, what about him?"

"He's the white boys' daddy."

"What?" Tristan said. "What do you mean by that?"

"Never mind."

They were quiet again.

"You know, my grandpappy just doesn't have rhythm," she said. "He's too dignified."

"The Montgomery bourgeoisie."

"He's only a dentist, like my father," she protested. She did not know why she was protesting, or against whom. "God," she added.

"Does he think Jesse's too pushy?"

She replied in her grand voice. "Your syllogism is fractured."

"He's for Jesse?"

"He was for Dr. King before everybody, right there in Montgomery. Before the whites canonized him and he became de Lawd. He just didn't approve of hippies and all that new life-style. The black bourgeoisie is way ahead of the white."

"I agree."

She laughed. "Of course he's for Jesse, but I think he wishes Jesse hadn't started things up again."

He did not say anything about that.

She did not let too much time go by before she said, "Come on, tell me, what're they doing to you down there?"

He told her. Not all. Only about the wake.

"It's humiliating," he said, and he stopped because his throat had gotten tight again.

Nanao said, "And you think it's sordid?" A favorite adjective of hers. "Do you—"

This time it was Maggie who interrupted. She yelled, "They said it's coming on after the commercials—" She threw out her arms beseechingly. "You gotta come and see it. Ybor City author passes on, they said. Do it as a favor to me, sweetie pie."

"Who's that?" Nanao said.

From the dining room the children, led by that boy who had stood on the veranda, chanted, "Cousin Tristan, come and see it! Cousin Tristan, come and see it!"

"You gotta see yourself!" Maggie said. "And me too! Come on or I'll miss it."

"What's that?" Nanao said. "What's going on?"

Tristan explained.

Maggie listened to him on the phone and her eyes widened as she imagined the girl at the other end. His explanations dwindled into diffidence as Maggie's interest grew. He feared he was blushing.

"You on TV!" Nanao said. "Holy, holy, I'm hanging up. You go see it." Then she screamed, "And call me back!"

"You want me to see it?" Tristan said.

Maggie replied, "Of course."

Nanao replied, "Of course!" And she hung up.

When he called back, she picked up the phone in the middle of the first ring. "How was it!" She did not wait. "Oooh, I wish I could've seen it. Why aren't you telling me?"

She laughed; she knew she had not given him a chance.

"I don't know," he said, his all-purpose reply.

She said, "First, tell me how you looked."

Maggie came into the study with the second glass of beer

and the dish of thin, crisp plantains he had left behind in the TV room. She placed them at his elbow.

"Talking to her again," Maggie said. "Tell her I love you."

"What's that?" Nanao said. "Who's talking to you?"

"That's my cousin Maggie," he said. He giggled; the first beer had had its effect. "She says to tell you that she loves me."

"Your cousin Maggie!" Nanao said. "How old is she?"

He giggled in a less strangled manner this time.

"Come on, tell me," Nanao said.

"I never ask a lady her age." He winked at Maggie. "But I can tell you she's beautiful."

Maggie retreated to the door. "Hey, I'm leaving. Tell her I'm an old bag and I love her too." She threw him a kiss and closed the door as she left. He knew she was thanking him for the set of Wedgewood demitasses he had told her she could have.

"She sends you her love too and she is gone now," Tristan said. He took a first sip of the new glass of beer Marina had sent with Maggie. Marina thought beer before dinner was good for the appetite.

Nanao said, "You been talking about me?"

"They figured out I was talking to a girl," he said. He controlled his laughter and it came out a chuckle. "The rest is pure conjecture."

"Tristan," she said.

He waited, but things kept bubbling inside him. He had never felt this way. Was he drunk? He allowed himself to chuckle some more. He liked the rippling careless sound of it.

He told her he had discovered you could put together film shots of real life and turn it into fiction.

Joe Sorrento had taken all that footage of quarrels, yelling, boasting, his own diffidence, and out came a homespun story. Aunt Clem, sweet and beatific, welcoming him to the ancestral home; Uncle Tom-tom looking solemnly, authoritatively into the camera, saying, "He was the greatest man ever came out of Ybor City"; the professor saying the same in academese; Maggie saying, "I want justice for him, justice!"; and then he, the grandson, announcing he was here to make all the arrangements, quietly, proudly.

"God," he said to Nanao, "it sounded like Grandpa was being nominated for sainthood."

The door of the study opened and Aunt Clem looked in. She put a finger to her lips to show she was not going to talk, and handed him a piece of paper. She winked and quickly left.

Nanao said, "I think it sounds nice."

The paper said, *I want the rockn chair & the tv if you threw it out. I got black white only.* He chewed the plantain slivers; he sipped the beer. Sure, she could have them. He found the mute button on the phone and tapped it and called loudly, as if he were Tom-tom or one of the cousins, "Aunt Clem, Aunt Clem!"

"What're you eating?" Nanao said.

He explained. Aunt Marina had made them from Aunt Mama's recipe and they beat potato chips.

"Those names," Nanao said. "They sound like what Grandpappy calls poor white trash."

Aunt Clem looked in, her eyes full of hope.

He muted the phone again. "Sure, you can have them."

Aunt Clem skipped to him and hugged him and he fell off the Balans chair onto his knees. "Oh, my goodness."

She skipped back to the door. "I leave you, honey, I leave you," she said and turned around at the door and like Maggie blew him kisses. "God love you."

"What's that?" Nanao said.

He did not tell her. Instead, he continued with the recipe. Unripe plantains thinly sliced—paper thin, in fact—and fried in lard, real lard; then the grease quickly sloshed off by placing them in a paper bag and shaking them, and then they were salted. "Whoosh, whoosh," he said, imitating the sound of the paper bag being shaken. "Delicious." He took another swallow of beer.

"Ummmh," she murmured.

He chuckled.

She sang, "Don't make no difference what nobody says."

He spoke the next line, prosy bass to her alto, "Ain't nobody like to be alone."

She said, "I'm not convinced by Bruce's accent. There's something nowhere about it."

"You said last week he was too gumbah."

"That's true too," she said.

He chuckled.

"Don't you see? Where do all those accents come from?"

He belched, but she did not hear him.

The door opened a bit at a time and then Horacio's head peeked through. "Hey," he said, just as his father Anselmo had said he would. He held out a note. "This is from Cookie. She's too shy, you know."

Tristan muted the phone.

Nanao said, "All those white Northern boys when they sing rock, those accents are not genuine."

The note said, *Maggie says I should tell you now. I would like the full-length mirror on the reverse side of the door in the front bedroom. I believe there is another one in the bathroom. But I am only asking for one. I am so ashamed. Of course if you have some use for it, please forget this note. Tear it up. Also, I want to thank you for introducing me to Joe Sorrento. Cookie.*

What full-length mirror?

Tristan had not yet said anything to Horacio about Cookie's note when Dewey looked in too. "Tristan, old man," he said as nonchalantly as he could, "I want to buy that TV off you."

Tristan said to Nanao, "Hang on a moment."

"Sorry to butt in," Dewey said, "I just happened to think of it now."

"I can't do it," Tristan said. "I'm sorry, but the TV set is Aunt Clem's."

Nanao said, "What're you doing—holding an auction?"

Tristan muted the phone.

Dewey said, "Shit. That's the story of my life. Too late."

Tristan took a deep breath and said to Horacio, "Tell Cookie of course."

"I told her it'd be all right," Horacio said. "She's saving you trouble taking it off your hands, right?"

Nanao said, "I'm hanging on."

Dewey said, "What's Cookie getting?"

"Jesus," Horacio said.

Maggie returned and neither Horacio nor Tristan had to reply. Behind her, holding a hand up to cover her eyes—for shame—was Cookie.

"I gotta tell you, I gotta make it clean," Maggie said. "I can't take the demitasses just like that. They're Ainsley bone china, didja know that? Queen Elizabeth's favorite china company!"

Tristan did not know what to say. He took a sip of the beer. "Uh-huh," he said.

"They were Celia's," Maggie said with great emphasis, her voice rasping bottom. "Your own grandma from Boston gave them to her. Years ago. You can imagine what they cost now!"

"Well?" Tristan said.

"Oh Tristan!" Maggie threw herself at him and again he fell to the floor in a kneeling position. "Oh, you're so good and I'm such a bitch! Look at the way I yelled at you! God almighty, the names I called you!"

"What about the names you called me?" Dewey said. "Did ya ever apologize to me? Never!"

Dewey held out a hand to her to help her up and she

grabbed it and pulled, intending to get up, but he fell to the floor, knocking his head against Tristan's arm. The phone flew away from him, but he caught it in midair.

"Hang on," he said to Nanao.

"Oh, oh, oh!" Cookie called.

Dewey and Maggie got up from the floor together, and she hugged him. "I'm sorry, Dewey," she said. "Today, I'm apologizing to everybody."

Horacio got hold of Tristan's chair but could not figure out how to set it straight. Tristan watched him from his kneeling position and could not for the moment direct him either.

The beer had not spilled, and Tristan finished it before getting off his knees. "Cookie, I said yes to . . ." He pointed to Horacio; he could not recall his name. "You can have the second mirror too, if you want it."

"Oh, oh!" Cookie said. "How can I thank you. I'll get you more beer."

She ran off with his glass.

"What about Pinpin's shoes?" Dewey said to Tristan. "I think we're the same size. There's a pair from L. L. Bean he wore the last time—cordovan and black, very sporty. You know L. L. Bean? It's legendary, man."

In the doorway were Anselmo, Eloisa, and Manuela.

"Is there anything left?" Anselmo asked. "I know these youngsters—they're vultures. They probably asked for everything in the house already and there's nothing left for us old folks."

Anselmo stopped. "What's that?" he said, pointing to the Balans chair as Tristan carefully lowered himself into it. "A chair!" He laughed short, snorting exhalations. "I gotta try it, I gotta!"

He stepped over to Tristan and proceeded to elbow him away from the chair. "Now, instruct me, I'm a dumb old man," he said. "Where does my ass go?"

He figured that out and then began to raise his feet to rest them on the knee supports. He fell sideways to the floor and there was a loud thud.

The noise of the thud brought Tom-tom and Marina. Tom-tom roared from the doorway. "Whaddya doing here! Out! Out! I gave instructions."

Anselmo laughed. "He gave instructions!"

"I said Tris was making a phone call," Tom-tom said, raising his voice higher than Anselmo's. "And he was not to be disturbed by nothing."

God. Nanao. Where was the phone. "Uncle Tom-tom, where's my phone?"

Marina began to tap each person on the shoulder. "Leave the boy alone," she said and repeated it with each tap.

There it was—under the work surface. He got down on his knees again, and before he reached the phone, he could hear squeaking sounds coming from it.

The squeaks turned into shattering yells as he brought the phone to his ear. "Help! Tristan! Help!"

Tristan's heart constricted. "What's happening, Nanao? What's the matter?"

"Nanao," Maggie said. "What a funny nickname."

Tom-tom pulled at Dewey and Horacio. "None of you heard about privacy? I'm gonna stand at the door from now on."

Marina repeated, "Leave the boy alone."

"Aunt Marina, the good set of demitasses are mine and I don't want anyone drinking out of them," Maggie said. She gave Marina time to protest, then she added, "You can check with Tristan if you don't believe me."

Dewey stopped at the doorway and called back to Tristan, "I'm going to try them on now and let you know."

"What's that? What's that?" Tom-tom said.

Tristan repeated, "Nanao, you all right?"

"Are you?" she screamed.

He said, "I'm sitting on the floor, but that's all. I'm talking to my cousins. I mean, they're talking to me."

"Shall I get off?" she said.

"No, no, please," he said.

"From what I hear there's a lot of them," she said.

Tristan looked around. Maggie and Cookie were gone, but the room was full. He was sitting/kneeling in the chair again. He did not know how he had managed that.

He saw Tom-tom hanging on to Dewey, not allowing him to leave the study. Tom-tom said, "Stay away from his shoes. I'm not gonna let you get out of here until you promise you'll leave them alone."

Dewey looked to Tristan for relief; he threw out his arms as if surrendering.

"Uncle Tom-tom, please," Tristan called. "Let him try on the shoes."

Tom-tom let go of Dewey. That cleared the doorway, but one of the kids got in. "Wow, what a place," he said, looking around and pointing at Tristan's chair. Marina had to tap him on the head and lead him out before she could start on moving Eloisa and Manuela out of the study.

"Hang on," Tristan said. "I got an idea. I'll make a list."

Anselmo began on a wave of laughter that could not be stopped. It drowned all talk and made everyone, including Tristan but not Tom-tom, want to laugh. "A list!" Anselmo finally said.

"Anselmo, there's nothing to laugh about," Tom-tom said. "Go inside and eat something and act your age."

Anselmo laughed at that, and this time when he came to a stop he said, "Young fella, you're going to have to face it—everybody wants a souvenir of Pinpin. Or Aunt Mama. You can't make that list by yourself. You better just let everyone line up and tell you what they want. I'm numero uno. I want the rocking chair belonged to Aunt Mama."

Tristan shook his head, "That's Aunt Clem's."

"Shit," Anselmo said and laughed a short laugh.

"Anselmo," Marina said. "You should be ashamed."

"You better go out there, Marina—it's already begun,"

Anselmo said. "They're opening up the cabinets, they're looking everywhere, they're taking inventory." He turned to Tristan. "Then they're going to come in here, young fella, and ask you for everything. They won't steal but they sure going to ask."

"That's all right," Tristan said and belched. "That's what I meant by making a list." He discovered he had to speak very slowly to get the words in the right order and that made him giggle. "I'll make a list and then there won't be any mix-up."

There was a silence full of wonder.

Dewey came back with a pair of shoes in one hand. He had heard what Tristan said and now wished he had not settled for just shoes.

Anselmo laughed. "Well, that beats me," he said.

Maggie said, "He's a prince."

Dewey called into the living room, "Hey, everybody, he's giving the whole house away!"

Tom-tom roared and for a moment there was quiet.

"Hang on," Tristan said to Nanao and sat up on the Balans chair again. When he looked round once more, the doorway was jammed with cousins. The quiet Tom-tom had imposed still held, but the suspense was so taut with expectations that even Tom-tom said no more. Tristan said to them, "Tonight? How about tonight? I'll make a list, so there won't be any confusion later on."

The kid who had stood on the veranda said, "What about us kids? Don't we get souvenirs?"

Tom-tom said, "Eloisa, teach that boy some manners."

Anselmo laughed.

As calmly as he could, for he could hear the squeaks from the phone again, Tristan said to the adults, "All right? It gives you time to pick out what you really want." He did not think he should answer that kid without thinking it over.

Manuela said, "I know what I want—the sofa couch in the TV room."

Tom-tom had to roar again to silence the hubbub that followed. "Tonight," he boomed.

The study emptied.

Marina and Tom-tom stayed with him.

Marina wanted to apologize. "I don't know what's come over everybody," she said.

"Greed," Tom-tom said. "That's what Pinpin used to say. Greed, Tom-tom, the world is eaten up by greed. That's why he spent most of his time with me. I didn't want nothing."

Marina breathed deep, then said, "None of them is on welfare. I have never seen them like this."

"You ain't been giving anything away, that's why," Tom-tom said. "They finally got the chance to be on one of those game shows and it has gone to their head."

Silence came over them. No one knew what to say.

Finally Tom-tom spoke in a flat tone unusual with him. "You don't have to give them anything."

Tristan said, "I promised. I want everyone to have a remembrance of him."

"Promises, who cares? So you promised, so what?" Tom-tom said. "Always say yes until you have to say no."

The phone squeaked.

Nanao said, "You're busy. Call me back."

The phone went dead before he could answer. He belched, he felt low. Real low.

Rosita came in carrying a beer. "Cookie said I should bring you this. What's going on out there?"

"Foolishness," Marina said.

Tristan took the glass of beer, but he knew he had to speak now before he drank it and began to look at everything in a happy, optimistic way.

He looked from one to the other, his trio of Ybor City parents, and said, "I heard the old man out there . . . I'm sorry I can't remember his name. I heard him—"

"Anselmo?" Tom-tom said. "Who pays attention to Anselmo? Ask Marina. Nobody pays attention to him."

"I heard him say there's going to be a funeral at some place—"

"Oh, that," Tom-tom said.

"Yes, and I have to tell you there isn't going to be any funeral for Grandpa. A wake, that's enough." He took a sip of the beer. "No funeral; I'd have to tell Dad and he wouldn't approve."

"You want me to speak to him?" Tom-tom asked confidentially.

Marina and Rosita appeared to lean forward to catch Tristan's reply.

So he said emphatically, "No, I do not approve either. Grandma did not approve of any such practice. And I'm sure Grandpa, I'm sure Grandpa . . . and at that place down here."

"The Centro Asturiano Cemetery?" Tom-tom said. "I better explain. Marina, don't ya think I better explain to Tristan?"

Marina nodded without looking anywhere in particular.

"It's this way," Tom-tom began. He looked around for a chair impatiently, but there was only that skinny chaise and he had to settle for a semicrouching position in order to talk to Tristan person to person. "The Centro Asturiano Club on Nebraska Avenue has always had a cemetery for its members. So did the Centro Español. And the Italian Club."

Tristan made a vague motion with his head.

"The idea was a very reasonable one, they didn't start a cemetery to make money, they didn't want to." He touched Tristan's arm to point out that this was important. "In fact, Celia and Cuco bought a large plot forty, fifty years ago." He turned to Rosita and Marina. "There's plenty of room left in it, am I right?"

Marina said, "You know there's room for three more."

"And so naturally Anselmo got the idea—wouldn't you get the same idea?—that Pinpin would be buried there with his father and mother and sister and her husband. It seems so natural and it don't cost anything, did ya know that? It was all paid for years ago and the Centro keeps up the grounds."

Marina said, "You wouldn't have to worry about it in the future."

Tom-tom placed a hand over his heart. "And I promise every Easter to take flowers. And the others will do their share."

Marina said, "There doesn't have to be a funeral. He could just be buried there without any fuss."

"Yeah, sure, no one even has to be there when they do it—Puig arranges it with the people at the cemetery," Tom-tom said. "No one's talking about a funeral. Ask Rosita. Rosita, you heard anyone talking about a funeral?"

Tristan looked at Rosita, but she neither spoke nor gestured. "Anselmo," Tristan then said, hesitantly, ashamed he was not pronouncing the name right.

"Forget about Anselmo, he don't know shit from Shinola," Tom-tom said. "We was talking about the plot. The plot in the ground. It's bettern a cremation, bettern a plastic bag with who-the-hell-knows what's inside."

Tristan shook his head, and for courage sipped some more beer.

"It occurs to me," said Rosita, "that there is another way of looking at it. What do your parents plan to do with the ashes? Did they ask you to bring them back with you?"

Tristan could not remember. It had been taken for granted, he was sure.

"Did they keep your grandmother's ashes?" Marina asked.

"Not exactly," Tristan said.

"Naw, they threw 'em out in the woods," Tom-tom said. "They did! Tris told me himself!"

They did not really throw them out in the woods; it was not like that. It was difficult to explain.

"So what's the difference if we keep 'em here," Tom-tom said, "and we put 'em in the Centro Asturiano Cemetery?"

Tristan turned to Rosita and Marina: they would see his point. "Grandma's ashes were scattered in the woods of our old family place in Maine," he explained. "She used to go walking there all the time in summer."

They waited.

He added, "That's a funeral too in a way, but without religion."

Marina said, "Oh, there's no religion involved here either."

Rosita tacked on, "Unless the family wants it."

"And arranges for it themselves," Marina said. "The Centro Asturiano has nothing to do with religion. It's a fraternal society."

Tom-tom gestured all that aside as if to get to the real subject. "So what's wrong with leaving Pinpin here? Here, he's right at the Centro Asturiano with lots of family and people he knew and that knew him. He won't be scattered around like dust the women sweep outa the house."

Why didn't they understand? Why wouldn't they understand? How long could he tell himself it was a cultural difference? God.

Tristan told them he had to think it all over. He had learned that ploy from Yale bureaucrats. A delaying action, and he could tell they knew but strangely enough were too polite to say so. If he had to resort to ploys, it must mean he was wrong about the funeral or, rather, the burial, or whatever it was. Actually, he wanted to call Nanao.

A whole ring and just the beginning of a trill before Nanao picked up the phone.

He was quiet after he said hello. Why was he calling her?

After a while she sang, "Go to the window," and skipped all of the lines, a long elision, until "You gotta raise your hand!"

She laughed, then said, "I'm sorry. What's wrong?"

He could not remember how much she knew: lying messes you up. So he began with the wake.

"You did right," she said. "Nothing's wrong with that. They'll come and their friends and talk and meet you. Just a sad, friendly gathering."

"I thought it was right," he said. "The wake, that is."

"Well, of course."

"But I'm not telling my folks."

"Why not?"

"They wouldn't go for it," he said. There were more reasons, but he could not articulate all that now.

"Why not?"

He exhaled deeply. "They'd think it was tacky."

"All that kind of thing is tacky," Nanao said. "Sweet sixteen parties, engagements, showers, marriage ceremonies. But you have to do it."

There was a long silence. These were things they had never discussed.

He told her about the cousins' proposal for a burial.

Nanao thought it over a moment and said, "If you don't want to tell your folks, you could always say you forgot the ashes."

"Forgot?"

"Or the airline lost them," she said. "How does that strike you? If they're so sophisticated they wouldn't be very upset."

"And let them go through with a burial here?" he said. "They might bury the body, actually, not the ashes. I've come to the conclusion they're not very forthright—tomorrow they're going to say, what's the difference whether we bury ashes or the body? They have their own way of putting a point across. I've thought it over, Nanao, and it would not surprise me if they did just that. They say they'd just bury him and not go through a whole ritual, but I don't know if they mean that either. They're sneaky."

He took a deep breath and let it go. Only Nanao could get him to talk that long without a stop.

"Tristan?" she whispered.

"Yes?"

"I think they're right, honey, not sneaky." She paused and he could hear her breathe. "They care, they do, I think. So let them have the burial. You don't want to bury ashes, you bury the body. Your family doesn't care and they do, so right's on their side." She stopped and he heard her breathing again. "Oooh, oooh, I'm sorry, I'm sorry!"

One more word from her and he would cry.

Maggie sprung open the door. "Come on, you're gonna eat! You should see the list! I been making sure someone doesn't put in a bid for your clothes!"

She laughed her deep laugh and got him off the chair.

He told Nanao he would think over what she had said, that he really would give it thought, and hung up without the usual farewells because Maggie was there.

"You gotta tell me about her," Maggie said. "Is it serious?"

She led him to the kitchen and on the way he thought, how would it be if he told the cousins that Nanao was a black girl from Montgomery and that, yes, he was serious. Except he did not know if he was serious. And except, except, except he did not want to know how bad they were. How racist, that is.

There was an enormous spread on the kitchen table. All the dishes everyone had brought and several that Marina had cooked there since he arrived. No one had yet touched any of them. They were waiting for him. There was only one place set at the table. There was no room for more.

They came in from all the rooms to watch him sit down to eat. They held their breath.

"Aunt Marina, Uncle Tom-tom," Tristan said. He had to clear his throat to say the rest. "I think you should plan to bury Grandpa's ashes at the Centro Asturiano Cemetery. Did I pronounce it right?"

Nine

TRISTAN HOLDS A FAREWELL PARTY

There might be something to Aunt Marina's theory—or was it Maggie's?—that beer opened up your appetite: he ate more than at the shore picnic last summer in Maine, his all-time record high. Marina stood quietly by, refilling his glass on occasion, seeing to it that he had a clean plate for each dish he tasted, and shooing off cousins who came too close; but Maggie was something of a cheerleader. She called out the cook for each dish, brought her forward, and made sure to elicit from Tristan at least one compliment as he ate her dish. Tristan listened to recipes for the *favada,* the Galician meat pies, the chicken and saffron rice, the shrimp and saffron rice, the black beans, the *picadillo,* the ripe plantains, the *yuca* in

Seville orange sauce, the baked fresh ham in a sauce with Seville orange juice and paprika and garlic, the red snapper in tomato and onion sauce, and of course Maggie's *pote.* "Delicious," he said about every dish and meant it, and some cousin or other sent out the word, "He says it's delicious," to those who could not fit into the kitchen. He took a swallow of beer between dishes—they could not be called courses, for there was no order to their presentation—and he paused often to belch. At home he would have apologized for the belches and suppressed many, but here he thankfully did not find it necessary.

Throughout, he could hear, sometimes loudly, sometimes dimly, Aunt Clem on the phone extension in the kitchen reporting on what he was eating to her sister Lila. Tom-tom tried to get her off the phone and so did various others, but Aunt Clem always protested that it was not fair. "Lila's stuck there with Olivia," she said. "She's missing out on everything because Tom-tom won't go home."

"Tristan wants me here," Tom-tom muttered each time, and no one laughed or objected, for he was carrying around the list that had been compiled by Maggie of the souvenirs the cousins wanted. No one had been able to persuade him to make additions or changes in the list, but some still had hopes and hung around him.

Finally Elmira and Elvira succeeded in getting Aunt Clem off the phone. She shrieked when she saw them enter with their home-made *turrones.* "Dessert, Tristan!" she announced, and to Lila explained, "I'm sorry, Lila, I'm getting off! I want to get a close look at 'em. Oh Elvira, oh Elmira!"

"Close look!" Maggie said. "Watch out, Aunt Elmira. You too, Aunt Elvira. You know what that close look means!"

Elmira and Elvira did not need to be alerted. They were not entrusting their fine china cake platters with their carefully piled pyramids of balls and squares of hand-rolled *turrones* into anyone's hands until they personally showed them to Tristan. That done, they might then pass them on to Marina but to no one else.

"Tristan, honey, you know what *turrones* is?" Aunt Clem said and did not wait for an answer. "It's the most Spanish dessert there is. No, candy. Anyway, we eat it at Christmas—you sure you haven't tasted it? Imported from Spain. All almonds crushed very fine—"

Maggie said, "The good ones."

"Yeah, the cheap ones got flour and stuff mixed up in 'em," said Aunt Clem and heard Elmira and Elvira draw breath. "Not Elmira's, not Elvira's. The idea! Elmira and Elvira are the only persons in all Ybor City and West Tampa knows how to make it themselves—"

"Our mother came from Spain and she taught us," Elmira said.

Tom-tom growled, "Spain, Spain," but no one paid attention.

"Oh yes, it's the real thing," Aunt Clem said. "None of your manufacturers can make it as good, you know how it is, and Cubans don't really know how to make it." She stuck her tongue out at Tom-tom. "I know I haven't got any Spanish blood, honey."

"It's very simple," Elmira said.

"Anyone can make it," Elvira said and smiled graciously at Tom-tom. "Hard work is the only thing required. Not a bit of intelligence."

Everyone who heard—and the kitchen and the TV room were quiet in deference to the two sisters—demurred. Loudly. Elvira and Elmira smiled as if begging Tristan to discount the others' exuberance. Tristan's wide-open glazed eyes showed, the sisters thought, that he was impressed. He took another swallow of beer.

"Try the round yellow ones first, my favorites," Aunt Clem said, pointing to the one at the top of Elmira's pyramid.

"That's made with egg yolks and almonds—oh my!"

Maggie said, "Watch out, Aunt Elvira!"

"Oh Maggie," Aunt Clem said and slapped her arm lightly. "Cousin Elvira's very generous!"

Tristan fell asleep. That must have happened in the middle of the *turron* recipe. The cop pointed the gun at him and yelled *freeze!* but the glass of beer did not fall out of his hand. He came to. All over the house people were eating. No one had touched the two platters of *turrones.* They were sacrosanct, though Elmira and Elvira were no longer there. The two pyramids sat in front of him at the table. Aunt Clem was back at the kitchen phone, reporting this time to her daughter-in-law in Plant City. "Oh, he's so-o-oo good-looking!" she said. "But he's got a girlfriend. He calls her all the time, it's so cute!"

Marina stood watch over him and the *turrones,* her arms crossed under her bosom. Elmira and Elvira had been escorted to the living room.

Tom-tom sat at the other end of the table. Between him and Tristan all the food was on show, and the cousins were permitted to approach and serve themselves but not to sit at the table. Periodically, Tom-tom said to Aunt Clem, "Get off the phone," but it still had no effect.

Nevertheless, the tone of good feeling prevailed in the house. It laved Tristan. At first it had exhilarated him, then with the help of food and beer lulled him. Soothing it was to luxuriate in the warm bath of family affection. Yes. Everything had come out great, yes great.

No, some things were still unresolved. What?

He brought up the glass to drink more beer, and remembered. Two things needed to be cleared up.

One: had he made clear that they could bury Grandpa's ashes at the Centro Asturiano Cemetery but with no fuss, as they had at first suggested?

Two: he had consulted his own feelings, ignored his parents', but forgotten Grandpa's own wishes—rather, never tracked down what they were definitively. He had taken for granted that Grandpa's wishes were one with those of Dad and Uncle Crispin and all the family that had gathered with him in the woods beyond the barn in Maine to scatter Grandma's ashes. But did he really know? Maybe he didn't even want that.

He emptied the glass of beer. He stood shakily, gestured to Aunt Marina that he was going off to the study, and made his way, past hugs and slaps on the back, to Grandpa's sanctum. It took him a minute to sit/kneel in front of the Toshiba. He kept a hand on the edge of the work surface in front of him to keep from toppling forward. Funny. It was funny.

He called up the WordStar directory. He was going to talk to Grandpa. He'd find out.

There on the screen were the three long lists of entries. He moved his head back and forth to focus on them and he pondered each title. Most were names—of cousins now in the other rooms, eating, laughing, slapping shoulders and hugging one another, discussing Joe Sorrento's TV report, eulogizing Tristan—but some entries he was not too sure about. *Boob.* What was that?

One short paragraph: *I turned into Nebraska on the way home and at a red light stopped on the outside lane. An old man musing. The car door was opened by one of the girls who walk up and down that avenue looking for johns. She stepped in beside me and unleashed one of her boobs from the trifling halter she wore. It was immense. It took ten bucks to get her out of the car. Is there a story in the several funny propositions she made (all indecent) before she settled for the ten-dollar bill? No, the one promise I've kept in this life of mine is not to write stories about the wholesome worldly wisdom of whores. Maybe there is a story about why whores are no longer either worldly (they were never wholesome) or wise?*

God. That was unsentimental. He'd never want a funeral, the man who wrote that.

Had he been true to Grandpa?

What should he do now?

He spoke aloud to the Toshiba, "Give me a clear signal. Yes or no. True or false."

He closed his eyes and once more addressed the Toshiba, "I think you are drunk."

He instructed the Toshiba to abandon *Boob* and he stared at the directory when it came on again. He waited a moment and looked at the orange screen for an answer or an inspiration, maybe even a voice. Talk it over with Nanao, he told himself. He reached for the phone and heard the door to the study open. Tom-tom peered in, but he also heard Aunt Clem on the phone.

Tom-tom said, "I come to bring you the list," before he noticed that Tristan was phoning. He dangled two sheets in front of him. "That Clem—I'll get her off."

"Please," Tristan said.

Tom-tom bellowed, "Clem, get the hell off! Off!"

This time she did, and Tom-tom placed the list on the work surface. "Nobody's taking anything till after the wake," he said. "I told 'em."

Tristan began to dial, but stopped when Tom-tom said, "I'm not taking the car either till then."

Tristan hung up, then shook his head hard to make his point. "You take it now, Uncle Tom-tom, there's no reason to wait."

Tom-tom grabbed Tristan's shoulder and squeezed it with passionate gratitude. "Go ahead, call her," he said. "She goes to that Yale too, your girl, right?"

Tristan nodded. He wished he would leave.

But Tom-tom really wanted him to talk. "A high-society girl, I bet, eh?"

If Uncle Tom-tom only knew how he needed her. Instead, he smiled diffidently and answered quickly, "She's from Montgomery, Alabama."

"A Southern cracker!" But of course Tom-tom did not mean it: the girl couldn't be that.

On impulse—not really; in response, actually, to a deep moral imperative—Tristan said, as if on a dare, "She's the daughter of a black dentist."

Tristan believed he saw Tom-tom wink, but he was so taut waiting for the outburst he expected that he could not be sure. In order to act natural he once more reached for the phone. He gave Tom-tom one last look, but he could not tell if he had understood that Nanao was black.

The phone rang like an alarm and he withdrew his hand in shock. He took a deep breath and picked it up and forgot he had dared to tell Tom-tom about Nanao.

He heard Aunt Clem say, "Don't be surprised, it's Clem! I'm here helping take care of Pinpin's grandson. Who's this, honey?"

He heard Dad speaking, enunciating with such clarity the number he had dialed that it took Tristan a moment to understand Dad did not know Aunt Clem. "Dad, it's me," he said, and Aunt Clem exclaimed, "Tristan! Where you calling from!"

"I beg your pardon," Dad said.

"Aunt Clem," Tristan said.

"What?" Dad said.

"What!" Tom-tom yelled and ran out of the study.

"It's me," Tristan said.

Aunt Clem said, "I know it's you, honey. Why'd you call? Let go, Tom-tom, let go!"

Tristan simultaneously heard Tom-tom's bellowing all the way from the kitchen and also over the phone. A screech from Aunt Clem. Then the receiver there was slammed down.

"Dad?" Tristan said.

"That was odd," Dad said.

Tristan began, "One of Grandpa's cousins—"

"No need to explain. Indeed, it's better never to explain

things of that sort. It gives you an air of mystery and does no one any harm. Girls, especially, will find you intriguing." Dad paused, but Tristan knew he did not want an answer. "I have been calling you for several hours, but the phone has always been busy. I daresay you now have completed all arrangements, and all by phone. Of course, I thought you might call me first, but you're right to tend to the arrangements first."

This time he wanted an answer.

"Dad, I haven't really gotten everything done yet," he said. "I was waiting until I had something definite to tell you."

"Oh," Dad said. "Oh?"

God. What had he done wrong? That Dad knew about, that is.

"You didn't care for my bit on 'All Things Considered'?" Dad said. "Not up to your expectations? Well, the fact is, we've been swamped with calls from the moment it went on the air."

Dad laughed as nonchalantly as he could, not a signal that he, Tristan, could speak yet. "I understand I am all the rage at Buxton. Your sister told the headmaster and the whole school stopped to listen."

"Gee, Dad, I'm sorry," he said. "There're people here and I didn't get to it."

"You didn't hear it!" Dad said. "No radio? The old man got so reclusive, I can see how it could happen he had no radio—I hardly ever listen to it myself. In fact, never. Except today. The old man really got down to the essentials of living, and he was right—I must remember that."

Tristan dutifully asked, "How did it sound, Dad?"

"Rather good, though I prefer to have others tell me than to say so myself. Indeed, it's gotten me all fired up, as they say up in Maine, and I've decided to go down there and open myself up to some impressions for the piece I'm doing for the *Times*. I told you about that, haven't I? I'm trying to be cool about it, but I find that I am telling anyone and everyone—volunteering it to passers-by willing to listen to more than one sentence from me. And since we're on strike, for those lowbrow television writers, and we can't even be seen having lunch with a producer or director, it gives me something to do that I really want to do with a whole heart. It will give them all pause to see me in the *Times* and to be reminded that I come of a literary family to whom Hollywood is ephemera and that I am not tied solely to the whims of stars and studio executives. Let them know I've got something more on my mind than residuals. Your mother, incidentally, is coming too. Down deep, she was fond of the old guy. Not, of course, to the house. Are you staying there tonight? We'll be at a hotel, I don't know which yet, and we'll take a suite. Your mother is asking our travel agent to book us at the most expensive. I understand that since I last saw Tampa there is such a thing as the most expensive. I'll want, naturally, to come over and take a look at the house—he wouldn't let Crispin and me come down there, you know, he so much prized his privacy, and that answering machine was all I ever got when I called. If you want to leave a message, leave a message, bark, bark! He was a great old man. Maybe we can drive around Ybor City. We might even look in on one, maybe two, of the cousins, if there're any around. And that Marina, of course. I hope she's been helpful. I don't need more than one or two quotes from those old Latins, that loamy soil from which he sprang. Not that you can dismiss them as some recently arrived Central Americans—they are something of an aristocracy too, if not exactly Boston, then, well . . ."

It took Tristan a moment to hear there was silence on the line: there was so much on his mind.

Dad and Mom were coming to Tampa!

There was no way they would not find out about the wake. No way.

No way they would not ask then for Grandpa's ashes, no

way they would not find out that he had only pretended to forget the urn or whatever it was they put the ashes in. No way.

"When?" he blurted. "When?"

"When?" Dad said.

"When are you coming? Right away?"

"No," Dad said. "Not until tomorrow."

No way.

The unbudgeable fear he felt was a first for him. He was pinned down to the mat. He could not even contemplate reasoning himself out of his problems. Problems? No, his panic. There was no turning to himself and finding the answer there. Nanao. He must talk to Nanao.

His hand was once more poised over the phone when he was interrupted by Tom-tom. Tom-tom wanted to know if the person on the phone had really been his father.

"I don't listen in," Tom-tom explained. "I respect an individual's privacy. But Clem is nosey and she heard something — she's telling everybody."

Tristan nodded and kept his hand on the phone to shoo him off. He did not even look his way.

"What'd he say? You tell him anything?"

Tristan found his voice and told him his father and mother were coming tomorrow. "I've got to make a phone call," he added.

Tom-tom did not unstick easily, and his intrusion into Tristan's worries gave Tristan time—and ease enough—to notice that Tom-tom was glad Dad was coming. How come?

"When we gonna pick them up?" Tom-tom asked. "What airline?"

Tristan shrugged and went so far as to pick up the receiver.

"Ya don't know!"

Tristan shook his head. He felt an overwhelming impatience to be rid of Tom-tom.

"What!"

Tristan said, "They're going straight to the hotel. They'll call when they get there."

Tom-tom's jaw dropped.

"Uncle Tom-tom," Tristan said, relenting enough to plead, "I must make a phone call now."

Tom-tom's shoulders sagged too now. At the door he turned around and with a sad wave of one hand and drooping bovine eyes said, "I don't wanna criticize, but your folks got strange ways."

Later—he would think about what Tom-tom had said later.

Again Nanao picked up the phone on the first ring. "I'm packing and drinking coffee," she explained.

He was quiet. This time he could hear himself breathe.

"I'm getting bad vibes," she said. "What's wrong?"

He told her. It took a while. She had to question him to get the details.

"You decided to let them have the ashes!" she exclaimed when he got to that part. "I love you, Tristan, I love you! I didn't think you'd do it, to tell you the truth."

"You never said that before," he said and believed it.

"Of course I said that before," she said. "One has to love somebody and I love you. You just interpreted it away. Sometimes I think you're more of a therapist than a friend."

"But there's nothing wrong with you," he said, his way of apologizing. "You wouldn't have gotten into trouble like this."

"It's my fault, I told you to do it," she said. "O-oo-oh, Tristan, I love you."

He did not say anything. He let her statement work its way inside him.

He was now somewhat less anxious, but anxious nevertheless.

"I'll tell you one thing more," he said. "I'm so upset that I tried to talk to Grandpa on the Toshiba."

"There's nothing wrong with that," she said. "Why shouldn't he send you an electronic message?"

"You don't think I'm crazy?" he said. "I tried to talk to him even before Dad called and said he was coming. Tomorrow. God."

"Neo-voodoo, that's all it is," she said. "You know us Africans. We go to the keyboard now instead of the drums."

"I looked for something in WordStar." He turned on the Toshiba, not hopefully but for something to do. "There's no hope," he added.

"And what did you find?" she asked.

He was looking at the WordStar directory now. "Names."

"Names?"

"The cousins down here," he said. "He wrote about them."

"You looked at his floppies?"

God. He had forgot to check on that. "Wait a minute," he said and went to the wall cabinets.

He came back to his chair feeling foolish as well as anxious. "He didn't keep any floppies," he said. "There are no copies of anything."

"Just on the hard drive?"

He did not bother to reply. But it did remind him to try the hard-drive directory. Had he looked at it before?

Nanao said, "Does WordStar carry everything? What about the hard-drive directory?"

"I'm looking at it," he said. "No hope."

"Why do you keep saying no hope?" she said.

He scrolled the directory and the funny program titles went on parade. Autoexec. Eglin. Hideaway.

"You know, you can just tell your folks that's the way *you* want it," she said. "Tell them your grandpa's cousins wanted the wake first, but you also want it, now that you've had a chance to think about it . . ."

He stopped the directory and went back. "Nanao, do you think the same thing I do when you see Hideaway?"

She said, "Encryptation?"

"Uh-huh," he said.

They were quiet.

Nanao said, "Did you ever read the Hardy boys?"

Tristan heard himself say, "I'm going to try it," a foolish thing to say, he knew, but his reasoning powers were no longer in control.

"Keep your fingers crossed," Nanao said. "Keep hoping."

"Wait," he said. "What file do I want to read?"

God.

"Burial?" she said.

Tristan knew he should look for it in the directory. So did she. They did not have to tell one another about these things.

"It's not there," he said.

He exhaled loudly, a desperate sigh.

She said, "This *is* just like the Hardy boys."

"Credo," he read from the list. "That must be it."

She said, "Try it."

"It comes up blank," he said, elated at first. "Maybe it's just blank and doesn't mean anything."

"No, it means encryptation," she said. "Awesome. I got goose pimples."

Tristan did not have to explain the problems ahead. The one big, big problem: the code word for running the program. It need not be a word, in fact, simply four letters. He closed his eyes to bring to mind all he knew about encryptation programs.

After a while, she said, "Look in the manual."

"I did," he said. "There's no manual for the encryptation."

"I've always thought that was foolish, anyway," she said. "If you go to all the trouble to get an encryptation program, why announce the code in the manual where everybody would look?"

"It's no use," he said.

"Don't give up hope."

"We're not very big on hope in my family."

"No?"

"Grandpa came down here after Grandma died because he'd run out of hope."

"That's sad."

"My first year at Buxton, so I didn't much notice what was going on."

She breathed harder, so he would hear and know that she sympathized.

"Dad was not happy about it, I remember that. Grandpa cut off all ties and came down here to live. Probably stopped writing too."

"You make it sound like it was a century ago."

"Four years is a long time."

Another silence.

Nanao said, "Well, if he's got a credo, that means he had hope."

"Credo just means I believe."

"Listen to me, I believe people write credos to say something positive."

"Maybe."

"Something that holds out hope."

He would not say yes, he would not say no. Nor would he sigh either.

"Tristan," Nanao said in a small voice. " 'Hope' is four letters."

He did not hesitate. "Nanao, I fed it hope," he said in a voice punctuated with panting, "and it is asking me what file I want to read!"

"*Credo!*" Nanao yelled, louder than Aunt Clem.

She allowed him to be silent while he read the entry.

I do not believe in the father, the son, and the holy ghost. I take that back. I believe, maybe, in the father and the son, and I would unquestionably replace holy ghost with a grandson. Grandfathers and grandsons quarrel with sons and fathers, but all love one another. What am I saying? I am saying all there is is here on earth. In New York and Maine and Ybor City. And there is a line that continues, no matter what fathers and sons do to break it. Let me start again. I believe in continuity and revolution. Given my time, I must believe in the liberation of the working class. Just to see this on the screen makes me cry. That belief zooms towards me across the arc of half a century. I am a fossil, a time capsule, and I do well to encrypt myself, open only to the gaze of electronic stars. Everything has been muddied, blurred, slurred. We drown in the half-baked, imprecise, lying words of the mediocre and the hustlers. Has the line been broken? Will my grandson hear me? Do none of my categories work? Are there really no more workers and no more capitalists, no more oppressed and no more exploiters? I can see the supercilious smiles of those who have sold their asses to the English departments. They have compromised even the esthetics of the novel. They say to those young people still foolish enough to look to literature, as I did and damn-it still do, for love, knowledge, and guidance: The writer has to be above the issues, above vulgar ideas; he has to love all his characters if they are to live in the world of his invention. Did Shakespeare love Iago? Balzac, Vautrin? Dickens, Fagin? Harriet Beecher Stowe, Simon Legree? And this world that the writers are supposed to invent—isn't it our world, the real world, trimmed by them for goals that have nothing to do with invention and even less with imagination. The world compromised and made serviceable for the ruling class. It does not matter. I do not care. People will see through them. As they saw through efficiency experts and now ergonomics and human engineering. Talk about a world of the imagination! These are the luxury pimps. They will dress up power no end to hide its harsh bones. But if I see the skeleton of greed, so do others. That is my sin: to think, when I despair, that others do not see. I gladly repent. How good to feel assured then that the hustlers will not prevail. People are intractable. They hang on to things that, as we Americans say, work. Whether it's a car or a play. Or a girl. That's my ergonomics. I shall have no truck with any other. All else is the madness of despair. I have known it, trapped as I was in that left-liberal intellectual round. (They are all wise centrists now.) I try to recall just what sort of sympathetic face I made when some fucker said, Isn't it wonderful that Orville Schell has called for an end to the war in Vietnam! Or my delighted grimace at the reply from some cocksucking feminist, But Mrs. Schell is even more of an activist! That is real torture: to remember that I should at that moment have vomited right on someone's good rug and did not. I deserved despair. So I came here to deteriorate with my deteriorating hometown—this Ybor City that invented me—and instead I found continuity. Revolution and continuity. If you look at Ybor City or West Tampa, where those unfashionable anarchists and communists lived, you see mostly mugging and decay. If you look at me, you see a battered old has-been, visited now and then by cousins and their children, none of whom has read a single book of mine. I admit I enjoy these visits. I sit on the porch and sometimes think that I was wrong to believe that literature was my grand irreplaceable vocation, inseparable from my life, its aorta. I tell myself that it is not now and probably never could have been. What a liberating discovery to make on my old porch where all my interest in stories began! How fitting it should end here and that I should now join that mass of humanity whose interests and rewards are at their fingertips. But soothing as it is to think this before going over to Rosita's porch for espresso, I know it is not so, not only not so for me but for that so-called mass of humanity. It is not true for Tom-tom or Clem or Maggie or even the youngsters like Dewey: their pleasures are deeply implicated with what could be, might be, should be—with the future. That the mass vegetates happily is a literary conceit of the elite, their way of surviving their own humiliations. I prefer my way of surviving, I bellow it from the apex of my forty megabytes: I believe literature is the grand repository of our best feelings and ideas, I believe the working class will yet liberate us all, I live in hope and die here and mix my bones with theirs. Human goodness supervenes.

A few lines down, Grandpa had added a note to himself: *It's a bit circular, I must rewrite it, tone down the worst rhetoric, introduce paragraphs and an element of narrative, because even the most frenchified essay of abstract ideas must have a beginning, middle, and a tentative end. Should I de-encrypt it? No, let my grandson discover me—here encrypted, here entrenched, ready to pounce.*

Before Tristan read the entry aloud to Nanao, he checked the date Grandpa had given it, then said to her, "He wrote it eight days ago."

Late in the afternoon next day, on transferring, as he was always careful to do when changing clothes, his notebook and pen to the black jacket that Charlene's brother, a young man his age and size training in a special six-week course to become a firefighter, last night loaned him for today's wake, Tristan took a deep breath, his first pause in two days, alone in Grandpa's front bedroom, where he had passed out from beer and exhaustion the previous night and had thus had no time for aloneness and contemplation, opened the notebook, and read the list, composed in New York, of the things he was flying to Tampa to accomplish. God. He had done none of them.

What had prevented him? His Hispanic cousins? Life?

This was, he noted, a new development with him: these large, unspecific answers to the kind of realistic questions he customarily asked himself. He was acting like a character in an Italian or Russian movie. Why this imprecision, this Slavic heavy breathing rather than reasoning? What caused it? His Tampa cousins? Nanao?

Why was he worrying? Hadn't everything come out right? Miraculously.

Well, almost everything was resolved. There were still things Dad did not know and might not be prevented from finding out. He himself felt there were possibly other things he, Tristan, did not yet know either. He was tempted to make a list of his worries.

But the wake, that unseemly get-together, was out of the way. No problem. It was okay with Dad. He had called to warn Tristan that they might possibly arrive late in the evening, and Tristan quickly reached for the print-out he had made of *Credo,* ready to read it to him as the clinching argument, and told him about the wake.

"A wake?" Dad said. "For his relatives and friends? I guess they're mine too." A pause—should he read Dad *Credo?* "We'll take an earlier plane—I was only getting together with the *Times* editor for cocktails, anyway. I should be at the wake. It wouldn't be proper not to. In fact, it's great, great!"

"You don't mind?" Tristan said.

"Mind? Don't you see?—it's perfect for my article. Super, Tristan, you've done wonderfully."

Tristan did not read him *Credo.* Instead he said, "And Dad? The mayor is going to be there."

"The mayor?"

"Of Tampa."

His father laughed shrilly. "For a ghastly moment I thought you meant Ed Koch."

Tristan decided then to save *Credo* for the leaving-the-ashes-behind argument. What a conniver he had become! Had he learned this strategy from Tom-tom? Or was it a tactic, rather? Or had this slyness been passed on to him in some invisibly minute Hispanic protein.

The door opened and it was Tom-tom. He no longer bothered to knock. Tom-tom had, after all, undressed him and put him to bed last night, more or less. Less, Tristan hoped.

"Here," Tom-tom said and held out a shiny black tie. "I got it for ya."

Tristan had caved in on the dark jacket, but a tie? He said,

"Nobody wears a tie anymore, Uncle Tom-tom," but knew he was fated to capitulate, and he took the tie before Tom-tom said, "At funerals, yes. Lookit me."

Tristan looked at him and saw that he wore a dark gray and black checked suit, a black tie like the other he had brought him, and very shiny black shoes. There were beads of sweat across his forehead that made him appear aggrieved.

"I can look good when I want to," Tom-tom said.

Tristan nodded and tied on his black tie as best he remembered. Tom-tom turned him to him and tugged at the tie one way and then the other. "Now, one last word before we go over to your folks," he said and kept his hands on Tristan's shoulders. "Just us, Marina is not gonna go because she wants to stay here. Somebody in the family has gotta stay in the house until the body is in the ground—" He stopped, but did not shift his gaze. "You know what I mean."

He gave Tristan a reassuring slap on the shoulder. "But that's not what I wanna tell ya. I wanna tell ya"—he pulled Tristan to him and placed both his arms round him and squeezed hard and butted his head into his shoulder, all very quickly "—I don't want ya to go away and forget me and Olivia and my Junior over in Miami, no. And those fool sisters and brothers and cousins, even if they're a pain." He could not talk anymore without crying, so he butted Tristan again.

Tristan did not trust himself to do any more than shake his head. He did so firmly.

Tom-tom said, "I know you're a man of few words, Tris, but I wanna hear ya say it."

"Sure," Tristan said. "Sure."

"Okay," Tom-tom said and clapped Tristan's shoulder once more. "I'm going in my own car because I gotta go pick up my cousin Arcadio after and take him to Puig's. They don't let him drive anymore—he's too old." He stepped back and looked at Tristan. "I wish Pinpin could see ya today."

Except for Marina and Rosita the house was empty. "Don't worry," Marina said when she saw Tristan look about. "They'll all be at Puig's."

Rosita said, "Sonny's picking me up."

He looked at her and she saw his alarm.

"Don't worry," she said.

"I hope Anselmo doesn't come," Tom-tom said. "He's too noisy."

"If that's the criteria," Marina began and gave up and said no more. She hugged Tristan. "Urge your folks to stay at my house. We've got an empty bedroom laughing away."

What a strange outcome. In twenty-four hours it was Mom and Dad who were problematical and the Tampa cousins his colleagues. Mom and Dad would not cancel their reservation at a new luxury hotel downtown (Aunt Clem had spent much of last evening on the phone. "They're staying at Gasparilla!" she shrieked to each person she reached. "Where Cher stayed!") and they had called from it half an hour ago to say they would soon be ready to be picked up.

Tom-tom found a few things to criticize about the Gasparilla. As he and Tristan pulled up to the hotel in the Volvo, he said he thought the guests' parking lot was insufficiently guarded. Inside, he said it was not elegant to have self-service elevators. "A guest should feel that there is always someone at his elbow, you know what I mean?" He had worked as a dishwasher at the St. Regis in New York when he was nineteen, and he also thought it was inelegant to have no desk on each floor with a service clerk to keep the guests from bringing in their own whores.

Upstairs, Tom-tom kissed Mom's hand, threw an arm around Dad, then stood off and let them have a good look at himself. "You didn't recognize me when I come in, I bet," he said. "You never saw me all dressed up."

"Anywhere," Dad said.

Tristan smelled Mom's perfume, noticed the difference between her clothes and all he had seen lately on the Tampa cousins, the way they fitted, was that it? She wore a string of pearls. A cultural difference, that's what it was.

Dad pointed with his Malacca cane to a couch. "Do we have time for a drink, say?" he said.

Tom-tom looked around. "Where's the bed?" he said.

Tristan said, "I think we have to go, Dad."

"Jesus, you got a suite!" Tom-tom said.

Mom liked that response.

In one motion Tom-tom took Dad's cane and inspected the silver boar's head. "I been worried about your leg," he said. "This oughta help." He returned it with much care. "Everybody could use a cane like that."

"I'm fine," Dad said.

Tristan said, "I forgot to ask, Dad."

"I'm fine," Dad repeated.

"Listen, I can't go with you," Tom-tom said. "I gotta pick up Arcadio. But I can't go 'less I tell you this boy is a prince. A prince. When he finishes that Yale you gotta send him down to us. Generous! Don't be mad, Tris, I gotta tell 'em."

"Go ahead," Dad said.

"Tris told everybody in the family they could have their pick of a souvenir from Pinpin. But that was before you were coming, so I wanna tell ya the family has cancelled that out. No souvenirs. No one's taking nothing, unless you give expressed approval and your okay, check and double check."

"Tom-tom," Dad said, and Tristan could see he relished saying his name. "Tom-tom, don't be silly. Of course it's okay. Tristan is in charge and what he says goes."

"You sure?" Tom-tom said.

"Let us not mention it again," Dad said, but a light shadow fell on Mom's face and she laughed to chase it away.

"The other thing is this wake," Tom-tom said to Dad. He obviously liked Mom, but he did not bother her with important matters. "We put a lotta pressure on Tris to have it, and we oughta pay for it. We gonna pass the hat in the family—"

"I won't hear of it," Dad said.

"It's not fair," Tom-tom said. "We was the ones wanted it."

"We want it too," Dad said. "I'm grateful to you for thinking of it first."

Tom-tom threw out his arms to indicate he was helpless to thank Dad adequately.

"You're a brick, my boy," he said to Dad. He took a deep breath and when he spoke his voice trembled. "We want the wake 'cause Pinpin was a great man."

Dad's eyes clouded over.

When Tom-tom left them, Mom said, "I love that guy."

Dad said, "He *is* a character. It might yield some significance to contrast him and Father—they were about the same age—and point out what different paths they took." He looked at Mom. "It was just a thought."

In the elevator Mom asked Tristan, "What did they pick as mementos?"

Tristan said, "Just about everything. I said they couldn't have the stuff in Grandpa's study. He bought that himself and I figured you and I would want it."

Dad said, "His files etcetera?" and Tristan nodded.

Mom said, "Were you joking about the contents of the rest of the house?"

"There are a lot of cousins," Tristan said. "What would we want with a lawn mower, for example?"

Dad said, "What did Tom-tom pick?"

Tristan told him. He did not look their way and they said nothing. It was not until they got into the Hertz car that they began laughing about it.

"I love that guy," Mom repeated.

Now, Tristan thought, now was the time to tell them he had promised them Grandpa's ashes for burial without fuss in the Centro Asturiano Cemetery. He touched the print-out in his jacket pocket, but he was driving, it would be too awkward. Later, when the wake was over and they had met everybody, the mayor included, and they were back at the Gasparilla feeling good, Tristan hoped, he would tell them.

"I like Tom-tom," Dad said. "That suit he's wearing would sell for a fortune in Soho—if the trousers were as short as Michael Jackson's."

"Don't be a snob," Mom said. "He is likeable because he's straightforward and comes right out with what's on his mind. Like a good New Englander. I underrated them."

Tristan caught Mom and Dad both looking at his jacket and black shiny tie, but he did not explain: he knew that they would say nothing unless he did.

Puig's occupied a square block in West Tampa. The long, low stucco building—like a nineteen-twenties mansion, until you felt rather than saw the oddity of no windows and the lighting behind the bushes—was set far back from the street on too wide an expanse of lawn. The driveway led them to the back of the building where there was a parking lot as large as a supermarket's. The high, wide double doors and the walks along the sides of the building were filled with dozens of people standing elbow to elbow, all turned towards the entrance where television news crews waved their arms to keep people away from the main walk from the parking lot, reserving the entrance and its overhang to themselves.

There was Joe Sorrento. He peered at their car and so did everyone on the walks who saw him do it. He waved at Tristan, then at his assistant, snapping his fingers as he did so. Cookie stood behind him holding a large briefcase that said *Channel 7.*

"What's this?" Dad said.

Tristan said, "I don't know," and felt he was dissembling. But, in fact, he did not know what was going on and began to worry.

"It's quite a crowd," Mom said, "but more than one person a day must die in Tampa."

There were two parking slots right in front, but the young

man there said they were reserved for the mayor. Cousin Jack stood at the farther slot and he ran over and informed the young man that this was the family from New York.

"I'm your cousin Jack," he said to Mom and Dad with a big smile. "I made a couple of calls and everybody's here. Puig let the TV news hog the whole entrance 'cause of the mayor. And between you and me, my informants tell me that every channel has promised him to carry a longshot of the front of the funeral parlor in the story. Puig doesn't get a plug, they don't get inside."

As they walked to the entrance Tristan heard the silence. Even Jack stopped talking. Mom and Dad suddenly looked different. Their backs were straighter, their heads less mobile, their glances downward. Many on the walks were cousins Tristan knew, but not in this guise: their clothes were their Sunday best, their faces composed, and none spoke.

Bright lights suddenly came on, and a TV assistant skipped towards them. He enunciated with great care, "Walk slowly, slowly, so we won't ask you for retakes." He waved Jack away from the three of them, and then began walking backwards, motioning them towards him as carefully as a dance director at an early learning rehearsal.

Dad stopped. With his Malacca cane he beckoned over the TV assistant. "Young man," he said. "I only take direction from top Hollywood directors."

Tristan thought, that was just like Grandpa. If he had not read Grandpa in the Toshiba he would never have noticed that about Dad. Vinegary too.

The quiet persisted. The assistant retreated to the cameramen, but the TV lights remained on. Jack rejoined them. "You won't regret this wake," he whispered to Tristan. "Your grandpa looks great and it'll be great publicity for his books."

At first Tristan thought the man who now came up to them was Maggie's husband, and said so, but he turned out to be Puig himself.

"We Puigs have been around Tampa as long as the Granados, so we know each other," he explained. He was not the self-consciously gloomy person Tristan expected an undertaker to be. He started to introduce himself to Mom and Dad in Spanish but quickly shifted to that mixed Southern-Hispanic-Floridian English they all spoke. "Maggie and me are old friends."

Puig held the people outside and in the lobby at bay. "Let me take you to a reception room right next to the chapel where people can come over to you on the way to the chapel," he said. "I think it will be easier on you than sitting right there in the chapel while people are doing the viewing." Flashbulbs went off, and Tristan saw that Puig was pleased. Dad, too.

In the jammed lobby Puig did not entirely succeed in keeping people from them. Some there and others standing along the walls in the corridors to the reception room approached Mom and Dad and spoke quietly. Dad wore a serious look as he listened to them, but Mom seemed to be smiling slightly all the time. They joined Tristan too, but they were Tristan's friends now and most merely tapped him lightly and walked a few steps with him.

What would they be *viewing?* Funeral parlor jargon, he figured. Strange vestiges these words were of religious funerals, like chapel for hall. He followed Puig with his eyes in order to warn him not to talk to Mom and Dad about the arrangements. He did not want them hearing now that they were not going to be given the ashes. And then there was the matter of payment.

By the time they reached the easy chairs Puig wanted them to sit in, Tristan had greeted all the cousins he knew and others he must have met on the porch last night while under the influence. A strange lady in a black dress and black straw hat had been hanging on to Mom, and Mom held an arm around her affectionately. She took Tristan's chair.

"Oh honey, I haven't worn this corset in twenty-five

years," she said to Mom, and he recognized Aunt Clem's voice.

Tristan was glad not to sit. He got to Puig as he was politely melting away. Over Puig's head he saw Professor Wallingford talking to Dad.

Puig did not let him say more than a word. "I have all the information from your uncle. Please do not worry yourself or your parents."

Tristan said, "About payment."

"Tomorrow, after the funeral," Puig said. "No, no, I made a mistake. Come the day after, whenever you like. There's no problem—simply come by, all right?"

He was gone. Why did he say funeral? But he said he had made a mistake. Jargon, that's what it was. Why was he uneasy?

There was Sonny. Tristan was grateful for his blond hair standing out or he would not have recognized him either in his funereal clothes.

Sonny first grabbed his elbow. "Okay, man, hang on. They gotta do this kind of stuff, it's their thing, you know."

Tristan happily said, "Yeah."

Sonny put an arm on his shoulder and they stayed together without speaking. Several older women kissed the two of them.

The young girl cousin who had given Tristan goose pimples at the airport came up and wound an arm around his waist under his jacket. "You're in bad company," she said, again breathily in his ear. To Sonny she showed the pink tip of her tongue.

Sonny said, "Don't listen to her. I'm a good boy now."

She said, "Where's your wife?"

Sonny said, "I said I'm a good boy now."

She winked at Tristan. "When I said bad company, I meant me." She pinched a bit of skin under his ribs.

Maggie was the first to talk above a whisper. "Any mayor goes to a Latin's funeral gets my vote!" She wore a matching

dress and hat of large white flowers on a black background. "Christ, I wish I was you kids' age!" she said, but she left them quickly for Mom and Dad. She did not faze Dad: he was happily exercising his noblesse oblige.

The hum of voices that had begun when Maggie started talking stopped. Mayor Freedman had arrived. No fanfare, just a couple of aides and a cop with her, but it was enough to impress everyone. She was a trim woman of fifty or so, on the alert. She nodded to anyone who caught her eye.

Puig led the mayor to Tristan first, and she shook hands with him and Sonny and said precisely and with care, *"Los acompaño en sus sentimientos."*

"Uh-huh," Tristan said.

"Muchas gracias," Sonny said.

"Where's the son?" one of the aides asked.

Sonny took the lead in walking them over to Dad. While Mayor Freedman repeated her greeting to him in Spanish, Sonny whispered in Tristan's ear, "Shall I tell her I'm on the lam?"

Dad said, "Oh yes, *buenos dias,*" to the mayor, and she added, "We have to do something tangible about honoring your father. It is a way of recognizing the important contribution Latins made to the growth of Tampa."

"You're very kind," Dad said.

Professor Wallingford said, "A statue in Ybor City?"

"At least a bust," the mayor said and looked inquiringly at Wallingford.

He introduced himself and added, "We've formed a committee at the university to do something about it."

The mayor quickly interposed, "Let's talk about that," laughed a short laugh, and said to Dad, "The University of South Florida's budget is a state responsibility, so I'm not afraid that the professor will sneak in talk about a salary increase."

And she was gone. An aide lingered to make note of the professor's name and phone number. That done, he said to

Mom and Dad and Tristan, "Mayor Freedman has a dinner and a meeting to go to this evening. She hopes you will forgive her for not staying to view the body or attend the ceremony."

The aide left in the midst of a stunned, new silence. Dad looked at Tristan. Tristan looked strange.

"Shit!" Maggie said. "It's out."

Dad seemed not to hear her. He said, "Aides always get everything wrong—that's American politics."

The look on Aunt Clem's face told Tristan the aide was right. The jargon now made sense.

Of everyone there he could only trust Sonny, his contemporary, for a straight answer. "Is it true," he asked, "that Grandpa is on view over there—in the chapel?"

Sonny pulled a little on Tristan's shoulder to shake him up affectionately. "But they're gonna have the funeral like here tonight in respect of your wishes not to have a big burial tomorrow."

God.

Maybe he could get Mom and Dad out of there before it all began, without their knowing.

Sonny jiggled him again and leaned his head over close to his. "Listen, look at it this way—we're Latin kids, we gotta keep the old folks happy in their ways."

But his old folks were Mom and Dad.

Sonny kept his head close. "What's the big deal, anyway. It's not so terrible. No religious bugaboo in it."

That was a plus. He returned Sonny's insistent gaze and tried winking for the first time in his life away from the bathroom mirror.

Now for Dad.

Aunt Clem beat him to it. "You wanta see him, you wanta," she pleaded. "He looks so peaceful, all his worry wrinkles gone, so peaceful. I don't know how they do it!" She struggled up from her easy chair. "Come on," she said and held out a hand to Mom.

Dad struggled with his thoughts.

Mom said, "No, thank you."

"I know, it scares you," Aunt Clem said. "But I'll go with you. Maggie too. Maggie!"

Tom-tom announced his arrival in his usual manner. "Shut up, Clem," he said. The silence was ended.

As if he had cleared the stage, Tom-tom began again. "I knew you was gonna take it well, I knew it," he said happily. "I hurried here, but I had to pick up Arcadio and Panchito. I told Panchito—he's gonna deliver the eulogy—Pinpin's son is gonna take it well. You ever heard of a Latin boy let his father go out there like smoke in the wind?"

He remained three or four feet away from Mom and Dad, aware that victory was not in hand yet. The old conniver! He threw his arms out and made a trio with the two dressed-up old men on either side of him. "What ya say?"

Tristan called, "Dad, please!"

Dad turned to him. "Tristan?"

"I want it that way too, Dad," Tristan said.

He saw his mother look amazed, then his father smile.

"I too," Dad said, and he turned to his wife. "And you, dear?"

"Of course," Mom said, but Tristan heard the asepticism in her voice, uncontaminated with sentimentality, which would later on be her source of fun about all this. "Yes, of course."

Tom-tom heard it, too. In an aside, as he brought Arcadio and Panchito to meet them, he said to her, "What can you do, we're a bunch of crazy spics!"

Mom laughed out loud.

Panchito's father had been a reader in the cigar factories in the old days, and Panchito had heard him deliver many eulogies at funerals. That is how he qualified. Tom-tom left him with Mom and Dad and without excusing himself led Arcadio immediately to Tristan. He let no one get in his way. "Here, here!" he called out.

Arcadio was black and his hair was the whitest gray Tristan had ever seen.

Tom-tom said, "Tris, I especially want you to meet my oldest cousin, Arcadio. Arcadio Granados."

"So you are Aunt Mama's great-grandson," Arcadio said. "She was my favorite aunt."

And Arcadio was black!

Tom-tom leaned forward and whispered, "And he's still an anarchist!"

Sonny volunteered, "You haven't seen me in a long time, Arcadio, I'm Rosita's son."

"I know you, Sonny," Arcadio said, "and I want you to stop it."

"Yes, Arcadio," Sonny said. "I swear, I'm stopping."

Arcadio said, "There are better things to do in this world."

Dewey came up, wearing a cotton jacket in the new black. "I was afraid I wouldn't make it." He stood on the other side of Tristan. "Hi, Arcadio, how do you like our new cousin?"

Tom-tom said, "Arcadio, did I tell you he goes to that Yale up there?"

"And the school of life, I expect," Arcadio said.

They were led to the chapel. A large one. It was filled, and people also stood along the walls. They were supposed to walk by the open coffin and look at Grandpa. Since Sonny and Dewey came along with him, Tristan was able to hang on to them when they got to the coffin and without stumbling close his eyes and not see the corpse.

"Look at him," Sonny said. "A real guy."

Dewey said, "Geez, he looks great."

Tristan looked and saw a strange man, formally dressed and wistfully peaceful. Not the man in the Toshiba. A puzzle, a contradiction. He would have to think about that.

There were places on the front bench for Mom and Dad and him. Tristan chose to stand along the side wall with Sonny and Dewey.

There was a mike up front, but Panchito eschewed it. He

began, "My father used to say about those cigarmakers whose reader he was, he used to say, they did their work and now they are done. Antonio Granados, the son of a cigarmaker, went out into the world and became famous. Isn't it right that having done his work he came home?"

The tears rolled down Tristan's face. He cried in front of them all, but he was not ashamed, because Sonny and Dewey were crying too.

ABOUT THE AUTHOR

Jose Yglesias, a playwright and journalist as well as a novelist, lives in New York City and North Brooklin, Maine.